PRAISE FOR *Deal-Breaker*

"Both women are likeable, warm, and passionate. The chemistry between them...sizzles." —*Rainbow Book Reviews*

PRAISE FOR *Earth Angel*

New England Chapter, Romance Writers of America
Readers' Choice Award finalist for
Best Contemporary Romance of 2013

"A wonderfully imaginative novel...Abby and Gwynne are completely engaging." —Katherine V. Forrest, Lambda Literary Award-winning author

PRAISE FOR *Angel's Touch*

2014 Golden Crown Literary Society Award
finalist for Best Debut Novel

"A well-written romance with a slightly different plotline. The reader isn't required to suspend much belief to feel the story is realistic. The characters are interesting... Overall it was quite enjoyable." —*Piercing Fiction: Straight Arrow Reviews*

Also by
Siri Caldwell

Angel's Touch

Earth Angel

DEAL-BREAKER

SIRI CALDWELL

Brussels Sprout Press

Deal-Breaker
Copyright © 2016 Siri Caldwell

Cover design by Marianne Nowicki

ISBN: 978-0-9974023-1-5 (paperback)
ISBN: 978-0-9974023-0-8 (ebook)

Brussels Sprout Press
P.O. Box 42133
Arlington, VA 22204
United States of America

First edition: April 2016

DEAL-BREAKER

1

Rae Peters never thought a pink satin thong would be her downfall.

As a backup dancer for wannabe chart-topping recording artist Kaoli Morgenroth, Rae Peters knew how to stick her gyrating dance steps under blinding lights while dodging the bras and panties that flew onto the stage like colorful, deranged birds. She made it look effortless, too.

Biggest rule for looking good onstage: never look down. Look at the audience, look at the other dancers, look at the distant walls soaring up and up and up into the darkness, but do not look down—not unless she wanted the audience to think she was unsure of where her feet should be. After which she'd be out of a job.

She was not looking down as she sprang from the moving platform, leaped into space with arms and legs extended, landed on a scrap of slippery lingerie, skidded, fell. Snapped her ankle. Tore her knee. Didn't scream. Did not look down. Did her best to make it look like she'd fallen intentionally, like she was supposed to crawl offstage dragging one leg behind her, rolling out of the way of the other dancers, avoiding the musicians and the backup singers and the remote-controlled, steadily gliding, larger-than-life scenery. With all the adrenaline, it wasn't that hard to do.

The pain didn't hit until she'd made it offstage. As her strength failed and agony took its place, she made one last push to make sure she was safely hidden from the audience before collapsing in the shadows on an unyielding coil of electrical cables.

She shouldn't have worried. Three stagehands swarmed around her with urgent, efficient, this-show-is-planned-down-to - the - fraction - of - a - second - and - it's - my - job - to - keep-everything-on-track speed and hefted her sweat-drenched, Lycra-plastered body out of the way before anyone could trip over her. Kaoli continued to sing without a hitch as if nothing had happened. The stagehands were saying something about an ambulance, but the words didn't register. Rae craned her neck to check out her lower leg. Her ankle didn't look right.

But she would be okay, wouldn't she? She could dance through pain.

It wasn't until later, through a haze of painkillers, that it occurred to her that she wouldn't be continuing with the tour.

———

It wasn't hard to figure out who was outside Rae's hospital room harassing the nurse.

"No cameras. No recording devices. No nothing," commanded a man who could only be Kaoli's bodyguard, his testosterone-laden voice projecting down the hallway. He rarely spoke, but when he did, this was the sort of thing that came out. "I'm dead serious. If I find out you have a camera hidden on you…" He left the threat unfinished. Way more movie-star action hero that way than admitting there was very little he could legally do.

"Why would I have a camera?" the nurse said.

Ooh, a male nurse. That explained the hostility. If it had been a female nurse...well, suffice it to say, paparazzi were rarely female.

"Why should we believe you?" Kaoli countered.

"Oh no," Rae said quietly. "Please don't." If Kaoli alienated the nurses... She really didn't want her to alienate the nurses. After having her broken ankle set and her torn knee ligaments surgically sewn back together, the last thing she needed was an angry nurse controlling her pain meds.

"This is a hospital," the nurse said. "I have more important things to do than take photos. I don't know who you are, and I don't care."

"Kaoli Morgenroth."

"Never heard of you," the nurse said.

"Don't you listen to the radio?" demanded her bodyguard, like it was a personal affront that he didn't recognize Kaoli, even though his obliviousness meant the risk that the nurse would try to sell a photo of her to the tabloids was nose-diving. Her bodyguard did have kind of a short fuse.

"I listen to the radio. And like I said, I've never heard of you. You're not as famous as you think you are."

Yikes. That was not going to go over well. Rae cringed, waiting for someone to respond. She didn't hear anything. Maybe Kaoli was giving the nurse one of her angry glares and saving her voice for her next show. One could hope.

Some silent agreement must have been reached, because the next sound was footsteps approaching her door.

"Surprise!"

Suddenly everyone was crowding into Rae's room and Kaoli was smiling her professional onstage smile and Kaoli's assistant was setting a vase of purple and yellow irises on the shelf under the muted television. Rae sat up straight in her bed—as straight as she could with her leg immobilized—and tugged on her flimsy hospital gown to make sure she was decent.

"I wasn't expecting you to visit." She couldn't swear to how much time had passed—a day? Two? She'd been in and out of consciousness too much to keep track—but it seemed like the tour should have already packed up and hit the road. And spared her the embarrassment of being seen like this.

"Just checking on how you're doing." Kaoli moved the vase of irises to the tiny table by Rae's bed. How typical of her to do something nice like bring flowers and then choose colors that would remind Rae of her bruises. She was sure it hadn't been intentional, but that's how everything had always been with Kaoli. "Everyone's thinking of you. The dancers, the band, the tech crew…even Mr. Hard-Ass here."

Kaoli's bodyguard frowned like he didn't appreciate the nickname.

Ignoring him, Kaoli dropped a magazine in Rae's lap and leaned over to open it to the page she'd flagged with a sticky note. "Have you seen this? Hot off the press."

The magazine lay open to a full-page photo of Kaoli onstage belting out a song, but Rae barely glanced at it before she fixated on the smaller, inset photo in the lower right-hand corner. She picked up the magazine and drew it closer. It was a photo of herself, crawling across the stage, one leg dragging, her teeth bared like a growling animal in what she'd thought was a smile while the dancers behind her aligned in perfect formation performing the acrobatic moves of Kaoli's current hit, "Wildcat". Chloe and Sylvie looked amazing, captured at the peak of a split jump, toes pointed, arms outstretched. The caption read: "Kaoli Morgenroth backup dancer declares: 'I hate your choreography, Kaoli! I'll make up my own moves.'"

Great. Her first photo by a real news photographer and she couldn't use it on her résumé. And her face—she'd had no idea pain made her look so unattractive. At least they didn't print her name.

Was that because Griffin Broadnax, Kaoli's high school sweetheart, current boyfriend, and now high-and-mighty editor-in-chief of one of the best-known gossip magazines in the country, was doing Rae a favor? Or did he simply not recognize his teenage nemesis? Maybe he didn't review the pages before they went to press, or at least not the last-minute additions. She honestly didn't know what the job entailed, only that Griffin was impressed with himself for becoming the hotshot boss before the age of thirty—their youngest editor-in-chief ever—and made sure all his old classmates knew about it.

But that caption…

Rae let the magazine fall to her lap. "I wish Editor Boy had asked me if I minded."

"Oh, honey, why would he recognize you?" Kaoli said.

Rae's mouth fell open. She didn't know what to say.

"It's not like you were friends," Kaoli said.

"I think he knows damn well who I am."

"Ancient history," she said breezily.

Maybe to Kaoli, but not to Rae. Some memories never had the grace to fade.

And maybe calling to check his facts was not something he did with someone who had, back when the three of them were in high school together, come damn close to sleeping with his girlfriend.

———

Several weeks later, in the front row of the largest lecture hall on campus, Axel Nye finished scrawling his answer to the last question on the final exam for Advanced Financial Accounting Standards and flipped to the front of his test booklet to double-check everything. Some students chose Tonoloway College for its proximity to rural Pennsylvania's cross-country ski trails and autumn deer hunting, but Axel had chosen it for the academic reputation of its master's program in accounting. The fact that his parents lived a mere twenty minutes away had had nothing to do with his decision pro or con, although it had turned out to be convenient for laundry and free meals.

Mentally blocking out the sounds of anxious breathing and scribbling pencils, he slid down in his seat and stretched his large-and-tall-size legs out in front of him, taking full advantage of the legroom that came with claiming a front-row aisle seat instead of retreating to the upper tiers of the hall's stadium seating like the wusses who were afraid to make eye contact with the professor. The professor wasn't even in attendance today, just Vance What's-His-Name, his short little squirt of a teaching assistant who'd been unlucky enough to draw proctoring duty. He seemed to be grading papers to pass the time and not really keeping an eye on the room.

Axel sprawled his legs wider and nearly tripped one of his classmates as she jogged silently down the aisle to turn in her exam. Jori Burgess. Not just his classmate, but his ex-girlfriend and the mother of his child. Athletic-looking—one of those scary chicks some guys didn't want to work out with because they couldn't handle the idea she might outperform them in the weight room—but not a dumb jock. She might look like she should be starring in her own fitness video rather than trying to fit in with spreadsheet-obsessed nerds whose skin never saw the sun, but in class she blew everyone away with how smart she was. He wasn't surprised she was one of the first to finish the exam. Or that she'd smirked at him and cheerfully waved goodbye with her middle finger noticeably extended.

He *was* surprised that Domenic Eubanks was done early, dropping his completed test booklet on top of Jori's on the lectern a few seconds after she left. Maybe he'd studied. For once.

Domenic lingered at the front, whispering with the proctor. Whisper, whisper, whisper. Could they be any more annoying? Axel drummed his heels on the floor to drown them out. Some people were trying to pass an exam.

When the boys finally stopped and remained silent for more than two seconds, Axel glanced up to see what Domenic was still doing up there and immediately wished he hadn't. He didn't need to see them making out. They should learn to control themselves.

He stared at his answers. Couldn't focus. Glanced up again. Glanced away. What did Vance-the-Squirt see in that guy, anyway? Domenic was such a player. You could tell just by looking at him that he'd bang anything that moved—he had that yes-I-*am*-a-god attitude down pat. The confident hip swivel, too.

Not like Gus. Gus had an even hotter hip swivel, but Gus didn't parade it around indiscriminately. He only showed it off in private, which was the way Axel liked it. He liked knowing Gus was all his.

Axel glanced up at Domenic again, just to prove to himself the poser was nothing he wanted.

And wasn't that a mistake. The boys had moved on to dry humping as they kissed, getting off on some kind of exhibitionist fantasy. Domenic was not completely into it, though. Couldn't be. Not if he had enough brain cells and coordination to multitask and keep Vance distracted and neglecting his proctoring duties while Domenic reached behind him for the meager pile of test booklets on the lectern and peeled off the top two, which had to be his own and Jori's.

Domenic rolled up the two test booklets together and broke off the kiss. "I'm going to think about my answers some more," he told Vance in a hushed, test-appropriate voice, quickly turning his back so his body shielded the test booklets from view.

Axel sank lower in his seat. He should've kept his eyes on his own test, because now he had another thing to feel guilty about on top of all the lies he told his parents about his quote unquote "roommate" Gus.

Better to feel guilty than to create problems for himself, though. He didn't need to accuse Domenic of cheating and end up entangled in the backlash. Because backlash there would be, especially when it came to light that employee sexual impropriety was involved. He had only one semester left to go. This was no time to volunteer for a headache.

2

Feeling awkward and slow and sick of the smell of chlorine, Rae squinted against the glare of the early morning sunlight and bobbed upright at the deep end of a massive outdoor swimming pool nestled in the Pennsylvania woods, her body suspended by two flotation belts strapped one on top of the other around her waist. Despite the flotation belts and the steady bicycling motion of her legs, she sank enough that the hair at the nape of her neck escaping her short ponytail was getting wet. Ugh. It was the beginning of summer, but when the water hit her neck, it was cold.

She'd ended up at the Mountain Laurel Center because her older sister Connie had mentioned her injury to Sierra Mosier, one of Connie's best friends all through elementary school and middle school and high school. Rae suspected Connie had mentioned that Rae was in desperate need of housing, as the apartment she shared with another dancer in New York City was currently occupied since they sublet it while they were on tour. Her parents had taken her in for several weeks, but as much as she appreciated their help, she'd been on her own long enough that living under their watchful eye felt almost as confining as the cast on her leg. When Sierra graciously invited her to stay at the yoga retreat center she and the love of her life co-owned, Rae had wasted no time accepting.

Rae told her parents it would be nice and quiet and

relaxing to live with a bunch of vacationing yoga enthusiasts out in the middle of nowhere on the outskirts of some sleepy college town no self-respecting city dweller had ever heard of, but the truth was, she wasn't here to relax. She wanted to be back onstage, and she would have traded a windowless dance studio that stank of stale sweat for a swimming pool with a view of beautiful clear sky in a heartbeat. But that wasn't an option, so she was reminding herself to be grateful to be free of her awful plaster cast and jogging in the pool sooner than anyone had predicted. Challenging her atrophied muscles with water resistance wasn't dancing, but pushing herself to the point of exhaustion was close.

And at least being in the water meant she didn't have to look at her weak leg. The scars left by the surgery were bad enough, but the loss of muscle tone? Scary. The leg had shrunk to half its normal size, a visible reminder of how much work she had to do. She'd rather look at just about anything else.

Fortunately, while she exercised at the deep end of the pool, the shallow end provided the perfect distraction: water aerobics classes. Well, not the classes. The instructor. Jori. As usual, Jori strode along the lovely slate pool deck in a faded turquoise one-piece swimsuit, quick-dry shorts, and sockless sneakers and shouted instructions and encouragement, her voice hoarse from fighting to be heard across the water over blasting music. Not exactly what Rae expected from a yoga center, because weren't these places supposed to be oppressively silent and meditative? And teach nothing but yoga? But far be it for her to complain.

"Any questions?" Jori yelled. It was a sexy kind of hoarse—feminine and rough—the kind she wouldn't mind listening to all day. "Any questions besides how I manage to be so adorable?"

She *was* kind of adorable. Full of energy despite the early morning hour, throwing herself into her job, trying to get her students to have fun and maybe fall in love with her just a little bit. And that hair: a fauxhawk with a shock of blond flopping at the top and darker blond fuzz on the sides. Rae was sure she wasn't the only one in the pool who yearned to find out if it was as soft and touchable as it looked.

"Push those arms! Push those floats through the water like you mean it."

The twenty women at the shallow end of the pool churned the water with their foam dumbbells with varying degrees of enthusiasm.

Jori pumped her arms to demonstrate the level of energy she wanted to see. "Just because I can't see you cheating, doesn't mean you get to slack off."

Inspired, Rae jogged faster.

Jori must have noticed because she gestured in her direction, inviting her to come closer. "Hey, sunshine. Why don't you join us?"

Rae smiled and shook her head. Jori meant well, but her class was amateur hour. If she knew Rae was a professional dancer, she'd understand that waving her arms around and looking goofy was not on her to-do list.

"Come on. It'll be fun." Jori jumped into the pool with a splash and swam toward her in her sneakers and swimsuit, looking intent on a private conversation.

Oh crap, Rae was going to have to find a way to not hurt her feelings.

"What's your name?"

"Rae."

"A ray of sunshine. I love it! No one's ever come up with

that one before."

"Actually—"

"No, don't tell me. That's your name for today."

"Um…okay." Sooner or later she'd find out it was her name *every* day. "I'm doing my own exercises. But thanks for the invitation."

"You're welcome to join us anytime."

Rae was still figuring out how to make it clear that wouldn't be happening when Jori swam off. The class was Jori's focus, and she didn't look back.

Well, okay. That was easy. Jori wasn't offended.

"Ladies, no slacking. Everyone should be moving left now." Jori pointed to the side to give them a visual, but pointed the wrong way. Some of her students went left, others right, and a few were so confused they stalled out and did nothing. "Your other left," Jori corrected herself. "Right. Left. One of those."

Jori climbed back out of the pool. "Watch. This is how I want you to do this next move." She faced away from her students and kicked one leg behind her, in and out. "Don't be checking out my butt, though."

Now that she mentioned it…

Jori turned to face the class and added an arm crisscross. "Your arms don't have to be straight," she reminded them.

Several women snickered. Jori did the move again, hamming it up.

"Speaking of…" Jori fiddled with her music and Kaoli Morgenroth's first hit, "Alpha in Heels", came on.

Rae threw her arms overhead and whooped. The aerobics class would think she was one of those rabid fans who desperately wanted Kaoli to be gay, but really she was just happy anytime anyone played a Kaoli song, because it meant her popularity was on the rise. Kaoli Morgenroth was a big enough name that she could afford to put on extravagant shows with dozens of dancers and backup singers and band members littering the stage, but she'd never had a song reach number one, no matter how much her fans thought she deserved to. And that was going to change. Her voice was good, her shows were awesome, and one day soon she was going to write the hit song that would make her a household name.

"Who read her interview in the latest issue of *Celebrity Crush*?" Jori asked. "What was that quote? 'I'm not opposed to being with a woman?'"

"'I'm not opposed to being with a woman if things don't work out with my boyfriend,'" amended one of the students.

God, had Kaoli really said that? Of course she had—she'd say anything to get attention. Jori's students laughed, but Rae had no sense of humor when it came to Kaoli. It wasn't nice to dangle hope in front of the lesbian fans, to whisper promises like *I might be gay*, to rev them up with *someday…*, to say *I'm not opposed to being with a woman* when she damn well was. She'd had the opportunity to be with a woman and she'd turned it down.

Not that Rae would tell them that. Kaoli would have her fired. The fans didn't really think Kaoli was going to sleep with them, anyway. She was a face on an album cover. An image. A fantasy. They didn't care that sometimes she wasn't a nice person. Rae knew exactly how much of a jerk she could be, and even *she* didn't care. Dancing for Kaoli Morgenroth was a dream job, and Rae had promised herself long ago that who Kaoli did or did not sleep with was not worth wasting brain power on. Who Kaoli *said* she did or did not sleep with was not worth wasting brain power on. All that mattered was getting in shape and getting back onstage as soon as possible.

By the time the water aerobics class was over and Rae had aqua-cycled for another hour, her legs were shaking and refusing to do what she told them to. At the other end of the pool deck, Jori chatted easily with her students as they put away their foam dumbbells and flotation belts and left for the locker rooms in the small building beside the pool.

When the last student was gone, Jori walked to Rae's end of the pool and squatted at the edge. "Everything okay?"

"Yeah." Rae came closer so she wouldn't have to raise her voice, paddling mostly with her arms because her exhausted leg was pretty much useless. She stopped an arm's length away, momentum drawing her closer than she'd intended. "Don't worry about me. I'm not a real guest. You don't have to make sure I'm having a good time."

Jori balanced her weight on her hands, lowered her feet into the water, and sat and leaned forward, hands curled around the edge of the tile. Her nose was sunburned and peeling. "What if I want to?"

Her charming smile was hard to resist. Her legs were close enough that she could touch Rae with her toes if she wanted to. Too close. But Rae didn't back up. Was it objectification to notice how athletic but deliciously non-skinny she looked, or the way her modest one-piece swimsuit strained to cover her not-so-modest bust?

Not that Rae was staring. Staring would be rude, and she was a feminist and didn't do that sort of thing. Which kind of too bad, because now that she was getting the full effect of her...smile...really, her smile, not anything else...close up, she didn't want to look away.

But she did. Right into friendly green eyes that made her glad she was floating in the water and not trying to maintain her balance on land.

———

Jori had never once seen their new visitor out of the water since she'd appeared about a week ago, but it didn't take a genius to figure out that the pair of crutches leaning against a deck chair were hers. And claiming she wasn't a real guest? She had a feeling she knew what that meant—it meant her ray of sunshine was another one of Sierra's and Melanie's charity cases.

Took one to know one. When they'd learned Jori was putting herself through grad school and teaching fitness classes to put food on the table for herself and her four-year-old daughter, they'd immediately offered her free room and board at their lodge in exchange for being their resident water aerobics instructor, which was awfully generous for only a few hours a week of work. She was surprised Sierra hadn't asked her to keep an eye on her injured pet project, make sure she didn't drown, but maybe Sierra wasn't aware of Rae's plans for her pool. Not that Rae needed watching. She seemed to be quite…capable.

Ignoring the ladder, Rae swam to the edge of the pool a few body lengths away from where Jori was sitting and did a pushup to propel herself out of the water. She paused there, supported by only her arms, and waited for the water to sluice down her skin. Then she swiveled to sit on the tile coping, rolled onto her side, and from there got to her feet in a weird maneuver that should have looked a lot more awkward than it did before she straightened and limped toward her crutches.

Rae was all leg. Long legs, long arms, long everything.

God help her if Jori ever saw her in heels, because adding three or four or five inches to those legs would boggle the mind. She looked nothing like a bony supermodel, though. Muscles flexed in her back as she swung her arms to keep her balance. And her glutes. And her shoulders. She might be skinny—she had so little body fat that she actually had to pad herself with two flotation belts, not just one, like any normal person, to keep her head above water—but she was ripped. Everywhere.

Except for that one leg.

"What happened to you?" Jori asked, following her like the nosy ambassador of hospitality Rae had asked her not to be. She couldn't help herself.

Rae wobbled and grabbed her crutches. "Dance injury."

"Doing what?"

Rae was shivering in her swimsuit despite the weather, and no wonder—it wouldn't kill her to put on a little body fat. She wrapped a towel around her chest as best she could while holding her crutches. "Landing."

Gorgeous, but defensive. Although it could be that the pain from whatever was wrong with her leg made her irritable.

"Will you be here tomorrow? So I can annoy you some more with my charmingly intrusive questions?"

Rae's frustrated expression softened. She had nice eyes. Whoever loved her was lucky, getting to linger in the glowing apology and forgiveness that transformed her average brown eyes to shining warm mocha.

Jori blinked. Where had *that* thought come from?

Rae tossed her head in a flirtatious move that was meant to be done with luxurious long hair but worked surprisingly well with her stubby ponytail. "Come back tomorrow and find out."

3

Jori had visited Professor Walston—her Advanced Financial Accounting Standards professor—in his office many times during the course of her intensive, year-round, eighteen-month master's program, and she'd never seen him sit behind his desk. He always rolled his ergonomic chair with its ridiculous number of creaking knobs and levers away from his cluttered desk and crossed his ankle over his knee like he was following some rule he'd read in an industry journal for how to keep things informal with his students.

Not today, though. Today he sat behind his desk.

It seemed she and her classmate Domenic Eubanks had turned in identical answers, including identically worded essays, on their exams.

"After your excellent participation in class and the other work I've seen you do, I must say I'm disappointed in this turn of events," her professor was saying. He'd been talking for a while. Academic dishonesty was unacceptable, and he'd thought better of her, and of course he'd be speaking with Domenic, but his teaching assistant had nothing but good things to say about the young man, although she shouldn't worry about that because no one was going to show favoritism toward anyone.

"I have no idea what happened," Jori protested. "I already told you I wasn't sitting anywhere near him, so I don't know how he could have seen my answers. All I know is, I didn't cheat."

"The evidence says otherwise."

She tried another tack. "Can I retake the exam? Prove I know the material?"

Professor Walston stared down his nose over his glasses at her, using up all the air in the office. "I'm afraid not."

"There must be something I can do to prove I didn't copy his answers."

His face remained stony. "Go home and give it some thought."

"That's it?" His lack of suggestions was not encouraging. If his only plan was to wait for a confession, there wasn't a lot she could do.

"If I can't determine which one of you cheated, or how the cheating was accomplished, I'm afraid both you and Mr. Eubanks will have to be expelled."

———

Jori escaped the building taking extra-long strides and cut a diagonal path across the campus green toward the parking lot. It wasn't just her future hanging in the balance—it was her daughter's, too. As much as she loved teaching water aerobics, it wasn't enough to support the two of them indefinitely. She needed to move on to a better career. She'd invested a lot in this master's program and she needed to graduate.

She didn't see Axel with his bulky backpack slung over one shoulder until she'd crashed into the hard corners of the textbooks inside and he'd gone tumbling to the ground.

"Sorry," she spit out, rubbing her arm where they'd hit. What was he, invisible?

Axel scrambled to his feet and struck a casual pose as if nothing had happened. It would be bad for his image if anyone noticed he'd been knocked over by a girl.

She and Axel had met in undergrad, back when he thought he was straight. They'd dated for two whole years before he lost patience and blew up at her for not having sex with him and accused her of being gay. She got scared she'd lose him, and Baylee was born nine months later. He broke up with her anyway, but he never really disappeared. Now they were in the same grad program together. Axel joked that she'd chosen this school because she couldn't resist following him, but that was so not true. Her mother thought she'd done it for Baylee's sake, but that wasn't it, either. They'd shared the same favorite econ professor junior year, and it was that professor who'd convinced both of them that Tonoloway College had everything they were looking for. Nothing personal about it.

Axel hiked his backpack onto his shoulder. "Having a bad day?"

"You could say that."

Jori spared a glance behind her at the building where Professor Walston had his office. Axel would hear about it soon enough, so she might as well tell him. "Walston thinks I let Domenic Eubanks copy off my exam. He can't figure out who cheated, so unless Domenic comes clean, we're both expelled."

Axel's face went blank with that kind of vacant, slightly panicked look people had when they were about to get in trouble. But he had nothing to do with this, so why would he panic? Was he that alarmed that he couldn't come up with a snappy, sarcastic comeback? A moment later, he shook it off and resumed his usual blasé expression. "Who except one of his boy toys would want to help Domenic?"

"Yeah. I don't think I'll try that argument. Walston is convinced it's me, and anything I say against Domenic will make me look bitchy, and with my luck, guilty."

"What did Domenic do, copy your essay word for word? He's not wily enough to switch things up?"

"Apparently not."

Axel played with the strap of his backpack. "I know you didn't do it."

Jori spluttered. Of course she didn't do it. She and Axel were two of the best students in the class. And if for some inexplicable reason she were to copy off anyone, it would be off Axel's exam, not Domenic's. Axel at least would have the right answers.

"You're taking my side? I'm touched."

"Don't get all gooey on me. It's just...I saw Domenic pick up your test booklet after you left the room. It had to be yours. You turned in your answers right before he did."

Oh God. Oh *God*. Axel could save her butt. This was perfect. *Perfect*.

"You saw him copy my answers?"

"I didn't say that."

Wait...what? He didn't want to help her? "You said—"

"I said I didn't see him copy your answers. I saw him pick up a test booklet that might have been yours."

"Same difference," Jori said impatiently. She should haul him into Walston's office right this minute before he decided he hadn't seen Domenic pick up her exam booklet, either. Honestly, Axel was a good friend, but when the shit hit the fan, he was always the first one to duck.

"Who knows what he did with it? He could have picked it up by accident." Axel shook his head in that irritating know-it-all way that she frequently wished professors would put him in his place for. "You know I always sit in the front row. I can't see what goes on with the rabble in back."

The urge to yell was overwhelming, but yelling would get her nowhere. Yelling didn't work for women, not unless they wanted to be accused of hysterics and labeled mentally unstable. It certainly didn't work with Axel—she knew that from personal experience. What worked with Axel was helplessness and falling apart—two feminine skills she'd never excelled at.

"If you tell Professor Walston what you saw and clear my name, I'll do anything you want." Damsels in distress didn't grit their teeth, so she tried to relax her face into something approaching a smile. "Anything short of having sex with you," she added, just in case one disappointing night hadn't been enough for him. She knew he was sleeping with men these days, but sometimes she got the feeling he still wanted to bang her because that would be guaranteed to miraculously transform him into a respectable straight guy. After all, it had worked so well the first time. "Please. There must be something you want."

She hated to sound desperate, but desperation was what was called for. Desperation worked. Begging worked. It wasn't even an act—she *was* desperate. That should make it easy to be convincing, convincing enough to make him respond the way he usually did to desperate females, which was to think he was in control, and when he thought he was in control, he felt safe enough to be magnanimous. She really wanted to get her degree, she had only one semester left before they gave her a piece of paper that would help her get a good job, and she'd be damned if she got kicked out of school so close to the finish line. Especially when she'd done nothing wrong.

Sure, she could probably transfer to another school, but what school would take her once they learned she'd been expelled for cheating? And even if she did manage it, it would mean retaking some classes if all her credits didn't transfer, or taking additional classes to meet the new school's requirements, not to mention moving to another town and finding money for not only tuition but also rent, because she would no longer have Sierra Mosier's generous part-time job that came with free housing. She had friends here, too. And babysitting, which was essential, since Axel was unwilling to spend any time at all taking care of their daughter.

"Home-cooked meals?" She wasn't a bad cook, and he'd mentioned that his off-campus apartment had a decent kitchen she was sure he rarely used. But she doubted he'd be interested. He was familiar with her cooking and she couldn't remember him ever raving about it. His mother's, yes, but not hers. What could he possibly be tempted by? Not water aerobics classes, that was for sure. He'd teased her about her choice of moonlighting occupations more than once. Easy for him to be critical—he didn't have to hold down a part-time job. "Help writing your résumé?"

"Maybe…" Axel frowned and rubbed the back of his neck.

Jori perked up. "Maybe help writing your résumé?"

"I have a better idea."

He didn't look too happy about this so-called "better" idea of his. Which made her crazy. What could he possibly want? And how repulsive and damaging to their friendship was it going to be?

"Spit it out. You tell Professor Walston I'm innocent and in return I do what?"

"I need a date for Sunday dinners with my parents. Preferably someone good-looking who's not an annoying ditz." He looked her up and down like he was trying to decide if she qualified. "That could be you."

Sunday dinner? That was too easy. She'd admit she'd been lax about making sure Baylee spent time with her grandparents, but he didn't have to force her to do it. "I already—"

"Not this once-a-month thing you're doing for Baylee's sake. Every Sunday."

"Okay…" There had to be a catch.

"I'm talking a real date."

"What does that mean? I have to dress up?"

"It means you pretend to be my girlfriend."

4

Most people who emerged from the massage room on the ground floor of the lodge at the Mountain Laurel Center had the dazed look of having just woken from a good nap, but Rae was positive she wasn't one of them. Getting a massage was more fun than killing herself with leg exercises, but it hurt just as much. She'd just spent her whole hour clenching her mouth shut so she wouldn't curse out loud as the massage therapist broke down the scar tissue that would limit her ankle's range of motion if left untreated. Excruciating, but she was making progress, and that made it more than worth it.

Now she was alone in the massage room getting dressed and testing her ankle's newfound flexibility. She strapped on her knee brace and her ankle brace and opened the door, and the massage therapist returned from wherever she'd been waiting, ready to see her off and set up the room for her next appointment.

As Rae maneuvered her crutches through the doorway to leave, voices carried from across the expansive lobby. One of them was Jori's voice. Rae paused and adjusted her grip on her crutches, unsure why she didn't just continue on her way out. Her stomach grumbled, ready for dinner. And then she saw her. Jori was making her way through the building with a lumbering bear of a man, her hand in the crook of his elbow, laughing up at him like an adoring girlfriend.

Because Jori was…straight?

Rae's heart sank. Not another one. How many times was she going to find herself attracted to someone who was fundamentally unavailable? Jori had been so charming when they met, so irresistible. Rae had been more attracted to her than she'd realized.

"Ready for this?" the man was saying.

Jori swatted him on the arm, still laughing. "This is the stupidest idea ever."

"You like it. You're already enjoying yourself just thinking about it."

"If it weren't so hilarious…"

Rae couldn't move.

"Do you need help getting back to your room?" the massage therapist asked, misunderstanding the reason for Rae's motionlessness, standing there blocking the door.

"Gus is very grateful to you, by the way," the man told Jori. "As am I."

"How grateful is he?" Jori gave a flirtatious hitch of her shoulders.

"Hey, none of that sex talk before dinner. You'll spoil my appetite. Save it for when it counts. You know, later."

"Rae?" the massage therapist said gently. "Do you need help?"

"I'm… No. Sorry." Rae planted her crutches and propelled herself forward and out of the massage room.

Jori noticed her and waved as she passed, but didn't stop to say hi. It was just as well, because Rae needed a minute to process this new information.

Jori was straight. Well, why not? Just because she worked for lesbian employers who attracted hordes of lesbian guests didn't mean she couldn't be straight.

Besides, Rae needed to get her leg functional as soon as possible and get out of here and rejoin the tour and start dancing again. She didn't have time to waste dreaming about a sunburned nose and a blond, sun-bleached fauxhawk and a perky voice misunderstanding her name. It was better that Jori was straight.

————

If this place were all yoga, all the time, Jori would be stuck teaching underwater yoga, not water aerobics. Was underwater yoga even a thing? She didn't mind learning new skills, but she'd put herself to sleep if she had to teach quiet stretching and wasn't allowed to bounce around to loud music and yell.

She did like the yoga barn, though. The spacious, free-standing studio was located in the woods a short walk from the lodge. It had once been a working barn and retained some of its rustic feel, but now had huge windows on three sides and a polished oak floor. Non-yoga events were held in the lodge's multipurpose rooms, not the barn, which meant that what with all the watercolor painting and memoir-writing and whatnot offered between week-long yoga retreats, Jori often took advantage of the barn's quiet space to study.

But when she got there, the barn wasn't empty. Rae, that constant presence in the pool, was already inside exercising. She was lying on her back in footless black tights, a black leotard, and a baggy gray sweatshirt and had her legs extended up a bare wall, weighted cuffs strapped around her ankles, toes pointed. Clearly there had been a few too many ballet classes in her past. Jori should have guessed that earlier when she'd seen her leave the pool, because no one moved with that kind of ethereal, athletic grace—limping on crutches, no less—without intensive dance training. As if to prove her point, Rae chose that moment to open into the splits, sliding her legs impossibly far apart against the wall. She drew them back together, out and in, ankle weights dragging against the wall with a rough whoosh of protest, again and again and again. It wasn't the way bodybuilders did that exercise—they used weight machines and their knees weren't obsessively straight. Had to be a dancer thing.

"Come. On!" Rae ordered her legs.

Even from across the room, standing in the doorway, Jori could see her legs were shaking. If she'd stop locking her knees she could cheat it a little. It wouldn't look as crisp and perfect and svelte, but it would help her crank out another rep. Jori should know. She'd worked her way through undergrad as a personal trainer and by working the local gym's front desk, keeping a textbook open on the lower ledge of the long counter where gym members couldn't see. Trainers might talk about maintaining alignment and proper form, but hardly anyone paid attention. Straight legs? Please. Lifting the heaviest weight possible the most number of times was all anyone cared about. Making it look good no matter what, even if it meant making the exercise as difficult as possible and sacrificing bragging rights? Had to be another dancer thing.

Rae's ribcage heaved up and down and her legs came together once more, then dropped open, still perfectly straight, toes still pointed, like she was doing everything in her power to pretend she wasn't on the verge of collapse. She let out a sound of pure frustration and smacked her thighs. "One. More!"

Guess floating across a stage in gauzy fairy-wing crap

might be more work than it looked.

Hovering in the doorway, half in, half out, Jori could have left without Rae ever knowing anyone had been here. Instead, she slipped into the room. Pushing hard was important in weightlifting, but this was more than physically pushing herself. This was anger. Which should have made her think twice before approaching. But something made her edge forward, some deeper part of her that couldn't bear to watch Rae struggle and at the same time couldn't look away.

She knew better than to startle her and risk causing an injury, so she waited until she was sure Rae had sensed her presence before she spoke. "How many reps have you done?"

Rae angled her head to look up at her, but didn't move her legs out of the splits. "Not enough."

"Are you seeing a physical therapist? Did they recommend this?"

"My physical therapist," Rae spat out, attempting to squeeze her legs together one more time, "assigns me exercises that would get a car accident victim into excellent shape to walk to the driveway and get back behind the wheel."

So Rae was designing her own rehab, apparently. There were probably lots of reasons that was a bad idea, but Jori couldn't really blame her. A physical therapist who was great at patiently dealing with the average couch potato wouldn't necessarily know what to do with someone this fit and this driven and this stubborn.

"At least try my water aerobics class." It would be good for her to relax a little instead of smacking her own legs. And her boss, Sierra, liked Jori to encourage the guests to participate. The classes were early enough that anyone who wanted to could join in, even if they were attending a workshop. "People see old ladies doing it and think it must be easy, but it'll kick your butt." People made stupid assumptions about age. "Promise."

Rae's legs made it only part of the way up before they got stuck. Grimacing with disgust, she used her hands to force her legs all the way together. "I need to focus on my own training."

Yes, she was clearly focusing. Maybe a little too much.

"Keep it in mind if you ever want a change of pace. Because I'm telling you, my class is a lot of fun."

It wasn't until she had already cocked her head that Jori realized she was flashing her most flirtatious grin. She had a whole collection of them, but this particular one she hadn't used in a long time. She saved it for special occasions, and special occasions rarely came up.

And this was not one of them. What was she doing, using that grin on a guest?

She opened her mouth to repair the damage, but no words came out because Rae's answering smile was an unexpected blaze of mesmerizing sunshine. Jori forgot what she'd meant to say. Do. Think. Some distant part of her brain clamored that she was on the verge of being late to her study group, but for the first time she could remember, being on time seemed unimportant.

Until Rae's smile faded and she turned away and flung her arm across her forehead, using her sleeve to blot the sweat that rolled down her face. It was a great way to avoid eye contact, if that was her intent.

Maybe Jori had come on too strong. Yes, definitely. Rae was a guest, for God's sake. She probably assumed Jori was hitting on her. And why shouldn't she? Jori had taken that smile much too far.

"Gotta run." Jori backed away, raising her hand in farewell, a gesture she'd been told more than once looked much sexier than waving. Damn, she needed to stop. Not that she did it on purpose. Flirting was something that happened naturally all on its own when she was around people who made her smile, and it seemed her ray of sunshine was one of those people. Even growling at her legs in frustration, Rae seemed like someone she could be friends with. It didn't mean anything deeper than that.

Not unless Rae was planning on flirting back.

Rae's arm remained flopped across her face as if she was too tired to open her eyes.

Yeah. It wasn't the first time Jori's flirting had fallen flat, but she always took it in stride. Not everyone was going to flirt back, and that was okay. She couldn't remember it ever bothering her. It didn't bother her now. She just felt...even though she shouldn't...disappointed.

5

When Axel had struck his deal with Jori, he'd almost hesitated. He often had these moments when he knew he should do the right thing, but then his mind would move on to the next thing and he'd forget. And then she started saying things like *If you tell him what you saw and clear my name, I'll do anything you want. Short of having sex with you.* Which got him thinking that yes, actually, there was something he wanted. And no, it was not sex. Not with her, anyway. Back when they were dating, her refusal to sleep with him had driven him insane. But not now. Now he knew that women had zero sex drive and men were what he secretly craved, and the idea of sex with a cold fish in bed like Jori no longer appealed. So no, he didn't want sex from her. But he did want something else. He wouldn't have come up with the idea if she hadn't offered, but hey, if she was going to offer…

She ought to hate him for forcing her into a deal. He didn't know why she didn't. Maybe she'd convinced herself that dinner with his parents was just a thank-you and that he would have spoken up and cleared her of cheating even without their deal, but the truth was, he didn't know if he would have. Because as much as he believed what happened to Jori was unfair, he didn't want to get personally involved. In the end, it was the promise of personal gain, not his sense of right and wrong, that made him agree to say something to Professor Walston. Meaning his mother was finally going to lay off pressuring him to bring home his imaginary long-distance girlfriend, whom he'd conveniently retroactively broken up with that very morning, to meet the family.

And now here he was with Jori, having dinner with his parents around the big formal dining room table and pretending to be reconciled and dating each other again with their kid at their side, while his brother, who was either older and braver or older and approaching senility, sat across from them with his own boyfriend, a living example of why coming out to your parents—when your parents were his parents—was not a good idea.

They tolerated Murray. They hadn't disowned him or barred him from their home. They even invited him to dinner.

And never failed to remind him there was no need to drag Hadad along. They didn't like having to buy extra food for his guests and they didn't understand what Murray saw in that young man anyway and would it kill him to consider his parents' feelings? Murray seemed to think that if he wore them down, they'd eventually get used to it, but Axel didn't know why he bothered. Being tolerated wasn't the same as being embraced.

Even Jori did more than tolerate him. Or maybe she did hate him and was just really good at hiding it. He didn't think so, though. He didn't appreciate her refusal to wear anything nicer to dinner than her fitness geek uniform of shorts, sneakers, and a tank top—she claimed she didn't own anything aside from the weirdly feminine business suit she kept for job interviews, and he wouldn't be surprised if that were actually true—but otherwise, everything was great. Jori seemed to genuinely enjoy spending time with him and his dysfunctional family, and the best part was his mother got to fawn over her granddaughter every Sunday instead of once every month or two, which was all Jori had made the effort to do since Baylee's birth, even though he'd told her often enough that his parents didn't mean the anti-single-mother slurs. Jori had pointed out for years that there was no reason he couldn't borrow the kid and take her to see her grandparents himself, but he'd done it a few times when Baylee was a baby, and his mother had hassled him about how he was doing everything wrong, so he'd stopped trying. Baylee wasn't a baby anymore, but he had no doubt his mother would still find plenty to criticize, no matter what age the kid was. It was easier to just pay child support and let Jori be in charge. Jori was a good mom.

A good person, too. She was easy to like. Hell, he wouldn't have dated her for so long if he didn't like her. Which was a good thing, because it would be hard to pretend to reconcile with a woman he couldn't stand. Not as believable, either. Or would that make it more believable? He and Jori had debated that, with Jori arguing that couples in romantic comedies always hated each other and him arguing that he didn't need to give his parents yet another reason to suspect he had zero interest in the female sex. Gender. Whatever he was supposed to call it.

He also would rather she stopped poking him with her pointy elbow. She seemed to be enjoying it a little too much.

Poke. Jori passed him a platter of his mother's fantastic roasted asparagus drizzled with butter and balsamic vinegar.

"Can't you tap me on the shoulder, instead?" he hissed.

"I'm holding this dish with both hands," she said loudly, not even trying to whisper. "I need a free hand if I'm going to tap. Poking is easier."

Everyone looked at them to see what was going on. Jori

chose that exact moment to demonstrate her point with a jab to his ribs. It didn't hurt—he was a man, and something as insignificant as a woman's elbow, even if that woman could bench press more than a real woman should, did not hurt—but it was annoying. When she'd said she thought they should fight, he'd assumed she meant fight with words, not limbs.

"How about you just say 'Axel, heads up. Food's coming.'"

"How about," Jori countered, "you stop daydreaming about all your other girlfriends and pay attention to what's going on at the table?"

His mother beamed at her.

Axel blinked. Mom was happy? How did Jori do that? Wow. Jori was brilliant at this faux girlfriend shit. Next his mother was going to compliment her on her dykey fauxhawk—excuse me, her unusual hairstyle—as a sensible choice for a young mother who didn't have time to devote to shampooing long hair.

His mother turned to his brother and he could almost sense everyone at the table stop chewing their food.

"Murray," she said brightly. "When are you going to bring home a nice girl like Jori?"

Murray scooted his chair closer to Hadad's and draped his arm over his shoulder. "Don't hold your breath."

"I want more grandchildren." She busied herself with the corn casserole to avert her eyes from the unseemly display. "My friend Annette from Pilates class has five already and I can't stand her yapping about how wonderful they are."

"Maybe Axel will give you more grandchildren," Murray said with a brotherly smirk. Murray knew the score. He wouldn't come right out and out him to their parents, but he never wasted an opportunity to make him squirm.

Axel scowled at him. He didn't mind taking his share of the parental heat, but Jori shouldn't have to, especially when she already had her hands full with Baylee and was doing an excellent job taking care of her all by herself, never demanding anything of him, leaving him free to live his life. If she had a second or third kid, that might change. But his mother didn't see it that way. She saw it as her job to push her sons to pass on their DNA, which she thought of as her DNA, which was of course better than anyone else's DNA and therefore urgently deserving of life regardless of how many needy mouths they had already spawned.

Parenthood. Ugh. Baylee was cute when she was well-behaved, but two hours a week was about all he could stand.

"Don't get ahead of yourself, Mom," Axel said. "I never said we were getting married."

"That didn't stop you the first time," his mother said.

Murray snorted. "Can we talk about *my* sex life next?"

"Yes, let's," Axel said. "I'm sure my five-year-old daughter would love to hear it."

"She's *four*," Jori corrected.

"I'd love to hear it," Baylee piped up.

"It's exciting stuff, Baylee." Murray swished his shoulders, which never failed to make their generally silent father cringe and order him to knock it off.

"Knock it off," their father said, right on cue.

Murray did it again, swishing his shoulders in a way that was possibly even more gay than the first time. "But not as exciting as watching your grandmother pressure your parents to get it on before they get married."

"Don't be ridiculous, Murray," their mother said. "Axel and Jori will…" *Cough, cough.* "…marry…" *Cough.* "…when they're ready. It's you I'm worried about."

"Of course it is," Murray said.

"Which is why," his mother continued, "I have arranged a date for you with a nice young lady I met in Pilates class."

"I'm not going on a date with her, Mother. I'm with Hadad."

"I'm not telling you to break things off with Hadad. You can just…live separately."

"You want me to marry this girl and keep Hadad on the side? This is more acceptable to you than me being gay?"

"You're the one who insists on having a man in your life," his mother said.

"Let's talk about something else," his father suggested. "Shall we?"

"Murray, I'm giving you the girl's phone number," his mother said. "You can at least meet her. For me."

"No." Murray clasped Hadad's hand, raised it above the table where everyone could see, and kissed it.

"Knock it off," his father growled, stabbing a hunk of steak and chewing hard.

Axel was afraid to look at his mother's face. She always tried to seat someone between Murray and Hadad—presumably because she disapproved of their relationship and not because she imagined there might be hand-holding or worse under the table—but most of the time Murray rebelled and picked up his chair and squeezed in next to his boyfriend and forced everyone to scoot over to accommodate him, giving no thought to their mother's blood pressure.

"Gu—Jori and I went to the gym yesterday," Axel said loudly, trying to draw his mother's attention away from Murray, who was rubbing his thumb over Hadad's hand and looked like he might be about to suck on his fingers next. Murray did not know when to quit. "We were lifting weights and he—*she*—" Man, he had to do a better job watching those pronouns, or his mother would have a stroke. One gay son was already more than she could handle. Why was he screwing this up tonight? You'd think the word *she* would roll off his tongue after all this time, but thinking about Gus at the gym in all his masculine glory—well, not *all* his masculine glory—and what a sight *that* was—tripped up his brain.

It would be easier to not say anything and not tell any of his stories, but he was too much of a talker to stay mute for long. So he switched pronouns. And pretended to his mother that Jori was Gus. And pretended he didn't see Murray and Hadad roll their eyes at him from across the table for being a coward. Besides, how could he convince his mother of his faux relationship without providing details?

Axel began his story again. "We were lifting weights, weren't we, Jori, darling?"

Jori put her fork down with a noticeable clink. "Can we back off on the mushy terms of endearment?"

Great. Now Jori was annoyed. He kept a wary eye on her elbow. "Whatever you say, darling."

Jori kicked him underneath the tablecloth. A small grunt of pain somehow escaped his throat. He covered the embarrassing sound with a manly, hacking cough.

Jori looked down her nose at him. "You were saying?"

His mother smiled indulgently at them both and exchanged a glance with his father. Maybe Jori was right about her theory that acting like they hated each other made their relationship more believable. It certainly seemed to be working on his mother.

"Do tell," Murray said, failing to acknowledge Axel's masterful redirection of their mother's focus and saving Murray's sorry ass from further maternal questioning. It had to make Murray crazy that they could almost hear her counting down the days until the anticipated engagement with the nice girl from Pilates he hadn't even met. "What fascinating thing happened at the gym yesterday with *Jori?*" He leaned hard on Jori's name, harder than necessary.

Axel glared at him, sorely tempted to toss him his own version of his brother's patented shoulder swish, but the impulse passed before he did something he'd regret.

"Jori works out." Anyone with an ounce of intelligence could see that neither one of them fit the scrawny, scarecrow-ish accountant stereotype.

"With you?" Murray said.

Axel ignored him and continued his story. "Jori was spotting me on a bench press when this guy brushes past her and mumbles a suggestion to meet him in the locker room. I nearly dropped my barbell. I mean, he hit on her right in front of me. I was right there. I could hear him."

"The nerve of that man," said their mother. "And did he really expect you to follow him into the men's, Jori?"

"I think he did." Jori smiled. She seemed to be enjoying herself. "Unbelievable, isn't it?"

"I'll say," Murray drawled. "I'm certainly finding it hard to believe."

"I tried to turn him down gently," Jori said.

"Actually, she told him to fuck off," Axel said.

Jori coughed in surprise. "I did, didn't I?" She pounded on her chest like something had gone down the wrong way. "I am such a good girlfriend."

"Are you choking?" his mother asked her.

"I'm okay." Jori gave herself another few thumps on the chest and excused herself from the table, still coughing.

"Axel, did you infect her with that horrible cough of

yours? I want you to take some of my Echinacea cough drops home with you."

His-and-her fake coughing fits. Why hadn't he ever thought of that? It was perfect, just the right amount of commotion to make everyone forget about his dumb weightlifting story before they realized it really didn't make any sense.

Jori was the best faux girlfriend he ever had.

————

Jori rushed through the door into the classroom where her Information Technology for Accounting exam was being held and slid into the seat next to Axel's. She'd have to relocate farther away once the exam began, but the proctor hadn't even arrived yet.

"When are you going to talk to Professor Walston?" she whispered, leaning close so the other students trickling in wouldn't overhear.

"Soon."

"I don't have forever."

"I'll get around to it."

"They're going to expel me if you don't say something," she hissed into his ear.

He jerked away, holding up a hand to ward her off. What did he think she was going to do, lick his ear? Gross.

She gripped the back of his seat and kept her face in his personal space. "I did my part, Axel. Now you do yours."

"Okay, okay."

"Today."

"Only if you promise to be my date at my cousin's wedding."

Jori wanted to kick him. Obviously she'd done too good a job of being nice to his mother. It was good for Baylee to spend time with her grandparents, and lying to them was actually kind of fun, in a sick sort of way, especially when they started slinging the anti-gay bullshit. But that didn't mean she didn't expect Axel to respect the terms of their blackmail agreement.

"Being your date at your cousin's wedding was not part of our deal."

"You're my girlfriend. My girlfriend has to be there." Axel slid down in his seat and sprawled out with his long legs and ape-like arms. "No wedding, no deal."

Jerk. She should have known he was ethically challenged. "When's the wedding?"

"End of the summer."

"I'll have to check my calendar."

"You do that."

"I'm not going to date you indefinitely, you know." She felt one of their classmates in their row staring at them, but whatever.

"My mother signed me up for 'learn to dance at your wedding' lessons at the dance studio in town. You should attend those, too."

"Dance lessons." She gave him the evil eye. As soon as he talked to their professor and cleared her name, she was going to put a stop to all these extra conditions.

"Unless you already know how to foxtrot?"

"Do I look like someone who knows how to foxtrot?"

"How would I know?" Axel muttered something under his breath about women never answering the damn question. "Yes or no?"

She was glad he was annoyed. He deserved to be annoyed

for not holding up his end of the bargain. "No."

"Sassafras Dance Studio. Fridays at seven. Be there."

"Fine. But keep this up and we may not be friends after this is over."

Axel shrugged, apparently unwilling to show concern over the fate of their friendship. "Ballroom dance is a useful skill. You'll thank me for this one day."

"Don't count on it."

6

Jori was at the shallow end of the pool hauling a lane divider out of the water in preparation for water aerobics class when the sound of a guest skittering on the slate floor in pool-inappropriate shoes made her glance over. The tight strip of black leather that was meant to be a skirt exposed more bare thigh than she'd seen in her bedroom in far too long, but it was so miniscule that the woman didn't dare take anything but the tiniest trotting steps. She couldn't imagine how uncomfortable that had to be. Women were meant to move, not be trapped by their clothes.

Whatever. Axel had finally talked to their professor and convinced him not to kick her out of the program, and no belt masquerading as a skirt was going to distract her from savoring her victory. He'd done it. And she didn't have to take his word for it—Walston had called her into his office to assure her she was in the clear.

The visitor continued to the far end of the pool where Rae, as usual, was doing her deep-water jogging and yawning. It was too early for sunbathers and there was no one else around, just Rae at one end of the pool and Jori at the other, so when the woman stopped and relaxed against the wrought-iron fence that marked the limits of the extensive patio and pool area, it was obvious that Rae was the one she was staring at.

Rae's back was turned to them both, and she didn't turn

around, either not realizing or not caring that anyone was there. The woman in the leather skirt kept watching, waiting for Rae to notice her. After sixty, ninety seconds of being ignored, she shifted her weight so her breasts pushed subtly forward in Rae's direction.

Jori wasn't sure their visitor was even consciously aware of what she was doing, but she did not want to watch. It was tainting her happy morning.

So why was she? It was none of her business who Rae was friends with. If they were even friends. Jori coiled up the lane divider, lining up the floats with more attention than she usually bothered with. Maybe the woman didn't know Rae at all. She looked familiar, actually. Could she be a confused guest looking for the aerobics instructor? Maybe she ought to check. "Can I help you?"

At the sound of Jori's voice, Rae spun around. And spotted their visitor.

"Kaoli?" Rae stopped her endless water jogging and swam toward the mystery woman.

Kaoli. That was an unusual name. Was that...could it be...Kaoli Morgenroth? Oh my God, it *was*. Kaoli Morgenroth's songs weren't overplayed on the radio as often as they ought to be, but she was a huge star. Jori glanced behind her toward the entrance to the fenced-in area, and sure enough, there was a bulky man—a bodyguard?—standing by the gate acting jumpy. The singer must have ordered him to stay back, because he looked like he wanted to be pacing the perimeter, not lurking behind a potted rosebush.

Kaoli approached the edge of the pool and gazed down at Rae. "Griffin asked me why I had to come down here to check on you and I was like, Griffin! You'll just have to deal."

She looked different without the heavy stage makeup and her trademark leather duster billowing behind her, sweeping the backs of her knees. But her voice—her voice she recognized. It was the voice that had Jori and half the lesbian population swooning. What was she doing here? And how did Rae know her?

Jori realized she was staring and adjusted her floats, trying to play it cool. She might have to check out the parking lot later to see if there was a long, sleek tour bus with Kaoli Morgenroth's name splashed across the side. That would be a fun thing to tell her friends about.

"We're sleeping in different cities anyway, so what does he care if I'm in my tour bus heading for Atlanta or here in Nowheresville, Pennsylvania with you?"

Rae stopped a few feet from the star and treaded water. "You didn't have to visit. That's quite a detour."

It was. Whatever city she'd started in, if it was anywhere near Atlanta, this swimming pool was not on the way.

Kaoli flicked her wrists dismissively. "There's no reason I have to stick with the group. Most of the crew won't even notice I ditched them until I'm back."

Really? They wouldn't notice their star was missing? A production the size of hers was sure to involve several buses to house the performers and crew and several more semitrucks to transport the stage sets, but still. She was the *star*. People probably kept track of her. Although as long as her performance schedule allowed it, maybe there was no reason she couldn't take a side trip and catch up to the group later.

Or maybe she just did whatever the heck she wanted.

"You didn't tell anyone?" Rae said.

"I told them I had a social event I couldn't miss. I'm sure

they thought I meant a party."

"You couldn't tell them the real reason?"

Kaoli leaned forward and teetered precariously close to the edge. "Did you know this dinky town you've hidden yourself away in has its own airfield? I think they have to chase the cows off the runway before people can land."

She had flown. Of course. She didn't have time to divert her tour bus for a two-day roundtrip. That meant no splashy vehicle to gawk at.

"Convenient, though," Kaoli said. "Because I need to talk to you. I have news."

Kaoli wiggled excitedly and Rae drifted closer as if the wiggling was doing something for her. The only thing it was doing for Jori was pissing her off, closing her throat with something that felt remarkably like jealousy.

Was Kaoli flirting with Rae? As far as anyone knew, Kaoli had a boyfriend, but her vague comments on the topic of her sexuality fed rampant speculation. If she ever did come out, the lesbian community would welcome her with open arms.

Rae reached the side of the pool and clung to the coping with both hands. She could probably see up Kaoli Morgenroth's skirt. Not that she would want to.

"It's a secret, but…" Kaoli bent her knees and sat on her heels, balancing on her stilettos and challenging the stretch of her microskirt to get as close as possible to Rae's ear. It was a miracle she didn't fall into the water. She paused to glance in Jori's direction, but with a turn of her head seemed to decide that the uninteresting pool employee wouldn't hear. She was wrong about Jori's auditory powers, though, because her voice was a lot louder than a whisper. Wouldn't be surprising if her hearing had been damaged by years of giving concerts and she didn't know the volume of her own voice anymore.

"Griffin and I are getting married. The ceremony's being held at a secret location in the Bahamas."

Married? So much for the rumors. Unless she'd misheard the name? No, she was pretty sure she'd heard her say *Griffin*, and Griffin was a boy's name. Too bad.

"Congratulations." Rae didn't sound particularly thrilled. "Griffin must be overjoyed. He's been waiting for this a long time."

He. Definitely a boy.

"So. Will you choreograph our wedding dance?"

"Me?" Rae ran a startled hand over her wet hair. "Why me? Don't you want Lorenzo to do it?"

"Lorenzo's a snob. Don't get me wrong, he's a great choreographer. He does a great job for the show. That's why I keep him. But it's no secret how he feels about my dancing abilities." Her voice dropped to a masculine register. "'Sing, Kaoli! Don't dance.'" She made a disgusted face. "I'm not going to involve him in my wedding if I don't have to." She rose and nudged Rae's arm with her toe. "I like you better."

"Thanks. I think. But you have plenty of other people you could ask."

"They're busy. You're not."

Because she wasn't working? That was kind of rude. Rae was busy doing other things, namely rehabilitating her leg. Which was more important than stringing together dance steps for a wedding she was surely not even invited to.

"What am I keeping you on payroll for if you can't perform? This way I get my money's worth." Kaoli paused, letting the threat sink in. "*Some* of my money's worth."

Rae worked for her. How had Jori not realized this? She'd assumed Rae's "dance injury" was something she got from goofing around, but it wasn't. She was a real dancer. For

Kaoli Morgenroth. Who was famous and could hire anyone she wanted. Wow.

"So will you do it? Will you choreograph our first dance?"

Did Rae have a choice?

"I've never done ballroom dancing," Rae said, apparently not ready to concede, despite Kaoli's threat to her paycheck. "Ballet and jazz and hip hop, sure. But none of that is exactly wedding dance material."

"It doesn't have to be real ballroom dancing. It's not like Griffin and I want to do an official waltz. Just throw some cool steps together."

Kaoli braced her hands on her thighs. The vibe she was putting out was very comfortable, very familiar, very I-know-you-want-me-but-there's-no-way-in-hell-I'm-getting-back-in-bed-with-you-so-I'll-taunt-you-instead. Very ex-lover. Could they be ex-lovers? Jori bit down on the inside of her cheek by accident. Ow.

"Please?" Kaoli said.

"I guess I could fake it," Rae said.

Jori shook her head. *Don't cave, sunshine.* She didn't know what their relationship was like, but it wasn't hard to figure out Kaoli Morgenroth was no good for her.

Kneeling in that damn skirt must not have been a problem, because there she went again. This time, Kaoli gripped the edge of the tile and kissed Rae on the forehead.

Rae shot back, away from her. A wall of displaced water splashed behind her.

Kaoli slowly stood, seemingly unperturbed by Rae's reaction. Maybe she knew Rae couldn't escape—that she had her trapped in the pool. And if Rae did try to leave, it would be in agonizing slow motion, limping on her bad leg. Kaoli smoothed the leather which had, against all probability, managed to stay where it was supposed to. "Will two weeks from now work? I should be able to drag Griffin out here the week after that, but I was thinking you could teach me everything first by myself, give me a head start. If I can get a room, that is. This place is surprisingly hard to reserve. How do they get so many visitors?"

"I think there's a hotel in town," Rae said.

"I saw it. It looks like a bedbug incident waiting to happen."

"Then crash on my sofa. Griffin can sleep on the floor."

Bad idea, sunshine.

Kaoli made a face. She'd probably never slept on a sofa in her life. "By the way, Griffin can only make it for one rehearsal. He's afraid he'll miss important breaking news if he's not at work."

"One rehearsal? Tell him he'd better be a fast learner."

Kaoli's pleased smile made Jori not like her very much. "I knew you'd do it."

———

What was she *doing?* Signing up to spend time alone with Kaoli? Rae splashed as she treaded water, less coordinated than she'd like.

And what was Kaoli doing? Why would she kiss her? On the forehead, yes, which was maybe not a big deal in Kaoli's mind, but Rae's body couldn't seem to tell the difference between a friendly kiss on the forehead and a passionate one anywhere else. There had been a time when she would have swooned for weeks over a kiss on the forehead.

She wasn't swooning now. More like squirming. The squirming was self-defense, an instinctual reminder to stay far, far away from this person she'd wasted too many hours on in high school, waiting for the next confusing peck on the cheek, the next secret smile, the next ambiguous touch.

Because Kaoli was straight.

More or less.

She'd hoped for *less* straight for a long, long time, but somehow *less straight* never meant *go all the way and have sex with my good friend Rae*, it only meant *flirt with her* and *lead her on* and *make her absolutely fricking crazy because I'm STRAIGHT*. Maybe straight.

It was all coming back to her, the way Kaoli would lie propped up on her elbows on the wall-to-wall carpeting in the Morgenroths' den with her trigonometry textbook open in front of her and Rae would sit cross-legged beside her, patiently explaining how to calculate the cosine while Kaoli sighed and tossed her shiny blond hair over her shoulder, sending whiffs of strawberry-scented shampoo her way.

"Can't you just let me copy off you?" Kaoli would whine. "It would be so much easier."

"That would be cheating," Rae would say. Not because of any moral conviction, but because she knew if she let Kaoli copy off her, that would be the end of their tutoring, and tutoring Kaoli was not something she wanted to give up. If it meant she had to sound like a nerd, so be it.

Kaoli rolled on the floor, obliterating the smooth lines in the carpet that were evidence of recent vacuuming, stretching like a cat and bumping against Rae's thigh. She pouted, looking up at her in entreaty. Rae held her breath, praying Kaoli couldn't tell that the feel of her pressed against her thigh was making her melt.

Except part of her was also praying she *could* tell.

Staying unnecessarily low to the ground, Kaoli reached

across Rae's lap for her guitar. Her budding breasts brushed against her leg.

Rae was dying. She didn't know exactly where she wanted to touch her, or how, but she wanted to. Not that she would ever get the chance. Kaoli would not be cool with it.

Cradling her guitar, Kaoli rolled onto her back and rested her head on Rae's thigh like it was her personal pillow, then adjusted another quarter-turn and settled in the crease of her hip. She felt perfect there. Rae stroked her hair. She was in heaven, staring into Kaoli's eyes, afraid to breathe for fear of breaking the spell.

This was so much better than helping friends from dance class pin their hair into a bun. This was real. This was...different. She was allowed to appreciate the silkiness of Kaoli's hair and touch it as slowly as she wanted, and no one was spilling hairpins into her hands and ordering her to hurry.

Kaoli nestled deeper into her lap and strummed a few chords. "No one will find out."

Find out what? That Rae had her fingers in her hair and Kaoli was rubbing her body against her in the den while Kaoli's parents were upstairs?

"Raaaaae," Kaoli complained impatiently.

The homework. Kaoli was talking about the homework. No one would find out if Rae let her copy the homework. But she couldn't let her do that.

"Do you really want to bomb the test?"

"Oh, all right."

Kaoli's parents loved Rae because Rae was the reason their daughter was suddenly getting A's in math. They thought Rae was a math whiz. Maybe one day Rae would look back on this and feel bad about not correcting them, but right now she was willing to pretend whatever the hell she had to pretend to keep Kaoli brushed up against her and not running away screaming. And trig was the perfect excuse. The longer it took to help her with the homework, the more time she got to spend with her stretched out on the floor. Alone.

So what if it meant Rae had to beg her older sister to explain the homework to her first and pore over the textbook for hours, praying that the numbers would start to make sense? Whatever she had to do, it was worth it.

Kaoli was counting on her. And Rae was happy to oblige.

Rae was over her now.

And Kaoli and Griffin were all grown up and getting married. Overachieving, self-important Griffin, the little shit who'd boasted all through high school that Kaoli would always be his, was marrying her. Well, good for him.

Rae hauled herself out of the pool and collapsed onto one of the long deck chairs. The chairs weren't the usual cheap stuff, but were instead these sleek works of art that looked like deep lilac bubbles. Rounded bottom, long curving leg…very feminine. Kind of made her wonder what Sierra and Melanie were thinking when they picked these out. She stretched out and made sure her injured leg was positioned the way she wanted it. Kaoli dragged over a chair for herself, scraping it across the slate and butting it against Rae's. Rae repositioned her leg, irritated with herself for being unable to look away from the practiced perfection with which Kaoli swiveled in her skimpy skirt to perch on her chair.

"Can Griffin dance at all?" Kaoli's own dance abilities were no mystery—Rae saw her onstage or in rehearsal every day. Kaoli might not have any advanced technical skills, but her sensuality combined with her crazy self-confidence and an ability to memorize steps meant she could fake her way through almost anything and her fans didn't know or care that she wasn't up to a real dancer's standards. Her fiancé, however…

"Griffin will do what I tell him."

"That's not what I asked."

"He'll figure it out," Kaoli said.

With only one rehearsal? Good luck.

"I'll keep it simple." Very simple. It was going to be interesting to see how she was going to teach anyone any steps at all if her ankle and knee weren't better. Which they wouldn't be, not in two weeks. How was she even supposed to figure out the choreography? It was hard to do that sort of thing in her head when she'd never studied ballroom dancing and wasn't sure which leg or arm was supposed to go where. But she couldn't tell Kaoli that. Kaoli was her boss, and if her boss wanted her to choreograph a dance for her, she'd do it, and do it without complaining.

"Simple is fine," Kaoli said. "Just make us look good."

"I'll do my best."

"Simple but flashy. You know what I like."

Rae resisted the urge to sigh. No wonder Lorenzo, their choreographer, was always snarling. "No limping or hopping, right?"

Kaoli frowned. Her gaze lingered on Rae's leg and Rae felt the urge to throw a towel over herself to hide the scars. At least she wasn't wearing her brace. Why had she made that stupid joke, anyway? The last thing she wanted was to remind her she was injured.

"How's the knee, by the way?"

Rae grimaced. Maybe part of her had wanted to force Kaoli to acknowledge that she was hurt. Because shouldn't this have been the first thing Kaoli asked, not some kind of afterthought? Sympathy had never been one of her good qualities, though. It wasn't huge for any performer. Faced with a colleague with a potentially career-ending injury, most performers averted their eyes, unwilling to deal with the fear that they could be next. Their own illusion of invincibility required it. The fact that Kaoli was visiting her at all was unusual.

"Improving. I should be on my feet real soon."

"And dancing?" Kaoli leaned forward, even though their chairs were already close enough to be touching, and rested her hand on Rae's thigh.

Rae tensed. It wasn't just her thigh that tensed— everything tensed. "Soon."

She missed dancing. The physical therapist she'd abandoned when she'd left for Pennsylvania had talked about getting to the point where she could walk again, but Rae didn't care about walking. Walking was for losers. She was going to run. Jump. Spin. Dance. If she couldn't dance, why bother? Since the minute she'd dropped out of high school and begun her professional dance career, she'd never dared jinx herself by considering what she'd do the day she had to stop dancing, and she wasn't going to start now. She wasn't going to wonder if trying college at her age with a bunch of eighteen-year-olds would be better than being stuck for the rest of her life teaching ballet to kids whose healthy young bodies would remind her every day of what she'd lost, or whether she'd have the money to even have that choice. She wasn't going to think about it because she didn't need to. She had a job. She was a backup dancer for a rising star destined to become one of the biggest names in music, and in a few weeks her knee would be healed and her ankle would be all better because she'd make sure of it, and then she'd be back at her job, proving what she could do in front of thousands of screaming, panty-throwing fans.

Kaoli squeezed her thigh a little too hard. "I don't want to be an ogre and remind you your contract is up for renewal in a few weeks, but I can't keep you if you're not ready to perform. I've got an empty bunk in the dancers' bus with your name on it that I can't afford to keep empty."

"I'm working on it." A few weeks? She had all summer and through early fall before the tour ended and contracts were renegotiated. That was more than a few weeks. It wasn't long, but it would be enough. It would have to be. "I'll be ready."

"Mmm." Kaoli's hand on her leg, which had felt so threatening a minute ago, now felt warm and concerned. Intimate. Gentle. Kaoli's warmth seeped into her skin. Oh no, not this. Not...

Too late. All the feelings from high school came flooding back. She'd thought she was over her, but all it took was one touch to show her she wasn't.

Damn body. Why now? She'd been dancing for Kaoli for two seasons and not once had she allowed herself to imagine that getting too close to her was a good idea. A few minutes of fantasizing was acceptable. A flush of excitement when Kaoli went onstage and turned on the charisma, or when the entire audience fell into synch with her and sang along? Harmless. But Kaoli had kept her distance, and Rae had done the same, and somehow, despite being old friends, they'd never been alone together, never gone out for coffee by themselves or hung out in Kaoli's tour bus or had a private moment backstage. Which was how Rae wanted it. She didn't trust herself. She didn't want to ever give the other dancers a reason to whisper that the only reason she got the job was because she was a personal friend of Kaoli's. A *very* personal friend. Going out of her way to avoid bumping into her was the only failsafe solution.

And now? Now Kaoli was getting married, and Rae wanted to throw herself at her because of one flirtatious touch.

But she wouldn't. She was no homewrecker.

Her inner bullshit meter laughed at that, reminding her how hard she'd tried to lure Kaoli away from her boyfriend when they were teenagers.

But was it really poaching if the girl's relationship with her boyfriend was shallow and passionless? Because Kaoli had never really had strong feelings for Griffin, not when she'd put so much energy into stringing Rae along on the side. And he was a boy, right? Automatic deduction of points for being a boy.

Kaoli rubbed Rae's thigh. "I miss you onstage. Let's have lunch. Dinner. I'd love to catch up."

"Of course."

Kaoli broke the contact and Rae could finally breathe. Kaoli wasn't usually like this these days. Never, as a matter of fact.

Think, Rae. Think. Remember what she did to you.

She glanced across the pool at Jori. Her aerobics students had arrived and she was splashing around waving a foam dumbbell to demonstrate a move, having fun. As tempting as Kaoli was, Rae had a feeling she'd rather have the imprint of Jori's hand tingling on her thigh.

Too bad she wasn't listening to that feeling right now. Instead, she was listening to her inner idiot, who wanted another chance with Kaoli. Her inner rationalizing idiot, who would obviously tell herself absolutely anything—like that Kaoli and Griffin didn't love each other—to convince herself this was okay.

The problem was, she'd wanted Kaoli so bad for so long, she couldn't turn it off.

7

After Kaoli left in the wake of Jori's water aerobics students, Rae counted down twenty more minutes before retreating to the locker room adjacent to the pool. The students had cleared out but the air was still heavy with warm steam from their showers. The only person who remained was Jori, who was pulling her gym bag out of an open locker three spots away and catching a thick textbook as it banged the metal wall of the unit and threatened to tumble out. Not that Rae was paying attention, but the title was something about corporate accounting. Huh. Math. That shouldn't be a turn-on, but it kind of was.

Rae leaned her crutches against one of the long wooden benches lined up between the walls of lockers and punched in the four-digit code that opened her unit. Her crutches slid sideways one after the other and clattered to the floor, the sound bouncing off the tile. She turned, but Jori was already there, her body able to act on reflexes that Rae's injury wouldn't allow, the crutches in her hands before Rae had even taken a step.

Smart *and* nice.

And all of it wasted on a boyfriend.

"Thanks," Rae said. "You didn't have to do that."

Jori propped up the crutches in a corner where they wouldn't fall. "How's the knee? Or…it's your ankle, too, right?"

"They both hate me right now." She was used to being exhausted and in pain all the time, but she preferred to be exhausted and in pain because she was dancing, not because she was injured.

"Do you need help getting in the shower?"

Only if you're not straight. Rae smiled at the thought. Two women hitting on her in a single day—that would be a personal record. Before she knew it, women would be waving their arms and screaming with joy and throwing panties at her like they did at her boss. Except Jori wasn't hitting on her. Kaoli had been, but Kaoli didn't count, either, because she hadn't meant her to take it seriously.

"Awkward, right?" Jori said when Rae didn't answer immediately. "I know. How about something less awkward—help getting back to your room."

Rae shook her head.

Jori clapped her hands over her mouth as if she could take the words back. "I didn't mean help getting back to your room like I was inviting myself in or anything. I meant drop you off at your door. No going in the room."

Too bad, because she was adorable. "I'll be fine."

"Okay," Jori said. "But tell me something. How long has Kaoli Morgenroth been conning you with that wiggle move?"

"What wiggle move?" Rae said, even though she suspected she knew. Kaoli did have a certain stripper-pole style. What surprised her was that Jori had noticed. And what did she mean, conning her? The days when Kaoli could con her into anything were long past.

"You know, the wiggle. She sticks her chest out, she wiggles what she's got, she kisses you on the forehead, and you agree to do whatever she wants, like create some cool dance steps for her and oh, I don't know, do her laundry. I'll bet it works on all the girls."

Jori was joking, but it didn't sound like a joke. Underneath her light tone she sounded angry, and Rae was not in the mood to be judged.

"How would *you* know? You're straight."

"I'm…" Jori looked at her quizzically. "What makes you think I'm straight?"

"I saw you in the lobby leaving with that guy, flirting with him." Touching him. Clinging to him, laughing up at him. There was no way Jori was going to pull that innocent act like Kaoli always had, convincing clueless Rae that her relationship with her boyfriend wasn't important.

"Axel? We're not dating. I'm just helping him convince his parents he has a girlfriend. I'm his stunt date."

Rae didn't believe her. Pretend to date a man? A lesbian would freeze men out, not flirt with them and pretend to be their girlfriend. Ah, but note she never said she wasn't straight. She only said she wasn't dating Axel. She was cryptically vague, and it was probably deliberate. Which normally would be a point in her favor on the gay side, but not this time. Rae couldn't afford to fall for another straight girl who thought it would feel good to soak up a naïve little lesbian's devoted attention. It wasn't worth it.

"I don't care if you're straight."

Jori's eyes widened. "That's very broadminded of you, sunshine."

"Straight, not straight, whatever. It's none of my business."

"It's not a secret. Axel did me a huge favor and I'm paying him back. I'm not sleeping with him."

"You don't have to explain." She didn't want her to explain. She didn't want to know.

Jori hesitated, then shrugged. "That doesn't mean I wouldn't sleep with him if I wanted to."

Straight. Just like she thought. A straight woman with a misleading gay vibe, but straight nonetheless.

Then why did she keep thinking Jori would never put up with being pinned beneath that bear? Or whatever man she really *was* dating.

"Men, women…we're all just people," Jori said.

Until it's time to choose, of course.

"Some more attractive than others," Jori added, still grumpy but showing no sign of leaving. "Especially when they give me the sexy death glare."

So maybe she wasn't straight. Maybe she was bi. Like Kaoli. Rae did not need a rerun of Kaoli.

Jori gathered up her shampoo and conditioner. "If you change your mind about needing help getting back to your room…to, you know, the hallway outside the door to your room…I think I'm right down the hall from you…Were you going up to your room right away? Because I was going to shower before I get dressed."

"I'm showering here, too. My room has a bathtub that's hard to step into. The showers here are easier." Easier, yes. But now she felt awkward about stripping off her swimsuit, suddenly acutely aware that the locker room was empty except for the two of them.

"I'll wait for you after you're done." Jori disappeared into one of the individual shower stalls and drew the curtain shut behind her.

Problem solved. Rae removed her swimsuit and hobbled into the empty adjoining stall, careful not to slip on the wet floor, cursing the pain in her leg.

"You okay?" Jori asked over the sound of running water.

Her knee, Rae reminded herself. Jori was asking about her knee. Jori was over there in the very next stall completely naked with her hands rubbing shampoo out of that sexy shock of hair, eyes closed, face tilted upward, and thinking about…Rae's knee.

"I hate how weak I am. My muscles are gone." She couldn't wait to have two calves that were the same size again instead of one that had wasted away until it was skinny and useless. She turned on the shower.

"You'll get your strength back."

She'd better. She needed to get it back ASAP or her job was history.

Jori raised her voice over the noise of water droplets splattering on tile. "Maybe if you went back to your physical therapist and let them help you…"

Her physical therapist? The one who had frowned at her ankle's range of motion and told her that her joints wouldn't be so unstable if she wasn't so excessively flexible, then sent her home with a printout of exercises to do on her own—exercises any decent athlete would already be familiar with? On her way out, Rae had thrown the printout in the trash. Dancers were supposed to be flexible. If her flexibility was off the charts—charts that had no doubt been designed with football or hockey players in mind—then something was wrong with the charts, not with her.

"She doesn't understand dancers." If she did, she'd have understood that being flexible didn't mean she wasn't also strong.

"Then find another one," Jori said. "One who can help you."

Rae glared at the shower wall. Jori had a lot of faith in those people, didn't she?

"One who specializes in dancers," Jori added.

Did people like that exist? She'd never really considered the possibility. Maybe she should have. After all, her surgeon had done a good job. Had treated her like a real athlete. Maybe there were other people who would, too.

Although at this point, she didn't really need help. She just had to keep working hard.

When she emerged from the shower, Jori had already changed into dry clothes and was blow-drying her fauxhawk. Rae hobbled past her and caught a blast of hot air from the blow-dryer. The smell of burnt hair mixed with a whiff of cocoa butter body lotion. She should have kept her dressing room blinders on and not looked, but Jori was dressed, and honestly, it didn't even occur to her to be good. With Jori's arms over her head and her comb pulling through her tuft of hair and her skin flushed from the heat of the shower, she looked soft and pink and blond and feminine, not at all the image she projected when she taught. Blond, yes. Huggable, yes. But not vulnerable. Seeing her like this made Rae want to reach over ever so gently and smooth her cotton tank top, slide her hands down her sides until she reached the hem, help her out of her top, and...yeah, that was inappropriate.

Rae toweled off and kept moving, whipping on a camisole without bothering with a bra. The cami stuck to her damp skin and the hem rolled under itself and jammed, leaving her navel exposed, but she was in too much of a rush to fix it so she just left it there. Underwear was easy enough to step into, but her pants weren't, even though they were stretch. She needed to get them on before Jori turned around and saw her sitting on the bench, struggling awkwardly to maneuver her weak leg into the leg holes. She hated being reduced to a toddler's skill level at getting dressed. If only she'd brought a skirt. A skirt she could pull on over her head and yank down to her waist instead of trying to guide her foot into a flimsy target without moving her knee wrong. Even shorts might have been easier, but she preferred not to have to see her surgical scars, even when the summer heat made shorts a logical choice.

"Wow, look at those abs," Jori said as Rae stood and finished pulling her uncooperative pants the rest of the way up. Apparently Jori didn't have the same qualms about looking, and didn't care if Rae knew it. "I know you just said you don't think you have any muscle, but…wow. And I'm not just saying that to make you feel better."

"Thanks." Maybe her abs were okay, but the rest of her?

Jori turned off the blow-dryer and kept her gaze fixed commendably on Rae's eyes. "That's a compliment, you know. You don't have to look embarrassed."

Rae zipped up her pants. Jori's gaze flickered downward for an instant and Rae's hand froze on her waistband, as aware of her as if she were *un*zipping her pants.

Jori was straight, Jori was straight, Jori was straight…

She so didn't believe that anymore.

"I'm not embarrassed."

"Now if you had a hairy stomach, that would be embarrassing."

"Excuse me?"

Jori was definitely not making an effort to look her in the eye anymore, but was quite blatantly checking out her bare abdomen. If only she'd been faster and taken the few seconds it would have taken to untwist her cami, she wouldn't look half-dressed. Rae yanked on her cami but couldn't get the hem free.

"I mean, of course you don't, you're a woman. You don't

have that trail of hair going down." Jori leaned closer and squinted. "You don't, right?"

Rae flushed. Jori did realize her head was unnervingly close to her waist, right? Which was right above her...her...

She could say the word. To herself. Just not when Jori was this close to...

"Some women have a few fine hairs," Rae pointed out.

Jori straightened. "But not like men. Which is a good thing, in my opinion. I don't get why women think that's sexy."

Rae debated whether she should answer that one or not. Surely Jori knew. "Because it's, like, pointing to...?"

Jori smiled and fluttered her eyelids. "You know it."

Rae flushed again.

"It's leading the way." Jori lowered her voice to a suggestive pitch that had Rae's abdominals clenching. "Personally, I can find it without help."

————

Beyond the yoga barn lay a network of dirt paths with please-do-not-enter offshoots to the owners' private cabin, the maintenance yard, and other areas of the property. Eventually the paths joined and became a nature trail leading farther into the woods. It was a good place for Rae to practice walking because the uneven ground challenged the stability of her ankle without actually being hazardous.

Her knee wasn't doing so great, but her ankle was feeling strong, so she ventured out into the afternoon heat without her crutches. She could do it. She wouldn't go far. And if she mastered her balance on dirt, the locker room floor would be easy. It had better be, because limping in front of Jori had been an embarrassing experience she didn't want to repeat.

It was cooler in the shade of the woods, but it was hard to enjoy it because her knee already hurt. Then her ankle, which had started out fine, weakened and throbbed and—God, no—wobbled. Her breath caught in her throat. She could *not* twist her ankle and set her progress back. She *would* not. She refused.

Best to return to the lodge before things got any worse and she was forced to crawl back. If crawling was even possible. Maybe she'd manage slithering. She really didn't want to find out. Perhaps leaving her crutches behind might have been a mistake. Well, not to worry—she hadn't reached that point. Yet. She had a massage scheduled in an hour, though, so she really did need to get back. If she was early she could hang out in her room or park herself in the lobby and wait. It wouldn't kill her to sit and do nothing but rest for a bit. She could always practice ankle flexes if resting became too tedious.

She spied a fallen tree branch a little way off that looked sturdy enough to use as a walking stick, so she slowly—cautiously—stepped off the path and grabbed it. It was a good height. The bark was uncomfortable in her palm, but the relief of having something to lean on was so great that she barely noticed. The stick was perfect, and with its help, she made it back to the lodge without cursing.

In the lobby, Sierra—her host—was on the floor playing Twister with a preschooler whose wispy blond hair was escaping from a ponytail that had started that morning on the top of her head but was now listing to one side. The girl's foot was sliding off one of the vinyl playing mat's red circles. Sierra, yoga teacher that she was, was balanced in a beautiful position that looked a lot like something she'd seen her students do. Downward-facing dog pose?

"Are you babysitting?" Rae asked.

"Just watching Baylee for a few minutes until her mother gets back." Sierra quirked her head up but didn't move from her upside-down position. "Are you coming to the party tomorrow night? Everyone's invited."

"What party?" In the short time she'd been here she'd learned the place was constantly abuzz with scheduled guest activities, but Rae had other things to worry about than keeping track of it all.

"It's a chance for the workshop attendees to show off the costumes they've been working on all week."

"Costumes?" Seriously, Rae could *not* keep track.

"For Creative Sewing?"

"Right." It was always something around here, and not just yoga: Painting the sacred journey. Songwriting for the soul. Drumming, which had been loud enough to hear across the entire property and made her miss dancing with an ache that had kept her in a foul mood for days. Apparently it went on all year, as each week a new group of women descended on the Mountain Laurel Center to feed their obsession with whatever the theme of the hour was.

"There are leftover supplies on a table in the back of one of the multipurpose rooms if you want to make something to wear."

"I don't think—"

"I made my costume yesterday," the girl—Baylee—said.

Great. The kid was going to guilt her into sewing something that wasn't a dance slipper's elastic.

"What did you make?" Rae asked. It wasn't the child's fault Rae was grumpy. It was her ankle's fault. And her knee's.

"It's a surprise," Baylee said.

"See?" Sierra said. "You'll have to come to the party so Baylee can show you her costume."

"Do you want to play Twister?" Baylee asked.

"Uh…" Rae stammered.

"You'd be good at it," Sierra said, all too eager to con her into joining them.

"I'm kind of having a little trouble with my leg right now." Rae lowered herself into an upholstered chair that was conveniently right there.

"If you can't stand on your leg you can do handstands," Baylee suggested.

"Excellent idea. Maybe next time." Rae rubbed her knee. Sitting had been a mistake, because sitting meant she would have to stand again if she wanted to continue to her room, and standing was the last thing she wanted to do now that she'd taken her weight off her leg.

Baylee snatched the spinner board from the floor and set it in motion. "Left hand on blue."

"I think that spin is for you, Miss Peters," Sierra told Rae with a smirk.

"Sierra—"

"I'm not getting *my* hand over to blue," Sierra said.

Right. Like Little Miss Yoga Instructor couldn't easily reach any spot on the mat.

"But I bet *you* could," Sierra said.

Rae sighed. She heaved her exhausted body out of the chair and gingerly lowered herself to the floor and placed her left hand on a blue circle.

A few spins later Rae was sitting in a semi-split with her right foot on red and her left foot on green, her legs comfortably straight so she wouldn't risk bending her knee wrong, and laughing as she tried to convince Baylee and Sierra there was nothing in the rules that said she couldn't keep her derrière on the ground—the game only disqualified players for falling, and since she'd started out on the floor, she hadn't technically fallen.

"Sitting makes the game harder," Rae insisted.

"Only for people who can't touch their toes," Sierra said.

"I can touch my toes!" Baylee jumped from her pose to demonstrate. She stuck her head between her knees and beamed with pride, oblivious to the fact that her knees were ridiculously bent.

"This is the last time I play Twister with someone as flexible as you, Baylee," Rae grumbled.

"Because you're not used to not winning?" Sierra said.

Baylee giggled.

"Your turn, Sierra," Rae said.

Baylee spun for her, but before she could call out her move she got distracted by something and popped up with a yelp of excitement. She barreled past on her little feet, heading for the double doors at the entrance.

Rae leaned back and looked over her shoulder to see what had caught Baylee's attention. It was Jori, sauntering toward them with a sexy grace that made it hard to believe she wasn't a dancer. Was Jori another one of Baylee's babysitters? Or…no, she couldn't be this girl's…

"Mommy!" Baylee shouted.

Jori scooped her up and swung her in a circle. Yes, apparently she *was* the girl's mother.

"Mommy, can we go now?"

Jori hugged her and lowered her to the ground.

"Oh hi," Jori said, spotting Rae. "I see Baylee talked you into playing." She turned to Sierra. "Thanks for watching her."

"Anytime." Sierra rose from another one of her yogic poses and retrieved the box the game belonged in.

Jori bent to pick up the playing mat, but Rae beat her to it, then busied herself folding the mat into a small square.

Jori had a daughter. She didn't know why it should be a surprise, but it was. She'd been so sure Jori was flirting with her. But flirting didn't mean anything. Not that having a kid meant anything, either. But then there was that man she'd seen her with... Not that *that* meant anything, either. But the signs were adding up, and even though part of her was urging her to ignore those signs, she knew what they meant.

When was she going to learn to stop doing this to herself? To become intrigued by someone she couldn't have? Someone she didn't *want* to have. Because even if Jori was working both sides of the fence and Rae maybe *could* have her, she didn't want someone who thought she wanted a lesbian relationship but really didn't.

She was too old for that. She really was. She knew better.

8

The party was in full swing by the time Jori and Baylee reached the pool. The patio area was packed with women in costume, and the shallow end of the pool overflowed with swimsuit-clad partyers chatting and drinking cocktails in waist- to chest-high water that glowed with purple underwater lights like a jewel in the night. Sierra was easy to spot by the makeshift bar, as was her partner, Melanie, who was chatting with a knot of guests. They were both dressed as poodles with a mop of yarn curls on top of their heads and a fabric, batting-stuffed tail with an oversize pom-pom at the end.

Jori had laughed when she'd seen the fabric and sewing supplies Sierra had invited her to use to make costumes. That was her—a mom who had time to sew. She'd found a discarded cardboard box instead and cut it into two triangles. Baylee had drawn the pepperoni and cheese with crayons and they'd turned Jori into a slice of pizza. Baylee's costume was just as sad—a Maryland blue crab with blue crepe paper streamers wrapped around her waist and pinned to her shoulders where they dangled loose as extra arms, a pair of blue felt-covered tongs—glued, not sewn—in her hand as a makeshift claw, and a profusion of shiny ribbons in her hair because crabs liked to be pretty.

"Come on," Jori told Baylee. "Let's see if there are any kids here you can play with." It was unlikely there would be, because the workshop people never brought kids, but there were always a few guests staying at the lodge who were passing through and weren't participating in whatever the workshop of the week was, and sometimes they had children in tow, so it was worth a look.

She scanned the crowd, guiding her daughter in close so she was pressed to her leg, protecting her from being jostled by people who might not look down and notice a little girl. A witch, an astronaut, a robot, a princess in an ornate ball gown…but no kids. That was too bad, but Baylee would be fine by her side for a while, and once she reached her limit, they could always leave. So, what next? Not the pool, not without their swimsuits. The bar might have snacks, but reaching the bar might be difficult with all the people packed in front of it. There were so many people…

Jori's gaze landed on Rae and stopped. Rae was balanced on the edge of one of the bubble-shaped lounge chairs, leaning back on her elbow in a comfortable, graceful pose, chatting with a woman in a cupcake costume. Rae was dressed as some kind of bird in a clingy white sleeveless, below-the-knee dress and a baseball cap she'd fitted with a cardboard beak and eyes made out of ping-pong balls. Her legs were crossed at the knee, and she swung her free leg in a lazy arc, dangling a flat sandal from her toes, skillfully maneuvering it on and off her heel. Jori leaned against the patio's wrought-iron fence and watched, fascinated, waiting for the sandal to fall to the ground, but Rae's foot and ankle were as coordinated and flexible as the rest of her. If Jori were that cupcake, she'd never guess Rae was injured.

Jori pushed off from the fence and approached, Baylee dragging at her side, before she realized what she was doing and came to a halt. Just because Rae was one of the only people she knew here didn't mean she had to go talk to her, especially when Rae was already having a conversation with someone else. She should mingle. Move randomly through the crowd. Keep Baylee occupied by guessing all the costumes. Jori was good at making conversation with strangers. Liked it, even. New people could be so interesting.

But before she knew it she had subconsciously made her way toward Rae. It didn't feel random.

The cupcake wandered off. Rae noticed Jori and smiled, and Jori forgot all about mingling. Rae slipped her feet out of her sandals and tucked one leg underneath her. It made her look like a model in one of those furniture ads where a barefoot woman, looking sexy yet wholesome, curled up on a spotless sofa and draped herself over the back of it like a man's fantasy that traditionally involved a woman on the hood of a sports car. Ads that had never done a thing for Jori besides make her laugh at how ridiculous they were.

She wasn't laughing now. Rae didn't look ridiculous. She looked sexy. And elegant. And stunning.

It kind of made her wish she wasn't dressed as a slice of pizza. An hour ago, allowing her daughter to smear borrowed red makeup on Mommy's face to look like tomato sauce had seemed like a great idea. Now she wished she looked like less of a mess. Because nothing said *dating material* like being dressed as a tomato massacre, especially in a sea of women in beautifully made costumes broken only by Sierra's and Melanie's goofy ones.

Oh well, par for the course. Even when she wasn't wearing a pizza costume, Jori was not exactly what anyone would call classy. Her wardrobe consisted of a ton of cotton and Lycra and not much else. Nice workout clothes, grungy workout clothes, non-workout clothes that worked with athletic shoes… She looked good, but there was something about wearing shorts for every occasion that, sometimes, when she was around people who dressed better, felt not quite presentable. But that was who she was. God knew what she'd do when she became an accountant and had to wear professional business attire.

"Hi, Miss Peters," Baylee said, looking up at Rae. Apparently Baylee was the only one able to speak. "I like your costume."

Rae smiled. "Thank you, Baylee, I like yours, too. Are you a…" She trailed off.

Jori held her breath, praying she'd get it right.

"…crab?" Rae guessed.

How in the world did she—

"I'm a crab!" Baylee waved the tongs that were her crab's claw.

"I love it!" Rae sounded like she really meant it, which made Jori like her even more.

"See my blue nail polish?" Baylee held out her non-claw hand. It was mortifying that a kid of hers would love nail polish, but if it made Baylee happy, she supposed a little mortification was a small price to pay.

"Nice," Rae said.

Baylee spun around to show off her dancing crab moves. Jori moved to protect the bystanders from Baylee's claw and was nearly knocked over by Melanie, who rushed in and swept Baylee off her feet. Baylee giggled and reached for the poodle yarn on top of Melanie's head.

"There's someone I want you to meet," Melanie told Baylee in a voice full of excitement, settling her on her hip and catching Jori's eye to make sure it was okay.

Jori nodded her permission. Melanie pushed through the

crowd to the far side of the patio and lowered Baylee to the ground next to a dachshund dressed as a ballerina with a tutu around its middle and pink ribbons tied to its tail. Baylee stared, then tried to give the dog a hug as it wiggled away from her.

Had Melanie snatched Baylee on purpose so Jori and Rae would be alone? No, of course not. Jori gave herself a mental shake. Melanie didn't know she'd been staring at Rae. Coincidence, that's all it was.

"Baylee's father's not here tonight?" Rae said.

Why would Rae think he'd be here? Was she fishing for information? Trying to figure out how available Jori was? That would be nice. But she'd already told her she and Axel weren't really dating. Oh, right. Rae didn't know who Baylee's father was.

"He wasn't invited," Jori said, staying purposely vague to see just how far Rae would go with her fishing expedition, if that was what this was.

Rae frowned. Jori hoped that was because she didn't like her answer and not because she disapproved of Baylee's father's existence, because she'd better not disapprove of Jori's choices. She'd had good reasons for everything she'd done.

Not that she didn't still find Rae more interesting than a full-time grad student and mother ought to have time for.

"What kind of bird are you?" Jori asked, steering the conversation to less personal ground.

"A seagull," Rae said. "I was trying to think of a costume where hopping with a not very functional leg would look natural."

"A peg-legged pirate," offered Sierra, appearing out of nowhere.

Dang, she'd forgotten there were other people here.

"Jori! Just who I wanted to see." Sierra took Jori by the arm and dragged her away, walking backward and parting the crowd with the tail that jutted from her belt.

Jori didn't know what was up, but she went along with it. She could always talk to Rae later. Or not. There was no need to act like a stalker.

"What's with the giant poodle tail?" Jori asked. "Kind of phallic, isn't it?"

Sierra stopped tugging on her arm for a moment and smirked. "It pains me to be the one to have to explain this to you, because you of all people should know this already, but that part of the body is located in the front."

"Shut up," Jori said. "I'm the only one around here who gets to make obnoxious comments."

"You're rubbing off on me." Sierra stopped in front of the bar, which was really just a long table holding drinks. "Listen, are you a Kaoli Morgenroth fan?"

Speak of the devil. She would have said yes without hesitation three days ago, but now she was wary of what this might be leading up to.

"Isn't everyone?"

"Want to see her in concert in DC in a couple weeks? I have an extra free ticket if you can put up with sitting next to me in the front row."

"Are you serious?"

She'd noticed the ads, but hadn't planned on going. Even if she could afford it, driving four hours for a concert was impractical, even if it was the closest stop on Kaoli Morgenroth's tour. But front-row seats... The invitation didn't include a ticket for Baylee, though, and unless Sierra was better at driving safely long past midnight than Jori was, it would be best to stay the night and drive back the next day. That would make finding a sitter a major challenge. Axel's mother might do it if asked, but Jori would rather not leave her child with someone who claimed to have no interest in being alone with her. Just because Grandma liked the idea of grandchildren didn't mean she wanted to get her hands dirty. Her childrearing days were over, she said, and Jori was fine with that. Axel's mother didn't owe her anything.

"I don't know if I can get a sitter."

"Melanie can watch her," Sierra said. "She loves Baylee."

"Isn't Melanie going with you to the concert?"

Sierra shook her head. "One of us needs to stay here to keep everything running smoothly."

"Then she'll be too busy to watch Baylee."

"She'll only be busy if there's an emergency," Sierra said. "Which there won't be. So don't worry about it."

"I can't ask her to do that. The two of you are already doing so much for me." Housing, a job, babysitting… "I can't accept the ticket. It's too generous."

"It didn't cost me anything. Rae gave us two tickets, and since Melanie's not a big fan and volunteered not to go… Did I mention Rae's going, too?"

Jori glanced across the crowd and found Rae, who was chatting with someone new. Would Rae want her there? She'd invited Sierra and Melanie—not her. "I really can't take the ticket."

"You really can."

"You could return it to Rae."

"I tried that. She won't take it back."

"Don't you have other friends?"

Sierra shrugged. "You're a friend."

Jori took a deep breath. Could she really leave Baylee

overnight with Melanie? Of course she could. Front-row seats were something she might never get another chance at. What the heck. "Okay. Thanks. But why me? I mean, I meant it about the friend thing. You see me every day."

Sierra turned so her unwieldy poodle tail didn't whack the glassware or the rows of glass liquor bottles off the table, angled her head in Rae's direction, and winked. "No reason."

Jori cringed. Did her boss think she wanted an excuse to spend time with Rae? How embarrassing. What did she do? Stare at her? Flirt too much? Wish Kaoli Morgenroth dead and not realize she was doing it out loud?

Sierra leaned across the woman who was taking care of the bar and opened the cash box and fished out the ticket. "Nice costume, by the way. Did you and Rae coordinate?"

"No, why?" Jori took the ticket—VIP seating, amazing— and stared at it. Coordinate? What did that even mean? Rae was an elegant black-and-white seagull and Jori was *not* a black-and-white pizza, but a sloppy brown and red pepperoni mess. There was no color coordination whatsoever.

"Seagulls eat pizza," Sierra said.

What? Oh no. "Promise me you won't say that in front of Rae."

"Too crass? Or too true?"

Jori blushed. She could feel her face burning. "I'm begging you."

"What? I'm kidding." Sierra backed away from the table, carefully maneuvering her tail. "Is something actually going on between you two?"

Great. Sierra had been kidding, and now Jori was going to have to explain that although Rae was intriguing, Rae was totally hung up on her rock-star boss, of all people, so Jori was focusing instead on pretending to date her ex-boyfriend.

Because of the two nonexistent relationships—with Rae and with Axel—the one involving blackmail was less confusing.

"Something *is* going on," Sierra said.

"No, really, it's not."

"I suspect we'll find out at the concert."

Just what she needed—a matchmaker. "If I didn't like Kaoli Morgenroth's music so much, I might give you back your ticket."

Sierra put her hands up, palms out, refusing to take anything back. "It's going to be fun. I'll make sure not to sit in the middle and get between the two of you."

Jori smiled despite herself. Even though nothing romantic would happen, it *would* be fun. In the dark, she could pretend she and Rae were on a date, soak in Rae's presence in the seat next to her, and wonder what it would be like to brush against her knee. It was perfect—she'd get all the excitement of the promise of a relationship with none of the complications. Because the last thing she needed was one more distraction. She already had her hands full with school and Baylee and now Axel. She didn't have time for anything else.

"Run along," Sierra said. "Hurry back to Rae."

Jori stuck the ticket in her pocket. "There's nothing going on."

"Go. Have fun tonight."

Sierra made a shooing motion with her hands and Jori stopped arguing and slipped into the crowd, back toward Rae. She thought she might have heard Sierra laugh.

But someone else reached Rae first.

"Rae Peters? Oh my God, you're Rae Peters." The female vampire in a plunging neckline was almost hyperventilating.

"Uh…" Rae smiled tentatively but politely, the kind of

smile a politician would put on when she met a constituent and didn't yet know whether she was going to be hugged or yelled at. "How are you?"

"You're Kaoli Morgenroth's girlfriend, right?"

Everyone within earshot turned to look, their faces full of curiosity. Jori stared, too, but not out of curiosity—it was more like shock. What exactly had happened after Kaoli's visit? Hadn't Kaoli said she was engaged to a man? Wasn't Kaoli her *boss*? And wouldn't Rae or Sierra or somebody have at least mentioned this?

"I'm…what?" Rae looked confused. "Uh…no."

"Oh." The woman's face fell. "You look just like her."

"I look just like…" She frowned. "What are you talking about?"

The vampire produced a smartphone from a pocket in her shredded skirt and swiped at the screen. "Here." She thrust the phone in Rae's direction.

Jori moved in to see. It was a photo of Kaoli Morgenroth kneeling at the edge of a swimming pool, hands on the tile for balance, kissing Rae on the forehead. The headline read: "Kaoli Morgenroth can't stay away from her secret girlfriend: visits to injured backup dancer threaten to derail concert schedule."

Wait. She'd been there when that photo was taken. That was their pool. This very patio. Their pool was famous. Wait until she told Sierra.

But the headline—that was wrong. A fraction of a second after that photo was taken, Rae had been halfway across the pool, flinching from the unwanted contact. Where was the real headline? *Thank-you kiss not appreciated.* Or how about: *Kaoli Morgenroth toys with struggling dancer's affections.* And how did anyone manage to take that photo, anyway? There had been no one else there but herself and Kaoli's bodyguard.

"A telephoto lens," Rae said, echoing her thoughts. "Kaoli is not going to be happy about this."

"You *are* Rae Peters," said the vampire. "This is so great! They're saying that song that's on the radio constantly—'Sex Goddess'—is about her new, first-time-ever girlfriend. You! She says now she understands why men like women so much." She threw her arm around Rae's shoulders and posed as she thrust her phone out. "Mind if I take a picture?"

"She...what?" Rae's face froze with the panicked look of someone who walks into a classroom and realizes the exam is not next week, as she had marked on her calendar, but today. "She...I can't believe this. She told the press I'm her girlfriend?"

———

As if living in a log cabin in the woods wasn't close enough to nature, Melanie and Sierra were building themselves a tree house. Baylee of course thought it was the best idea ever.

"Want to help paint the ladder?" Sierra asked Baylee when Jori dropped her off for a few hours of babysitting.

Baylee was off like a shot to find a paintbrush with Sierra, leaving Jori shaking her head in amazement as she stood next to Melanie watching them go. During the day she had access to daycare at the college, but it was unavailable for evening classes. Those were the hours when having friends like Sierra and Melanie to help out was a lifesaver.

Too bad she couldn't count on Axel to watch his own daughter once in a while. Sometimes she wondered if she should pressure him to be more of a dad, but then again, most of their classes overlapped. And she herself had grown up without a father and turned out just fine. Baylee would, too. The kid didn't even seem to notice she was missing a father figure.

Jori couldn't imagine what that would be like, to not even notice, but her situation had been different. Her mother had been confined to a wheelchair, and not in an I-can-still-play-basketball kind of way, and part of Jori's desire for a dad had really been a desire for an adult—any adult—who could help her mom.

Baylee didn't have that problem. When she got older she wasn't going to have to make dinner for a physically incapacitated mother and an older brother who not only made her do all the cooking but also the laundry, the housecleaning, and all the other little things their mother couldn't manage. She wasn't going to learn that all a boy had to do was whine that his sister was trying to turn him into a girl by making him do girl stuff and he was off the hook.

Maybe if her mother had been stronger…

But her mother couldn't handle the stress of hearing them fight, so Jori had learned to be cheerful and upbeat in her presence and to pretend nothing was wrong. It was easier to just do what needed to be done and escape to friends' houses, charming her way into their parents' hearts so they'd let her stay as long as possible.

"So," Melanie said, filling the silence. "Rae Peters. I saw the way you looked at her at the party."

Had she looked at her? Jori shrugged it off. "I didn't look at her."

"Didn't you?"

Jori glanced at the time. She should get going. Baylee was settled and she didn't want to be late to class. But if she ran across campus when she reached the school parking lot, rather than walked—which she'd done many times for less important reasons than not blowing off a friend—she'd make it.

"Weird that she's dating that rock star," Melanie said.

"Yeah, I don't get it, either." If Melanie was trying to warn her off by reminding her that Rae was already taken, she was wasting her time, because she was in no danger of forgetting that salient fact.

"Not that you're bitter or anything," Melanie said.

"What? I'm not bitter. It's none of my business if Rae wants to settle for someone like that."

"What makes you think she's settling? I mean, we're talking Kaoli Morgenroth. Dream crush of women everywhere."

"I don't think she's good for her." She left it at that, because if she told her the dream crush of women everywhere was about to marry some guy named Griffin and that Rae deserved better than to be someone's rebound, or worse, someone's mistress… If she told her all that, Melanie would think less of Rae, and something inside her didn't want that to happen.

Melanie said nothing and Jori looked at her more closely. A hint of a smile lurked at the corners of her mouth, making her look as smug as if she were about to win a bet with her girlfriend, as soon as her girlfriend had some time alone with her.

"You like her." The way Melanie said it, it wasn't a question—it was a statement of fact.

"She's dating Kaoli Morgenroth." Which meant it made no difference whether Jori liked her or not. As in *like* liked her.

"And you're dating what's-his-name," Melanie said.

Axel. Right. Her ex-turned-pretend-boyfriend. How could she forget?

"It's not the same."

"Hmm. If you say so." Melanie was grinning, though, like she couldn't help herself.

"Why are you smiling like that? Do you know something I don't know? Did she tell you something?"

"I have eyes."

"No, really, you can tell me." This was no time to keep a secret, especially if it involved Rae and who she was or was not interested in. And Melanie definitely didn't have to look so amused.

"How often does she talk about her girlfriend? Never."

"That's all you've got?" That wasn't proof. That was nothing. She'd been hoping for more. For someone whose girlfriend was supposedly a childhood friend of Rae's, Melanie didn't have a lot of insider information. "All that means is she's private. Or modest. She doesn't want us to think she's bragging about dating someone famous."

"Her girlfriend visits and doesn't spend the night?"

How did she know that? Melanie lived here in her cabin with Sierra; she didn't live down the hall from Rae in the lodge the way Jori did. "You keep track of Rae's visitors?"

"One of the staff noticed. She mentioned it to me."

Was everyone keeping an eye on Rae's love life? Or was it Kaoli Morgenroth's love life they were so interested in? "I'm sure rock stars keep a tight schedule."

Melanie laughed and shook her head. "Gotta sleep sometime. Might as well be in the loving, bony arms of her supposed girlfriend."

"Rae is not bony," Jori protested. "She can bench press as

much as I can." Probably. Or at least look good trying.

Melanie laughed again.

Yeah, she'd walked right into that one, coming to Rae's defense. But so what? So she liked her. Quite a bit.

And Melanie, however far off-base her reasoning was, was right about another thing: Rae didn't act like a person who had a girlfriend. It was possible that what Jori had witnessed at the pool between Kaoli and Rae had been the awkward interaction of a struggling relationship—and how could it not be struggling if one of them was about to marry someone else?—but she didn't think so. There'd been something about it, some lack of closeness, some absence of the little signs that two people coexisted in intense proximity, that made her think they were not a couple. But the fact was, Rae said they were dating, so the only respectful thing to do was to take her at her word. Melanie could speculate all she wanted, but in Jori's case, speculating would only make her want something she couldn't have.

"She's taken," Jori said.

"If you're going to lie to yourself," Melanie said, "far be it from me to stop you."

Jori glared. People who were right could be highly annoying.

But Melanie wasn't completely right. The truth was, Jori wasn't really lying to herself. She was just trying to stay sane.

9

"I think everyone's bi," Kaoli said.

She hadn't been supposed to return until Rae had her choreography ready, but when she showed up in the hallway outside the room in the lodge that was Rae's temporary home, her bodyguard nowhere in sight, Rae didn't turn her away. If she'd knocked twenty minutes later, Rae would have been asleep, but hey, who needed sleep? They were all night owls on the road, and Rae wasn't about to draw attention to the fact that her sleep schedule had changed.

When Kaoli learned that Rae didn't keep wine in her mini-fridge, they'd gone to the first-floor restaurant bar, and instead of sharing a drink there in public like boundary-respecting coworkers, Kaoli had ordered two glasses and carried them upstairs as Rae led the way on her crutches, all the way back to the privacy of her suite.

And then barely waited for the door to swing shut behind her to drop her bombshell.

I think everyone's bi.

Rae swallowed. Now Kaoli decides to venture into dangerous territory? Now, when she was about to get married?

Of course now. Late at night when she'd told her fiancé she had a business meeting to deal with the latest rumors—Rae really wished Kaoli hadn't shared that detail—was the perfect time to bring up dangerous topics with the woman who'd once had a crush on her.

Whose bright idea was it, anyway, to tell Kaoli she was welcome to crash in her suite anytime? Come on up and take a bow, Rae. When she'd made the offer, she hadn't believed Kaoli would take her up on it, showing up unannounced for no apparent reason, booking her bodyguard his own room and not bothering to get one for herself.

Rae gestured for her to sit at her small table, even though her leg was throbbing with exhaustion and she longed to stretch it out on the sofa. It needed to be elevated. But the table provided a barrier between them. The sofa didn't.

"Have you heard the word *bicurious*?" Kaoli said. "Such a great word."

"Have you heard the words *cold feet*?" If Kaoli was so bi, why hadn't she ever slept with her back in high school, back when it would have made a difference?

Kaoli didn't even blink. She'd always been good at not hearing what she didn't want to hear. "It's all a continuum. Most people aren't in touch with their deepest, truest desires so they deny they could fall a little bit in the middle, but not me."

"Are you kidding me?"

"Everyone's more bi than they'll admit. Don't you think?"

No, actually, she didn't.

"I'm not bi."

Kaoli looked taken aback. There was a time when Rae would have fallen all over herself to agree with her every word, eager and grateful to escort her down this road.

She wasn't that person anymore.

"Not even a little?"

"The heterosexual brainwashing from my parents had me

going there for a while, but no, I'm really not."

"I think I am. I think I'd like having sex with a woman," Kaoli said dreamily, raising her stemmed wineglass to her lips, taking an imperceptible sip, then gesturing with her glass in Rae's direction. Kaoli never got drunk, but she liked to keep a drink in front of her so she could claim the next day that she hadn't been sober. That had been her style in high school, and it looked like it hadn't changed. "I think I'd like to do it with someone like you."

Rae stared. She'd always wondered what it would be like to have sex with Kaoli. For years she'd wondered. But not like this. Not when Kaoli was pretending, once again, to be drunk.

Unfortunately, Rae's body didn't care about her opinion. Her body had waited for this for a very long time, and it didn't understand why she wouldn't give it what it wanted. And her mind…her mind was rebelling, too. In high school she'd never been sophisticated enough to figure out what to say to make Kaoli fall into her arms, and to finally have the chance to have her…

She wanted the satisfaction of knowing that after all these years she'd finally gotten what she wanted. That she'd finally *won*.

Kaoli stared brazenly back.

Rae covered Kaoli's hand, the one that was wrapped around the stem of her wineglass. The glass trembled, the way her body used to when Kaoli would bump shoulders with her accidentally on purpose in the hallway at school between classes. The smell of alcohol wafted up, crowding her living space with memories of a teenage Kaoli. They both guided the glass down and it hit the tabletop unsteadily.

Rae squeezed her hand. "You know you're full of shit,

right?"

"Everyone thinks you're my girlfriend. Why not make it real?"

Rae released her. "I agreed to pretend to be your girlfriend. Pretend. Not for real."

The photo had been a slip-up. Someone with a telephoto lens had captured Kaoli kneeling alongside the swimming pool kissing Rae on the forehead and sold it to some up-and-coming gossip site instead of to Griffin, who as *Celebrity Crush*'s editor-in-chief could have bought exclusive rights to the photo and blocked its publication. Having long and endlessly hoped for even the smallest sign that Kaoli Morgenroth was gay, her huge lesbian fan base had gone wild. When her entire concert tour had suddenly sold out within hours of the news, Kaoli and her publicity manager discovered that the rules of popularity in the music world were not the rules that governed real life, and they decided that this—rather than a non-attention-grabbing engagement to a boring, heterosexual magazine editor—was the image she needed. Kaoli was now officially cheating on her longtime boyfriend to be with Rae, and lesbian fans were salivating, taking bets on how soon she'd dump him.

And Rae agreed to go along with it. It would have been nice if the first she'd heard of it had been from Kaoli and not from a stranger at a party, but dealing with her boss's diva behavior was part of the job, and if it meant not getting fired? Of course she'd gone along with it. An injured dancer was an unemployable dancer, so it was important that she hang on to the job she had. Besides, she wanted Kaoli to perform to sold-out houses almost as much as Kaoli did. It was her career, too. And it was fun to see photos of herself trending online. Yes, she was vain. Yes, she lied to the public. But it was no worse than what any other celebrity did. If they were in the hospital, they were struggling bravely and not yelling at the nurses. If they were married, their marriage was blissful, right up until the moment their agent announced they were getting divorced. And what harm did it do? She didn't like lying, but if a little lie made people happy, who was she to tell them they were wrong? She hadn't purposely posed for that photo, and she wasn't kissing Kaoli on the lips for the cameras.

In private, though...that would be different.

"Don't you want to know what it would be like, you and me?" Kaoli leaned across the table, chest-first, just the way Jori said she did.

Rae felt a flash of heat, forgetting everything but the memory of how Kaoli had once gripped her by the waist and stared into her eyes and inched forward until Rae was pressed up against the wood paneling in the Morgenroths' den, enveloping her in a haze of strawberry fragrance as the creaking of Kaoli's mother's footfall overhead fell silent. When she couldn't get any closer without irrevocably venturing out of the platonic friend zone, their lips had touched. Kaoli had made a break for it and run upstairs. Rae had stood there, breathing hard, too excited to feel cheated. Of course she wanted it to go further—although she was a little vague on what "further" would be—but they were headed there, she was sure of it. Soon they'd be moving to open-mouthed kisses and losing their virginity to each other and life would be perfect.

When Kaoli returned with melting blue popsicles clutched in her fists and bright blue stain on her lips, and it finally dawned on her that she wasn't ever going to kiss her again, Rae had stomped home and hurled her trigonometry textbook against the wall.

She never imagined they'd end up like this. With Kaoli begging her.

"Give me a chance, Rae."

"I already gave you a chance. You ran away."

An emotion that might have been guilt flickered through Kaoli's eyes. "I didn't know what I wanted. We were so young. You're not going to forgive me for that?"

"I can understand being confused back then. What I can't understand is why you're still confused now. You've had plenty of time to figure it out."

"Everyone has their own timetable. We're not all lucky enough to know exactly who we are when we're a teenager, like you," Kaoli said. "It doesn't mean I didn't want you. Because I did. I did want you. I always wanted you."

"Not enough."

Kaoli was quiet and intent as she rubbed a fingertip up the stem of her wineglass. "If I could go back in time and do it over again, that day you tried to kiss me—I'd kiss you back. I totally would. Sleep with you, even. I wouldn't run away." She was taking forever to finish that wine. "You gave me a chance, and I was too immature to realize what I was giving up. I blew it. Will you let me try again? Please. Tell me it's not too late."

She sounded so sincere. In the years since high school, Kaoli had gotten better at choosing the right words and saying them with just the right delivery. She'd always begged, but never with this kind of finesse, like she meant every self-debasing word. Like Rae was a goddess and Kaoli knew she wasn't worthy of her but she wanted her too much not to try.

It felt flattering.

It was meant to.

Rae shook her head with a tiny, sharp jerk. She was not falling for this garbage. She was not.

Kaoli slid her hand across the table and stopped just short of Rae's in a silent plea, her eyes simmering with a seductive heat Rae remembered all too well. Rae curled her fingers around Kaoli's hand.

Oh hell, she *was* falling for it.

"You won't regret this," Kaoli said.

It was amazing how she could look so utterly sincere and not mean any of it.

"What about your husband-to-be?" Rae reminded her, reminded herself. It was disturbing how much part of her still wanted to sleep with her. "Don't you care about not hurting him?"

"He knows you were into me in high school. He won't care."

"You told him?"

"I didn't have to."

Had she been that obvious? She'd tried hard not to be. Perhaps only Griffin, who'd been just as in love with Kaoli in high school as Rae had been, had had the incentive to recognize what was going on. How embarrassing, to think he'd known. And Kaoli, of course, who'd trailed her hand along Rae's thigh, acting like there was nothing sexual about it, pretending that all she was doing was flipping through their yearbook, saying "Isn't Griffin cute?" when it fell open to the page with his picture.

"Hmm," Rae had said, too worried about keeping Kaoli's friendship to tell her what she really thought.

"Who do you think is cuter—Griffin or Antonio?"

"They're both so..." Rae closed her eyes and sighed dramatically to hide the panic she was sure Kaoli would sense. She hated not knowing the right answer. Schoolwork was so much easier than this—the answers were all in the textbook. Figuring out which boys were supposed to be cute was so much harder. She needed a mental cheat sheet to tell her who had the best dimples, the most amazing eyes, and the sexiest unappealing physique.

"It's hard to choose," Rae said at last. Which was actually true. Boys all looked the same. If they weren't in her class, it was sometimes almost hard to tell them apart. Not girls, though—girls were all unique. It was kind of weird. "I want to say...both of them?"

"I agree." Kaoli fanned herself, excited by hotness Rae couldn't see.

Relief rushed oxygen to her brain. She'd gotten it right.

But Kaoli had known it wasn't the whole truth, after all. She'd known what Rae was.

And Rae's older and wiser self was done deluding herself. Kaoli didn't love her. She didn't know what exactly Kaoli did want, but it wasn't love, and Rae didn't want anything less. Not from Kaoli; not from anyone. Sex meant something to Rae. It wasn't casual. It wasn't something she did with someone she didn't even like. Her body might disagree—certainly her fingers seemed to disagree, the way they were stroking Kaoli's hand—but her body wasn't in charge here. Her brain was in charge. And her brain was reminding her that she had a long-standing policy—thanks to Kaoli herself—never, ever to date anyone who was in the process of exploring, discovering, or deciding on her sexuality.

"I'm not doing this."

"You know you want to," Kaoli purred. "You want to know what it would be like. You want to know as much as I do."

No, thanks. Rae was not falling for another kiss-and-run.

But those lips…

She'd always thought those lips looked kissable—and they were. She'd always wondered, if that mouth-to-mouth encounter in the Morgenroths' den had gone deeper, how she'd taste. What would it hurt to find out? Just one little kiss. She didn't have to sleep with her, but God, would that be vindication. Sleeping with Kaoli after all those years of resentment. Finally. Revenge. She would definitely consider revenge sex.

No, she wouldn't.

"Come on, Rae. Say yes."

Kaoli Morgenroth wanted to sleep with her. Why would she say no to that?

"I—" Her phone rang. "I should get that."

She sprang for the phone, which lay a few feet away on the countertop in the kitchenette. Her body wasn't ready for the sudden move, and she found herself hopping on one leg to keep her bad leg off the floor. "Sierra. What's up?"

She glanced back at Kaoli, who slouched in her chair and pouted. Rae cringed. She shouldn't have acted so relieved at the interruption. She shouldn't have *felt* so relieved.

"I'll get more wine," Kaoli said, walking toward the door and letting herself out without waiting for a reply. She didn't look happy.

"Rumor has it you were seen in the restaurant with a hot babe," Sierra said. "Please tell me you didn't pick up the phone if she's with you right now."

"She's not with me right now. She's on her way down to the bar for an unnecessary refill on alcohol."

"Oh my God, you really are on a date. I'll call you tomorrow. I didn't expect you to pick up. I was going to leave an annoying message."

"No, it's okay. Really." She could use a voice of reason right about now.

"Tell me the instant she gets back and I'll hang up."

Sierra was way too excited about this.

"It's not a date." Except it kind of was a date. It hadn't started out that way, but... "Okay, we might be in date territory at this point."

Might? It had always been like this with Kaoli—so hard to pin down and label.

"Ooooooh. Who is it?"

"My boss."

"Oh." Sierra's voice fell flat. Had she been expecting it to be someone else? "I thought..." Her enthusiasm disappeared, replaced by caution. She cleared her throat. "I thought you said the rumors about you two dating weren't true. Besides, she's straight. I mean, your sister always said Kaoli was straight. I assumed she still was."

"So did I."

"What changed?"

"I'm starting to think maybe she's not that straight."

"Maybe she's not that straight?" Sierra echoed, a note of incredulity creeping into her voice.

A muted female voice in the background said, "Uh oh." Had to be Melanie, overhearing.

Sierra wasn't done. "Doesn't she have a boyfriend? What makes you think she's not that straight?"

"Most straight women don't tell me they think everyone is bi."

Sierra gave a snort of disgust. "Me neither."

"I'm trying not to take it too seriously, because the only reason she wants to jump me is I'm probably the only lesbian she knows."

"Wait. How did we get from *not that straight* to jumping you?"

Rae heard a whistle of encouragement in the background from Melanie. She wouldn't be so excited when she found out who they were talking about.

"She's exploring her options," Rae said.

"Are you going to be one of the options?"

"I haven't decided yet."

If Kaoli really was working through stuff? If she was seriously reconsidering her sexuality and was prepared to break off her engagement to Griffin? Then she deserved a chance. It wasn't a moral failing to be confused, no matter what age she was. It was scary and important.

But chances were, Kaoli was just screwing with her. Whether Rae was willing to be screwed was the question she had to figure out. Fast.

"And doesn't she have hundreds of lesbian fans who proposition her at her concerts? I mean, come on, Rae, you're not the only one who could help her with this little issue of hers."

Kaoli's powerful voice soared from down the hall. "Won't be watching the time, 'cause time don't mean nothin'…" She wasn't singing at full volume, but she was going to piss off everyone asleep on this floor of the lodge no matter how impressively on-key she was. "Time don't mean nothin' to a goddess, ooh, goddess, yeah, goddess…" There was a knock on the door.

"She's back," Rae told Sierra. "Gotta go."

She put down her phone and opened the door. Kaoli stood holding two glasses of red wine, her weight thrust onto one hip in a pose that Rae wished Jori was here to see so she could explain her strongly held opinion on how wrong it was to stand like that.

"Goddess, yeah, goddess…" Kaoli came in, still singing her brilliantly confusing song. No one could figure out if the lover in the song was a man or a woman, and Kaoli wasn't saying.

Rae let the heavy door swing shut behind her and turned the lock. Suddenly Kaoli was crowding her against the door, wineglasses sloshing dangerously.

"Miss me?" Kaoli said.

Before Rae could answer, Kaoli's lips met hers. No buildup, no warning, no nothing. And for one reckless moment, Rae kissed her back, unable to do what she needed to do, which was pull the fuck away. Because instead of lust and vindication and half a lifetime of pent-up desire, what bubbled up was rage. How dare Kaoli try to kiss her now? She should have done it years ago, when it would have meant something, when it would have mattered.

Rae jerked away from Kaoli's kiss.

"Wow, that's embarrassing," Kaoli said, laughing, waving the wineglasses around and raising both hands in surrender, as if overplaying it would help her save face. "You don't want to…" She laughed again, shook her head in disbelief. "Wow."

"I don't."

Which was, surprisingly, a relief. If Kaoli hadn't forced the issue, Rae might have stayed stuck in the past forever, thinking she was over her but always wondering what might have been.

She didn't want her.

She could have kissed Kaoli for that, for freeing her.

Better not, though. Kaoli wouldn't understand. She'd probably never received a thank-you-for-trying-to-make-out-with - me - and - making - me - realize - I - don't - want - you kiss. A now-I-can-go-on-with-my-life kiss. A what-did-I-ever-see-in-you kiss.

She also *really* didn't want to touch her wet lips again. They were kind of revolting.

"What happened?" Kaoli asked. "Did I scare you off?"

Rae bristled. "You scared me off in high school," she said. "You flirted with me relentlessly and never followed through. I wanted you, and you didn't want me, and I'm sorry, but I'm not going to forget that just because you finally changed your mind."

"Ouch. Can we tone down the excruciating honesty thing?"

"I don't know if I can."

Kaoli sighed as she finally set the glasses down. "You always were big on honesty."

She was? When? When she lied about being good at trig so she could tutor her? When she swore it was an accident that her thigh touched Kaoli's on her parents' couch under the chenille throw? When she pretended not to be in love with her?

"You were such a stickler about not letting me cheat on my homework," Kaoli said.

Oh. That.

"It was annoying," Kaoli said.

"I was *helping* you." And trying to get her to fall in love with her. Which Kaoli damn well knew. "At least I wasn't a tease."

"We can still do this, Rae. Just one night." Kaoli smoothed her own hair and stroked down her neck suggestively. "One beautiful night. No strings. I want to make up for what I did to you. Give you what you wanted."

Amazing how Kaoli kept turning this around, kept acting like Rae should be able to forgive her for what she'd done.

But Rae had had enough. "I'm not sleeping with you, Kaoli. Go play your games with someone else."

"Games?"

Really? "You're getting married. I don't want to have an affair."

"You know what? I don't either." Her eyes softened in that way that had always gotten to Rae, that way that made her think Kaoli loved her. Only now she knew better. Kaoli pursed her lips in the shape of a kiss and actually managed to look wistful. "I prefer to think of you as an adventure. So what do you say? Are you feeling adventurous?"

Was that what this was about? The thrill of getting away with breaking the rules? Well, newsflash, Rae didn't believe in those rules—rules that said sleeping with a woman was not okay.

"I'm not *adventurous*." Rae gave her a disgusted look. "I'm gay."

Kaoli pouted. "You're not seriously going to turn me down, are you?"

Rae held her gaze, silently daring her to ask again.

"There's nothing wrong with wondering what it would be like," Kaoli said. "With being curious."

Rae said nothing.

"Aren't you even a little bit curious?" Kaoli said. "I am."

"I'm not."

Rae knew what she wanted. And it was not Kaoli.

10

Axel was late. Pairs of adults who had given up a Friday night at the movies to learn to dance were spread throughout the low-ceilinged basement studio of Sassafras Dance, their bored chitchat a babble of background noise bouncing off the mirrored walls and competing with muted Big Band music coming from the studio above. But no Axel. He had ordered Jori to attend four weeks of ballroom dance classes with him to master the basics in time for his cousin's wedding, and now he couldn't bother to show?

She'd give him ten minutes. If by then he hadn't arrived, she'd leave and find something better to do with her precious hour that Baylee was at the sitter's.

That was fair, wasn't it? If she didn't believe in keeping her word, and if the wedding weren't such a great opportunity for Baylee to see the cousins and aunts and uncles she'd never met, Jori wouldn't be doing this at all. Because what could Axel do? Go back to their professor and say he'd lied about her being innocent? A stunt like that would get *him* in trouble, and Axel was too smart to do that to himself.

A middle-aged woman wearing skimpy white shorts, a glittery gold wrap top, and matching gold heels a drag queen would love glided purposefully toward the corner that housed the sound system, where she deposited a clipboard and her purse on a shelf. The chatter died down and the students clustered around her. Jori hung back from the group, contemplating her escape. She was the only one wearing denim cutoffs, and that might be a sign she didn't belong here, no matter how beginner level this thing was supposed to be.

"Hello, everyone. I'm Marcella," said the woman in the gold heels, turning to face the class. "Alicia had her baby yesterday so I'll be stepping in as your instructor for the next few weeks. She tells me this class is how to dance at your wedding. Foxtrot, waltz, a little Latin. Is that what everyone's here for?"

The students all nodded. Jori had forgotten the class had a theme. Not Axel's mother's idea of a hint, she hoped.

"Everyone's getting married?"

There was a murmur of agreement. Several of the couples nervously edged closer to each other.

Marcella looked around the room, nodding her head as she counted how many students she had. "Raise your hand if you're an even pair."

Everyone's hand went up except for Jori's. As if it weren't already glaringly obvious that she was alone.

Marcella nodded at her. "You'll dance with me."

"I signed up with a friend," Jori felt compelled to explain, "but he's late." Either late or a no-show who would live to regret it. He had eight minutes to prove which one it was.

The clatter of heels sounded outside the room, followed by a second person's quieter, less hurried gait. The non-heel-wearer did not sound like Axel, who now had seven minutes. At six minutes and fifty-five seconds, a student in a skintight top and a flippy dance skirt rushed in.

Many seconds later, the other person arrived, and it was not this woman's boyfriend—it was Rae. A simple white blouse knotted beneath her bust and ass-hugging black stretch pants made her look like the dancer she was. And no crutches—wow. And no brace? Rae was making unbelievable progress. She devoted herself to her rehab exercises with more dedication than anyone Jori had ever seen, but wow. There was no way a knee brace could be hidden under those tight pants, right? Because she walked without any sign of a limp. There did seem to be more hip swiveling involved than in a normal gait—very relaxed, very sensual—but if she hadn't known, she'd never have guessed Rae was injured, or that her slow, deliberate, sexy pace was masking caution.

Jori grinned and waved like she hadn't seen her in weeks and then felt stupid because maybe Rae wouldn't be as excited as Jori was to see a familiar face. Rae raised a hand in acknowledgement and then ignored her to remove her sneakers and change into heels. Heels? The woman was either trying to prove something or had no fear.

"Two extra women," Marcella told the new arrivals. "As usual, we're short on men, so you'll have to learn without a partner."

"I want to learn both parts," Rae said, testing her heels with an unselfconscious swivel in place. Unlike most of the students, who had hesitated at the door, unsure of where to go or what to do, she radiated self-confidence. Dance studios were her natural habitat, and her energy filled the room. "I can lead."

"Why?" Marcella said.

"Why not?" Rae said.

"What are you doing here?" Jori hissed across the room.

"Fine. Dance with her." Marcella pointed at Flippy Skirt, completely ignoring the obvious signs that Rae and Jori knew each other.

Okay, so Marcella had already claimed Jori as her partner,

but still. Not that Jori couldn't have ditched Marcella and run over to claim Rae without an invitation, but what if Rae didn't want to dance with her? She had a girlfriend. She wasn't dying to hold Jori in her arms.

Marcella turned her back on them both. "Now we start," she told the class.

Marcella was ten minutes into explaining the foxtrot before Jori remembered that she'd been planning to leave. With Rae there, she didn't feel like leaving anymore. And it would feel good to be better at the foxtrot than Axel.

Marcella's procedure was they learned a step, practiced it to music with all the couples arranged in a circle, and then everyone switched partners. This was, Marcella informed them, so that couples wouldn't adapt to each other's mistakes and learn bad habits. The about-to-be-married couples grumbled about it and one woman even looked like she might refuse, but Jori loved the idea because it meant she had a chance of ending up with Rae without making it look like she didn't respect her unhealthy relationship with her girlfriend. A few rounds in, when the music sounded like it was coming to an end, Jori dragged the guy she was dancing with halfway across the room and parked herself beside Rae. Now all she had to do was wait for the instructor to announce, just as she had each time before, that it was time for the ladies to move down the circle counterclockwise to their next partner, and Jori would walk straight into Rae's arms.

"Gentlemen stay where you are," Marcella said.

Counterclockwise, counterclockwise, counterclockwise, Jori reminded herself, her thoughts stuck in a whirling loop of anticipation.

"Ladies move…uh…let's see…clockwise to the next gentleman."

Wait…what? Clockwise? Jori had already started to take a step toward Rae. With the sudden change in direction she lost her balance and her foot landed with an abrupt, unexpected thump. Why would Marcella choose *now* to forget which way they were going?

As everyone took their new places, Rae, as a "gentleman", was stuck where she was, while Jori, as a "lady", had to change course and head in the wrong direction, away from her. They weren't supposed to go clockwise. The instructor wasn't supposed to pick a new direction; she was supposed to have a predictable system and stick with it so everyone got a chance to rotate through and dance with everyone else. And so Jori could game the system. Next time she was positioning herself on Rae's other side and working on her telepathic coercion skills to make Marcella pick the direction she wanted.

"Girls leading?" her new dance partner greeted her. "What is this world coming to?" Jori supposed she was the one he was addressing, but he was loud and belligerent enough that he clearly meant for Rae to hear—maybe for the whole class to hear. "Is there no male privilege anymore?"

It was a joke, of course—an attempt at a joke—and maybe if he had offered a friendly, sheepish smile it would have softened his words and made them less of an insult. Instead he widened his mouth in what some men thought was a smile but was really a pleased-with-himself show of dominance that was directly descended from a wild animal baring its fangs.

"Get over yourself," Jori snapped. She'd never been one to take the high road when it came to rudeness. Couldn't he tell that Rae—even injured—was twice the dancer he would ever be? Not just twice—a thousand times. And shouldn't the better dancer be the one leading? The whole ballroom dancing system was set up backward. If it weren't for the problem of women often being too short, even in heels, to guide a man's arm over his head, and men's weird ingrained reluctance to twirl, women would make much more competent leads.

Marcella turned on the music and was already barking out instructions, so even though she didn't particularly want to, Jori took her partner's hand and moved into position.

"Do you know what you're doing?" he asked.

"Not really. You?"

He glared. Apparently he didn't feel the need to actually say anything in response to a direct question. Whatever. She was only stuck with him for the next five minutes until they got to switch again, and this time, she was going to be next to Rae on the correct side. Jori purposely stumbled over her own feet several times, carefully orchestrating it so other couples would overtake them and pass them and she'd end up where she wanted to be. Next to Rae. On the side she hoped was going to be the lucky side.

Please say clockwise. She didn't know why she wanted this so much, but being foiled by a woman in a glittery gold outfit definitely brought out her competitive nature. *Please say—*

"Gentlemen stay where you are," Marcella said as the music ended. "Ladies move clockwise—"

Yes!

"Sorry I'm late," boomed Axel's unmistakable voice from the classroom door. "Jori, darling! Forgive me."

No, not now, not now, not—

Axel swept into the room and pulled her into his arms, intercepting her on her path between Jokester Guy—who had cooperated quite nicely, never suspecting that she was controlling their trajectory—and Rae. Damn it.

"You can't just—"

Axel guided her into a perfect spin without any hesitation. "Can't I?"

As the music started and everyone began the pattern Marcella had just taught them, it was immediately obvious that Axel had taken ballroom lessons in the past. He knew the steps, and unlike most of the students, he wasn't shuffling uncertainly or staring at his feet.

"You sound swishy when you call me 'darling,'" she muttered under her breath.

"I do it to annoy you," he said.

"You're succeeding." If it weren't for him, she'd be dancing with Rae right now.

Maybe Rae didn't want to dance with her, but she wouldn't have refused if she thought they'd been randomly paired. And then Jori could have touched her hand and closed her eyes and pretended it was real until the music stopped and reality intruded. "Why did your mother sign us up for this class if you already know how to dance? I could be using this time to hit the books." For her real classes. At school. The summer semester was well underway and she had work to do.

"She doesn't know. I picked up some moves from an old boyfriend and didn't feel the need to inform her."

"Why does this not surprise me?"

"And I figured you needed the instruction," Axel said. "I see I was right."

Jerk. Jori flashed him a fake smile and tripped herself, almost taking him down with her. When she recovered, the music had ended and they were standing next to Rae. Again. What a coincidence.

"Gentlemen stay where you are. Ladies move clockwise to the next gentleman."

At last. Axel released her and moved to welcome the woman to his right while Jori moved into place in front of Rae. She thought Rae would hold out her hands and take her into dance hold, but instead she gripped her arm and practically collapsed. It was costing her a lot to act like her leg wasn't bothering her. If only Jori could pick her up and take her home and park her on a comfortable sofa and not let her get up until she was fully recovered. But she knew better than to suggest it. Rae would be bouncing off that sofa or doing sit-ups or leg lifts on it, refusing to sit still.

"Knee?" Jori asked.

Rae nodded. "Ankle, too." She tilted her head in Axel's direction. "What's he doing here?"

"Twisting my arm." And inadvertently putting her in the same room with Rae and making her day. "What's with the heels?"

Rae sighed. "I'm sick of sneakers. I want to feel like a dancer again." She eased her weight off Jori's arm and let go, as if being reminded of her injury meant she had to prove to her audience that nothing was wrong. Like Jori wasn't a friend she could relax around.

"Lean on me. It's okay."

"I can stand on my own."

"You're doing more than standing," Jori said, refusing to let her off the hook. She'd seen her on crutches just a few days earlier. Dancing in heels did not seem like a good idea.

"This?" Rae swiveled her hips in a sexy move they had definitely not been taught in class.

"Don't—"

Jori cut herself off as Rae danced her ribcage side to side

with a sway of her shoulders, head, arms, and hips, fluid and natural and perfectly coordinated. It made Jori want to cry, because it was so beautiful and the rest of her was so broken.

"This beginner-level stuff isn't really dancing," Rae said. "It's more like walking in time to music. Not much of a challenge."

"Maybe not for you," Jori said, wishing she could say the same. "Why are you taking this class, anyway?" It had to be agony for her, dancing with clumsy beginners who had no idea what they were doing and would never, ever reach her level no matter how hard they tried. "Don't you already know all this stuff?"

Rae glanced over at the instructor like she couldn't understand why they were being allowed to waste time talking instead of getting back to work, so Jori looked, too. Marcella was busy fiddling with the sound system.

Rae balanced on her good leg and rotated her weak ankle a few inches off the floor as if all she really needed to do was stretch it, not rest. "When you tell people you're studying to be an accountant, I'll bet they ask you for help with their taxes, right? Even though your specialty might be, like, I don't know…"

"Managing a company's books."

"Exactly. Dancers specialize like everyone else. And I don't do ballroom. I'm here to pick up some ideas for a friend who asked me to choreograph a little something for her wedding."

A friend. Was that how Rae thought of Kaoli Morgenroth? Then again, she was in a roomful of strangers and wouldn't want to risk every word she said being leaked to the press. And she obviously didn't realize Jori had overheard when Kaoli asked her for this eentsy weentsy favor, so maybe she was just being circumspect when she referred to her as her "friend" instead of as her boss or her girlfriend.

Her girlfriend. What a fucked-up situation that must be, if it was true. She wanted to ask her if she really was Kaoli's girlfriend, and if she was, why in hell the wedding was still on. If she could figure out a way to ask without sounding like she didn't approve. Because what if it was true? Then she'd come off as a nosy, judgmental, disapproving ass. Which she supposed she was. Because the idea of Rae being in love with Kaoli was so irritating it couldn't possibly be true. She didn't want it to be true.

"I'll help you practice what we learn in class if you help me figure out my friend's wedding choreography," Rae said. "It's hard to do it all in my head. It would help to have a live body to figure out which arm goes where."

More dancing with Rae. Just what she needed. The thought of touching her without a roomful of witnesses made her heart hammer in anticipation. Or maybe terror. It was hard to tell which.

"A live body. You make it sound so tempting."

Marcella clapped her hands to get the class's attention.

Rae slid her hand across Jori's back to bring her into the proper dance hold. Her touch was electric, sending whispers of sensation across her skin in all directions.

"Is that a yes?" Rae said quietly, drawing closer.

They were the same height. Their bodies were just a few inches apart, and looking into her eyes was…well, let's just say that when she'd danced with the men in the class, meeting her dance partner's gaze at close range for more than a few seconds had been uncomfortable, and her gaze had skittered around the room, fixed firmly over her partner's shoulder. But looking into Rae's eyes was different. She remembered these eyes—warm, alluring pools of mocha streaked with amber and ringed with a dark border, shining with an intensity she couldn't look away from. All she could do was hold her breath and wait for the music to start so she could surrender to whatever direction Rae led her.

"And now it's time to move on to something more exciting," Marcella announced. "The tango."

"Oh God," Rae muttered, too low for Marcella to overhear but clearly audible to Jori. "Please tell me we are not doing the tango."

Why? What was wrong with the tango? Jori tried to dredge up a mental image of what it looked like and failed.

"You know this dance?" Jori whispered. "You, who doesn't do ballroom?"

"I've seen it done," Rae whispered back.

"First, the basic stance," Marcella said. "In tango, we stand close. The hips should touch. Ladies, step back with your right foot. Stay there. Split stance."

The hips should touch? What did that mean? Did that mean she and Rae were supposed to stand side by side or...

"Now, gentlemen, step with your left foot between the lady's legs."

She was starting to see the problem here.

Rae stepped between Jori's thighs, her foot landing with a thud that echoed in Jori's heart. From a distance it had to look like her thigh was jammed into Jori's crotch and that pelvis had made contact with pelvis, but they weren't touching—not quite. She didn't know how Rae was managing it on her injured leg—how she managed to stay in such complete control—but as close as they were, they were not actually touching.

She could feel the heat of her thigh, though.

"Don't be shy," Marcella said. "Right between her legs. The legs must touch."

Rae stayed perfectly balanced, their lower bodies oh-so-carefully not touching. If she was unhappy about their intimate not-quite-contact, she didn't let it show. She looked calm and unflustered, if a little grim. This was probably normal for her, to intertwine her body with someone she wasn't sleeping with. She touched other dancers all the time. It wasn't sexual. Denim cutoffs might not have been Jori's best wardrobe choice, but what difference did it make, really? Rae's legs were covered, and one layer of clothing was no worse than two. In theory.

"Good. Stay there while I come around and check."

Crap. Marcella was going to make them touch.

As the instructor approached, Rae moved almost imperceptibly closer until the illicit breath of space between them was gone and their thighs hit. Jori would have thought her own reflex would have been to bounce off, but instead, she was overcome by an instinctual pull toward her, a need to press closer. It took all her willpower to stop herself from melting into her like a lover. Honestly, what was wrong with her? Rae was not her girlfriend. The only reason she had her leg wedged into her personal space was because Marcella was going to make a fuss if she didn't.

"Hang in there," Rae said.

Could she tell that Jori was nervous? Jori searched her face and noticed beads of sweat forming along Rae's hairline. So she wasn't the only one.

Jori squeezed every muscle she could control to prevent herself from moving. Her feet pressed into the floor, her pelvis locked in place, her hand gripped Rae's. The pulse in Rae's palm pounded against her skin. Jori inhaled unsteadily, and Rae shuddered and closed her eyes. Rae's hair smelled faintly of chlorine. They were close enough that she could tell.

Marcella checked on their position and moved on to the next couple. As soon as she was gone, a rush of air escaped Jori's lips. Rae opened her eyes and extricated herself from their pose to hop toward the benches at the front of the room.

"My leg's tired," Rae explained, lowering herself to the nearest bench. "I can't control the shaking."

Was that what that was? Shaking from exhaustion? Jori didn't think so. Maybe she was being unfair, because it was obvious Rae really had been pushing herself to her limit, but in her opinion the trembling had very little to do with fatigue.

But if that was the way Rae wanted it? To pretend she didn't feel anything? Fine. Rae didn't owe her anything—not a relationship, not a dance, not even honesty. Jori might want those things, but Rae didn't have to give them to her.

Wait, did she say *relationship*? What she meant was…not a relationship exactly, she didn't know her well enough to want a *relationship* with her, just the fantasy of…oh heck. She didn't know what she wanted.

The rest of the class went by in a blur. When it was over, Axel was the first one out the door, in so much of a rush to leave that when he brushed Jori's cheek with a kiss, she didn't have time to react. Then he was gone and everyone else had gathered their belongings and escaped—all except for Rae, who stood at the foot of the stairs that led out of the basement studio to the street-level exit, her dance shoes in one hand and her other hand on the banister, making no attempt to move.

"No elevator," Jori commiserated, joining her.

"I should be able to handle stairs," Rae said. "I was doing really well. But now my leg's so useless I don't know if I can." She craned her neck to see the top of the stairs and her shoulders slumped in defeat. "Some days I wonder if I'm ever going to dance again. I mean, maybe this is it—maybe my career is over and I just don't realize it yet."

"Hey, don't give up." Jori sat on the lowest step and Rae sank down next to her. After watching Rae push herself so hard for so long, it was discomfiting to hear her express doubt in her own abilities. "Haven't you ever failed before?"

"Do you know how many auditions I've been on? How many times I didn't make it? They don't even look you in the eye. They just say thank you and wait for you to move out of their line of sight so they can reject the next dancer."

"And then you nail the next audition."

"This is different. This is bigger than one audition. This is my life." Rae curled her arms around herself. "It's depressing. To know my body can break."

"You can fix it." Rae was doing all that work on her own with no support. No wonder she was worn down. "Shouldn't your boss have someone on staff to help you, to make sure you're getting better? Someone she could send here?"

"If I were a big-time football player, then yeah, we'd have a doctor or a trainer or whatever those guys have. But I'm not a football player. No one's invested millions of dollars in me. No one cares if my career is over, because there's a long line of unemployed seventeen-year-olds willing to do just about anything to take my place and accept my measly salary. I'm expendable. If I recover, they'll take me back. If I don't, oh well, I'm just another artistic nobody whose career was cut short. Too bad. Shit happens. Life goes on."

Her shoulders shook, and Jori gently put an arm around

her, hoping to ease her shaking. The moment Rae stilled, she released her.

"If you've reached the point where the only thing left to do is admit to yourself that you're never going to be good enough to dance professionally again, no matter how hard you try, then okay. But if there's still a chance, if there's still hope, then don't you dare give up on yourself. You've come this far. Maybe it's going to take longer than you thought to get back on your feet, but so what? Let it take longer."

"Yeah, okay, enough serious talk," Rae said. "I haven't given up yet." She stared up at the banister. "Right now all I need to decide is whether I can drag myself up the stairs or if I should sit and do the reverse crawl. I'm thinking if I'm on my derrière I can't fall."

"I have a better idea."

Jori jumped to her feet, and without asking for permission—so Rae couldn't say no—she scooped her up, one arm around the middle of her back, the other under her knees. Rae screamed—a playful scream, not a scared one—and linked her arms behind Jori's neck. It was a wonderful sound.

"*Derrière?*" Jori teased, relieved that Rae had allowed her to pick her up. "Is that dancer-speak for *ass?*"

"Put me down. I'm too heavy."

"You're not." She was a lot heavier than Jori's handful of a daughter, of course, and lifting a human being was more awkward than lifting an iron barbell, but it wasn't impossible. And it was worth it. If she'd known all those hours at the gym were going to lead to holding this woman in her arms, she'd have trained even harder.

Reminded her of an old argument she used to have with Axel, back in undergrad when they were dating for real and he would make fun of her morning routine of a hundred sit-ups. "Crunches aren't functional," he would say, claiming they were old-fashioned and that there was no activity in daily life that involved that particular motion. But he was wrong. He'd never made love to a woman and made it so good that she jacked off the bed. When her abs were sore the next day, they both knew why.

Something she shouldn't be thinking about now, even if that was nearly impossible with the way Rae was clinging to her, dangling her shoes and purse from one hand and fitting the curves of their chests together like jigsaw puzzle pieces with only one solution. Good thing Rae couldn't read her mind or she'd think twice about getting so comfortable. The position wasn't necessarily sexual, but to Jori's imagination, it absolutely was.

She started onto the stairs and staggered under the load, almost sending them both tumbling to the ground. God, that was embarrassing. Rae didn't *look* heavy. Must be true what people at the gym said about muscle weighing more.

"Wait. This'll make it easier." Rae shifted position and hung on tight, swinging her legs and landing with them wrapped around Jori's waist.

Like *that* wasn't sexual.

Jori grunted from the impact and fought to keep her balance on the narrow step. Rae's lithe, sweet strength felt really, really good. Too good. No woman had ever braced her inner thighs around her without kissing her first and being at least partially unclothed, and Jori's body was flooding her with hormones to prepare her in case Rae decided to follow suit.

Rae wasn't going to do any of that, though, so Jori continued up the stairs, one careful step at a time. And Rae was right—her weight was better anchored, making her easier to carry. Not easier enough, though, because whatever advantage Jori had gained in weight distribution she was rapidly losing in strength thanks to the desire that pulsed through her with ratcheting intensity each time Rae shifted in her arms. With each jostling step, Jori had to pretend she couldn't feel Rae's heat burning through their clothing, because otherwise she would weaken too much before she reached the top, and she couldn't risk that. Dropping her was not an option.

"You're doing great," Rae said softly, her voice much too intimate.

Not helping, sunshine.

Because not having her in her arms was starting to feel like it, too, was not an option.

11

Two days later, afternoon sun filtered through the trees outside the yoga barn's huge windows as Jori sashayed across the hardwood floor, hugging one of the long wooden benches that belonged along the wall and spinning it around, practicing what she'd learned in dance class while she waited for Rae to show up. Chairs, fallen logs, small children who happened to be related to her and wouldn't complain—she was hoisting everything she could find, preparing for her next chance to carry Rae up a handy flight of stairs.

A flash of movement in the open doorway made her turn, and there was Rae, leaning against the doorframe, her crutches nowhere in sight. She looked like a dancer. Her walnut-brown top could pass for a camisole but was likely a leotard, her beige dance skirt hung long on one side and short on the other to reveal more leg than the average cellulite-fearing woman would want to reveal, and just in case that wasn't dancerly enough, she completed her outfit with dangerous-looking heels that couldn't possibly be good for her and that Jori wished she didn't find sexy because the whole concept of heels was just so wrong. She figured if Rae was leaning against the wall it was because she was bracing herself against the pain of putting weight on her leg, but then her arm slid higher up the doorframe, her upper back shifted subtly, and what had at first glance appeared to be a resting position had morphed into a come-on.

Jori snorted. What was this, National Stick Out Your Chest Month? Because this was exactly what Kaoli Morgenroth had been doing at the pool watching Rae, waiting for her to notice her. Kaoli Look-Up-My-Skirt Morgenroth. Rae's damn girlfriend. Why did women do crazy shit like date unavailable women? Or, if Melanie was right, *pretend* to date unavailable women? Love triangles weren't healthy, although the possibility did make her blood pulse a little faster. Because when she thought of Rae, she knew exactly why someone would be tempted to ignore good sense.

"That doesn't work on women," Jori said, setting the bench down. Had Rae seen her dance with it? Or did she think she was just rearranging the furniture? Crap. She wasn't going to let herself get embarrassed until she knew she had a reason to be. She was strength-training, damn it, not fantasizing.

"What are you talking about?"

"You know what I'm talking about. Draping yourself against the wall."

"Draping?" Rae pretended to look affronted. Right. Like she didn't know what her body was doing. "I'd call it *leaning*."

"Men love that sort of thing," Jori said. "Women don't. We don't notice."

Rae moved with a graceful ripple, drawing attention to her body while managing to make it look natural and unintentional. "It sounds like *you* noticed."

"Okay, I noticed. But I wasn't turned on." She didn't *want* to be turned on, not by a straight woman's trick. Not by a straight woman's trick performed by a lesbian, either. How many times had she seen a woman stick her chest out in a man's direction and felt nauseated? Men were simple-minded, visual creatures. Women needed more. "It's too blatant."

"Too blatant, huh?" Rae shifted against the doorframe again and arched her back into an exaggerated pose that no mere mortal ought to be able to achieve. She shimmied as she returned to a more normal position, graceful and effortless, putting her dancer's training to good use.

Jori watched, fascinated in spite of herself. Oh, who was she kidding? All those straight women who made her want to gag? She was just jealous they weren't interested in her.

"Look at you, all flustered and uncomfortable." Rae let her head drop back until it rested on the wood. "Relax. I'm not flirting with you."

"Why the hell not?" Jori said.

Rae laughed, brushing it off like it was a joke.

Which she expected, really, since Rae had a girlfriend. And thought Jori was straight.

"When I start flirting with you, you'll know."

When she started, not *if*.

She didn't mean it, though. Jori was reading way too much into it. Because Rae had a girlfriend. Rae had a girlfriend. Rae had a...

"When is that going to be?" Jori challenged her.

"Hmm." Rae touched the doorframe and ran her hand up and down the molding with daydreamy slowness.

Jori figured she should probably be offended that Rae was jerking her chain, but instead she laughed. "Is that the next step up after the wiggle?"

"What, this?" Rae rubbed the front of her body against the doorframe. "Inappropriate touching of the woodwork?"

If it were anyone else, she might have felt like she should look away, but Rae was having so much fun it made it all feel...not innocent, exactly, but not something that needed to be taken seriously. Not something that would require her to sternly remind herself that Rae was already spoken for.

"I don't know if I'd pick up on that," Jori said. "It might be too subtle."

"In that case, I may have to go straight to nudity."

"Too late." Didn't she remember? Jori certainly did. Ever since that day in the locker room, her mind had been stuck on an instant replay of Rae exposing her bare sculpted waist as she dressed. Each time she thought about it she was hit once again by a shot of need that squeezed something deep inside and made it hard to think about anything else.

"Right. I forgot that didn't work." Rae stopped rubbing against the doorframe. "Why didn't that work?"

"Because if I see one more guy salivate over a woman for no other reason than she's half-naked and gorgeous, I'll scream. Maybe that's all it takes to make a man foam at the mouth with lust, but—" Jori listened to herself spout yet another one of her theories. She didn't know where she came up with this stuff, but she seemed to have an endless supply.

"But…?"

"But not me." She'd seen Rae with nearly nothing on, and yeah, she had a nice body, but the mere sight of it hadn't made her fall crazy in lust with her.

Her breathing kicked up a notch, remembering.

Must be all that ranting, making her breath get all messed up.

Jori gulped for air and continued. "If I thought I was in love with every naked woman I saw, I'd either have to quit using the locker room or clear my schedule, because I'd be a very busy lady."

"You wish."

"I don't wish."

Rae contemplated the wall and lifted one knee in a balletic pose. "Of course you don't. You're straight."

Not this again. "The truth is—"

"Yes?" Rae slid her knee up the doorway as high as was safe in that skirt. Higher, actually.

She complained that her injured leg was still atrophied, but the difference between the two was growing less and less noticeable every day. Not that she was staring. Much. Even recovering from injury, Rae looked amazing, and it was becoming more and more difficult to react to her moves like they were nothing more than silliness.

Skirts were not her thing. Heels? No way. Yet skirts and heels on Rae? Somehow that was different. And that disturbed her. It wasn't like her to let a woman turn her head so much that she didn't recognize her own opinions anymore.

"For women, visual appeal isn't enough," Jori said.

"You're making kind of a big generalization, aren't you? Maybe some women are more visual but they learn to hide it."

"Okay, so *in general*, nudity isn't enough to make a woman crazed. In general, men get hit by physical attraction first and then emotional attraction grows from there. We're the opposite," Jori said. "At least I am," she added, so Rae couldn't accuse her of stereotyping. "First I fall in love with a person for their personality. Then their body becomes interesting."

God, she was such a hypocrite. She ogles—*admires*, she corrected herself—Rae's butt—*skirt*, damn it—and then claims women aren't visual.

"How civilized of you."

Jori frowned as she replayed what she'd said: *First I fall in love with a person for their personality. Then their body becomes interesting.* She found Rae's body interesting. Her eyes didn't skim past her without noticing, like with all the other naked female bodies she saw in the locker room every day. That meant…oh no. That meant she was already attracted to her and well on her way toward…

When did *this* start? Well, she knew when it started. It started the first time she saw her, a small determined guest in the deep end of the pool, squeezed into two flotation belts so she wouldn't sink, pushing herself to the point of exhaustion. All she'd been able to see was the tops of her shoulders and her head and her adorable stubby ponytail. It had been enough.

Rae finally took mercy on her and put distance between her and that doorframe, making her way across the floor with a slow, rocking gait that suggested she didn't quite want to bend her knee, despite what she'd just done to the woodwork. That slight hesitation in her stride as her heels clicked on the wood floor did something to Jori's gut. But then it got worse, because soon Rae was standing in front of her, closer than would normally have been comfortable if her nervous system hadn't decided the boundaries of her personal space no longer existed.

Rae held her arms out in invitation—not to embrace, but to dance—and somehow it was too much.

When Jori didn't respond, Rae dropped her arms to her side. "You really are straight, aren't you?"

"What? Why?" Jori gave a startled twitch and almost laughed out loud at the disconnect between her own line of thought and Rae's. What could she possibly have said that made Rae come to that ridiculous conclusion?

"You've obviously spent a lot of time thinking about what's wrong with men."

"Shouldn't that make me *not* straight?"

"Not necessarily. I mean, for me, I prefer to spend my time thinking about women. Why should I care what men think of the opposite sex? I leave it to the straight women of the world to figure out what makes men tick."

"Good point."

Rae held out her arms again. Jori shook herself out of her decidedly *not* straight train of thought and reached for her. Rae positioned Jori in a standard dance hold, one arm curved around her shoulder, their free hands clasped. No tango legs, thank God. But just touching her, standing in each other's space, was unnerving. And wonderful. And this time they were alone... Jori jerked her gaze down at her arms and memorized the correct pose.

"So you're not going to explain?"

Jori shook her head. They were in each other's arms—sort of—and that made it hard to focus. Talking and dancing at the same time was turning out to be surprisingly tricky. Or maybe the real problem was that it was hard to do much of anything when the only thing that mattered was the caring, supportive pressure of Rae's hand on her shoulder blade and the fact that she was standing close enough to kiss her.

But she had to reply. "I don't believe in labels. I believe in being willing to love no matter what form love takes." There were a lot of things she was less than honest about, but this wasn't one of them. She never lied about the important stuff.

Rae pressed her lips together the way people did when they disapproved of you but weren't going to say so, at least not to your face. "Just say it: *bi*."

"It's not that simple."

"One syllable."

"Still not that simple."

Rae looked amused that she wasn't going to win this one. She tightened her hold and stepped forward with the music, prompting Jori to step back. "I'll dance the lead and you dance the follow, straight girl."

Dancing with her was heaven, and arguing with her was…well, she'd never thought arguing about her sexuality could be so much fun. "Haven't you ever heard that it's all a continu—"

"Do *not* say it's all a continuum." Rae's grip on her hand and her shoulder blade was firm and unyielding. "I am so far at the end of the continuum, I'm not even *on* the continuum. I am so far at the end I've fallen off, and when people say it's all a continuum it's like they're telling me I belong on it, and I don't."

"And that means I can't be different?"

"As long as you're not dating *me*, sure." Rae gave her a warning smile.

Or was that a teasing smile? Before Jori could decide, Rae was moving again and leading her into a rapid sequence of dance steps.

Jori tried not to trip. Oh joy. But this was what she wanted, right? She wanted to be alone in a room with her, holding hands, standing close, breathing the scent of chlorine that seemed to be a permanent part of her, joined in a shared rhythm.

"Teach me something that'll make me look like a better dancer than Axel."

Rae adjusted her hold, sliding her hand from Jori's shoulder blade to her waist like she was trying to decide which was better. She gripped her waist, making her choice. Her touch burned through Jori's tank top.

"Is that why you're being so nice about helping me? To

learn stuff you can dance with him?"

Why, no. No, it wasn't.

Rae continued, oblivious. "I told you ballroom isn't my thing, right? That means this isn't going to be real ballroom dance. I'm making shit up. Do you want me to get someone else?"

"Of course not." Even if this wasn't technically real ballroom, whatever that meant, it wasn't like anyone could tell the difference. Rae was a professional dancer, right? Surely anything she taught her would be good. Not that Jori was going to learn anything useful, anyway, when instead of watching Rae's feet she was noticing that her leotard was so old and worn that its elastic had weakened, and that although it still hugged her body, the stitched edging at the neckline clung less fiercely than it should, revealing a hint of the tops of her breasts. Rae wasn't wearing a bra. Because she didn't need to. Some women might feel self-conscious about that, but not Rae, sticking her chest out like she had something to stick out. She owned it, and that made her sexier than anyone who met society's ridiculous standards. How amazing would it feel to touch her delicate skin, slide over the gentle swell of exposed temptation, and slip under the edge of that neckline with just her fingertips, aching to reach farther down? It was making her crazy to clasp her hand in a dance hold, to touch her and yet not touch her the way she wanted to.

"I'm just going to be creative," Rae said, blithely unaware of the direction of Jori's thoughts. "I told Ka—" She cut herself short. "I told my friend," she corrected. "But she doesn't care that what I teach her won't be a real foxtrot or whatever, so I have free rein."

"Kaoli Morgenroth. I know. I overheard her asking you to do it."

"Oh." Rae took an awkward step back on her injured leg and wobbled dangerously. "Did you hear the part about—" She let go of her and covered her mouth. "What else did you hear?"

It wasn't hard to figure out what Rae was worried about. "You mean the part about her getting married?"

Rae gripped her shoulder. "You won't tell the tabloids, will you? She'll think I'm the one who leaked it."

"I wouldn't even know who to call."

Her fingers dug into her deltoids. "She's fired people for less."

"I won't gab."

"You sure?"

"I'm sure."

Rae sighed with relief. "Thank you. I really, really, really—"

"—appreciate it?" Jori said, before Rae got carried away and started offering sexual favors. Yeah, right. That was Jori's approach, not Rae's. It was always a joke, of course. But it wouldn't be as funny coming out of Rae's mouth.

"I really do appreciate it."

"Is she planning on ever telling her fans? How does she expect to keep something like that a secret?"

"It helps to be engaged to the editor-in-chief of *Celebrity Crush*."

Was that who that Griffin guy was? No kidding. With the biggest, most credible tabloid in her lap, she must be under the illusion that she could control her publicity. She'd also never been quite as famous as she'd recently become, so no one had bothered to dig for dirt. That might be about to change.

"Are you and Kaoli really…" Jori trailed off. It was none

of her business. But she had to know.

"Dating?" Rae finished for her.

Jori nodded.

"I…" Rae hesitated, then took a deep breath. "Yes."

Jori tried not to react. Her heart dropped anyway.

Rae could have anyone she wanted. She didn't have to be someone's mistress. She could be with someone who would put her first. She could be with someone like Jori.

"Have you been dating long?"

Rae laughed uncomfortably. "Not long, no."

"Because I could have sworn you looked like you didn't want her to touch you, that day she showed up at the pool." Jori forced herself to stop talking, because if she said anything more, Rae would realize she cared, and she didn't want her pity. If Rae was unavailable, there could be no good outcome to her knowing how Jori felt.

"Um, yeah." Rae bit her lip. "It's only been a few days, but don't spread it around, okay?"

Her resolve to not say anything slipped. "Why would you—"

"We have a history," Rae said. "I've been waiting for this for a long time. Since high school, believe it or not."

Of course they had a history. There was something about the way they acted around each other, about the way they drifted toward each other and then recoiled. Maybe they learned to do the stick-out-your-chest thing from each other. Although Rae was *way* better at it than Kaoli.

"There are other women," Jori said. Other women who weren't jerks. "You don't have to date someone who's marrying someone else."

"She's not as bad as she seems."

Not exactly a heartfelt declaration of love.

But what could she do? Nothing. Nothing but be a friend and shut up.

Jori slipped her right hand into Rae's left and allowed Rae to draw her into position. And thought about what it meant that Rae had leaned against a doorframe to smile at Jori and arched her spine and her perfect, tiny breasts in her direction.

When she was supposedly dating someone else.

12

It wasn't until Rae, Jori, and Kaoli convened mid-week outside the yoga barn that Rae realized the space she'd been practicing in with Jori was in use.

"I should have checked the schedule," Rae said as the workshop attendees stretched their arms wide while Sierra urged them to relax their ribs. She *had* checked it, but when she'd seen "Freeing the Voice Workshop" on the calendar, she'd assumed the yoga barn would be available since the non-yoga workshops were always held in the lodge's multipurpose rooms, not here. She hadn't counted on yoga being part of a singing class, although it did make a weird kind of sense. Clearly she'd had no idea how far Sierra and Melanie were willing to push their creativity to reach new customers.

"Where to?" Kaoli asked.

"We could check the multipurpose rooms," Jori said. "Move the furniture out of the way."

Rae had tried to talk Jori out of joining them, telling her she didn't want to impose, but she'd lost. Jori wanted to help her demonstrate the dance moves they'd worked out together, she'd said, and she wanted to make sure Rae stayed off her feet. Both of which were unnecessary, but not unwelcome.

"Those rooms are already in use," Rae said. "I heard singing in there on my way here."

Jori pushed her hands through the shock of hair at the top of her head and continued down the fuzzy sides to rub the back of her neck. "How about we practice outside? On the grass somewhere. Or the parking lot."

"We can't dance on grass." She hated to be negative, but… "Or gravel. Our shoes have to slide." She was starting to think they might not have a choice, though. Maybe grass would work if she was careful with her ankle.

"Did I see a band shell in town?" Kaoli said. "That might have a wooden floor."

"That's a great idea," Rae said. Leave it to Kaoli to take note of anything resembling a stage.

"Okay then," Kaoli said. "What are we waiting for?"

"What about your bodyguard?" Jori said. "Don't you need him?"

"He woke up with a stomach flu." Kaoli touched her throat and shuddered. "I'm staying as far away from his germs as possible."

"What happens if someone recognizes you?"

Kaoli shrugged like Jori was overreacting. "I'm supposed to be on tour. The undesirables won't be stalking me here."

What did she mean, she wouldn't be stalked? Photographers had stalked her to this very location to take that misleading photo of her kneeling by the pool to kiss Rae's forehead. But Rae didn't bother pointing that out, because Kaoli knew better than anyone that if she wanted the public to believe they were dating each other, then they needed to be seen together. And that was the real reason Kaoli wasn't afraid to practice outside: she wanted to be seen. And it wouldn't be a problem. Maybe Jori didn't realize it, but most of the time, Kaoli didn't really need a tough-looking guy to follow her around. One day she'd be famous enough to need him around the clock, but for now, the bodyguard was more of an ego boost than real protection.

The bodyguard and his germs had the key to Kaoli's rental car and Rae didn't have a car, of course, so they headed out to Jori's ancient Corolla hatchback.

"Rae, you should take the back," Jori said as she removed Baylee's booster seat and stored it in the rear cargo space. "That way you can keep your knee straight and stretch your leg across the seat."

"Yeah."

Rae stashed her crutches behind the booster seat and scrambled into the back. The crutches were not just in case of emergency—she needed them, and she was not happy about it. It was only temporary, though. A day. Two, max. She'd overdone it—nothing serious. It had probably been a mistake to rush into heels. Her ankle had gotten tired, and then her knee had overcompensated, and now here she was, still not free of those damn crutches. But it had felt so good to ignore her sensible sneakers and slip into shoes that made her feel like dancing that she couldn't promise she wouldn't do it again.

"You can rest your foot in my lap," Kaoli said, opening the opposite door. "If anyone sees us, it'll look sexy." As if she really thought they'd be noticed driving into town, or that their seat selection would become a topic of discussion. Or that anyone outside the car could see whether Rae's foot was in anyone's lap or not.

Rae planted her good leg on the car's upper frame to block Kaoli from entering. There was no way she was going to subject Jori to thinking they were doing anything untoward in the back seat. "Take the front, Kaoli. My knee hurts and I don't want you jostling it."

Kaoli grudgingly got into the front passenger seat. Ten minutes later they were in town, parking in front of a row of shops and making their way across the freshly mown grass of the central square.

When they reached the band shell, it was empty. Rae sat on the lip of the low stage and braced her back against a wide post supporting the roof so she could stretch her legs out in front of her. She left her crutches below, propped against the edge of the stage. Kaoli hopped up beside her, still fixated on this idea that they should sit together.

It didn't look like anyone had recognized them. No one even glanced in their direction, even though Kaoli's skirt was so short she shouldn't be sitting in it, not without tights. Her legs dangled off the stage, bouncing and kicking with enough energy to show off her inner thighs, if not her panties— assuming she was wearing any—to any passersby who looked her way. Another vigorous kick accidentally made contact with Rae's crutches and knocked them over. Jori caught the crutches as they fell and repositioned them within easy reach of Rae, but out of range of Kaoli's careless feet.

"Shouldn't we be getting started?" Jori asked.

"I need a minute to rest," Kaoli said.

More like she needed a minute to see if anyone would notice her, but Rae's knee hurt too much after their brief walk from the car to argue. Jori met Rae's eyes. She must have sensed that Rae wasn't ready because she shrugged and sat on her other side.

A group of loud, boisterous, drunk college boys who somehow hadn't left town for the summer passed by on the sidewalk. There were at least ten of them, and several had removed their shirts in the hot weather. Kaoli fanned herself vigorously with one hand. Jori checked them out, too, and

Rae's heart sank.

"Shirts are overrated," Kaoli declared.

Jori scoffed. "Not on those guys, they aren't."

"Are you crazy?" Kaoli asked. "Did you see their chests?"

Rae closed her eyes, hoping the guys were being loud enough that they wouldn't hear Kaoli's comments. The last thing they needed was a crowd of drunk men believing she and her friends would welcome the opportunity to be hit on.

"I've seen better," Jori said. "They need to work out before they subject us to the view."

Of course Jori wasn't impressed—because despite Rae's conviction that Jori was straight or bi, anyone capable of flirting with women the way Jori did didn't honestly like men at all. She couldn't. Except the way she was staring, she wasn't exactly acting like she wasn't interested.

"Now that one..." Jori nodded in the direction of a man trailing at the edge of the group in a sleeveless black tee that exposed biceps that were significantly larger than the group average. "That's a man I'd enjoy seeing more of."

No. *No.*

Kaoli kept her gaze fixed on their retreating backs. "Bodybuilders don't do it for me."

"I doubt that," Jori said. "Have you seen the men who dance in your show? I assume you hired them."

"They're for the audience, not for me," Kaoli said.

"Because you might be gay," Rae reminded her. She wasn't sure why she bothered—if Kaoli wasn't more concerned about hiding the truth from Jori, why should she worry? Especially since it was going to be impossible to hide once Griffin showed up for rehearsal. And didn't scream at her for sleeping with his fiancée. Maybe that was why Kaoli didn't care.

"Gym rats spend too much time checking themselves out in the mirror," Kaoli told Jori. "Who needs that?"

"Everyone's entitled to their own opinion," Jori said.

"These guys may not be built," Kaoli continued, "but they give off that vibe. That irresistible male vibe. You're welcome to go for the buffitude, but I go for the vibe." She nodded knowingly, then remembered herself with a wince. "I mean, I used to be. Before I realized I liked girls," she amended, rolling her eyes at Rae like her new sexual orientation was Rae's stupid idea, not her own.

Rae shook her head and chipped at the flaking paint on the wooden floorboards by her leg. If it weren't impossible for an injured dancer to audition for another job, she might reconsider whether this job was worth putting up with her boss's personality.

"They don't have the vibe," Jori said.

"Of course they do," Kaoli said dismissively, apparently forgetting—again—that she wasn't supposed to find them attractive. "You can tell yourself you don't like their randy, half-naked awesomeness and pretend they're not a hell of a lot more fun than the guy who's surgically attached to his biceps curl machine, but I don't believe you."

Glaring, Jori pulled her reflective sunglasses off the top of her head and positioned them on her nose. Her silence was intimidating—Rae sensed it and it wasn't even directed at her. For someone who was purportedly a fan, she seemed a bit hostile. "They didn't do anything for me."

"Fine. You're only interested in girls and fully dressed, muscle-bound male morons. But if this is how you're hitting on Rae, by dancing with me—I mean, that's why you're here, right? Because our invalid wants you to dance with me?—I've got to tell you, I don't think it's a very good plan."

Kaoli was wrong. Jori wasn't hitting on her. Rae wouldn't mind if that changed, but for now, the reality was…

"I'm not hitting on Rae," Jori grumbled.

See? She was right.

Jori cleared her throat. "I'm not." This time her voice was flat and indifferent.

Wow. That felt like rejection.

Rae reached for her crutches and awkwardly maneuvered herself onto her feet. "How about we work on the dancing?"

Jori jumped up and held out her hand to Kaoli, their argument seemingly forgotten in her haste to get the point of the afternoon over with. Kaoli batted her eyelashes, and Rae wondered how she'd feel if Kaoli decided to slide her arms around Jori's neck and kiss her and find the answers she hadn't been able to find with Rae. It would never happen, but what if it did? Kaoli could satisfy her craving for adventure, Jori would get bragging rights for the rest of her life for scoring with someone famous, and they'd both understand when Kaoli moved on and decided women weren't for her.

This was going to be fun, trying not to picture them in bed together. Rae turned on the music and began talking them through the choreography while Jori did the physical work of showing Kaoli what to do. Watching the two of them together, it was hard to believe Rae had ever found Kaoli attractive. Kaoli was the one she was supposed to be teaching, but Jori was the one who held her attention. Jori might have trouble picking up dance steps and she might not execute them perfectly, but there was nothing clunky about the way she moved. The fact that she *wasn't* trained, that she didn't have years of dance classes behind her, made her swiveling hips seem even more sensual.

Kaoli wasn't perfect, either—she was a singer who knew

how to move, not a trained dancer—but it wasn't the same. Kaoli was too controlled, too calculating, too heartless. Her fans might be captivated by her charisma and want to sleep with her, but not Rae. Not anymore. Not even to prove to her teenage self that she could. The only person here who had that effect on her was Jori. If she had a doorframe she'd lean against it and stick her chest out just to watch Jori get flustered and listen to her come up with outraged, adorable explanations for why Rae shouldn't do things like that.

Instead, she contented herself with watching. Jori dealt with Kaoli like a pro, keeping her focused on the steps and deflecting Kaoli's diva attitude so they could get it done. Every move Jori made, every reach, every turn, every seductive glance over her shoulder set off an answering shiver in Rae's nervous system, reminding her how good it felt to stretch and flex, reminding her of everything she'd been deprived of by her injury. When Jori floundered on one of the more complicated moves, Rae gave in. She put aside her crutches and joined in to help, and Kaoli behaved herself, holding hands without turning it into something it wasn't.

Touching Kaoli wasn't quite the same as touching a stranger—maybe it never would be, given their history—but it was close. It didn't make her nervous. It certainly didn't turn her on. It was comfortable. It was like dancing with any of the other dancers she worked with every day. Like she'd always wanted to feel around her.

But it wasn't until she took Jori's hand to demonstrate the next part of the choreography that she felt not just comfortable, but free, and she let loose and really danced. She stretched her arms and twisted her ribcage and shimmied her hips with all the soul-deep emotion she'd pour out if she were onstage. She imagined the people passing by on the street were her audience, and she made her movements big enough and bold enough to be seen three blocks away. Her ankle was a little wobbly and her knee was a little weak, but none of that got in the way of turning the relatively simple steps into undulating waves of yearning and heat, or of showing Kaoli how amazing this choreography could be if Kaoli's stupid boyfriend weren't the one dancing it. But mostly she danced for herself, reveling in the pure joy of transforming music into motion, of feeling her muscles wake up, of returning to who she was meant to be after long weeks of losing herself to pain. She danced recklessly, just like she always did. It was the only way to dance.

After a while, a small crowd had gathered near the stage. They weren't watching Rae—she had no illusions about that. Kaoli was the reason they'd stopped to stare. They didn't climb onstage or shriek Kaoli's name or shout how much they loved her, though. Which was nice. Instead, they seemed to sense she was working and were satisfied to just observe from a distance, as if they'd been invited to an exclusive backstage event and would be kicked out if they didn't stay on their best behavior. But Kaoli would have to be deaf not to hear them on their phones gasping to their friends that they would not believe who they'd found.

An hour later, Kaoli announced that she needed to find a ladies' room and hurried off in the direction of the nearby shops and restaurants. That was when the rabid fan action finally hit. Half the crowd ran after her, pleading for selfies or shouting out offers to be her tour guide around town.

As the crowd dispersed, Rae eyed the floor, wondering how much it would hurt to bend her knee to lie down and rest. As usual, she'd overdone it. The floor looked far away. If Kaoli was fast, it might not be worth it to stretch out on her back—not if she was just going to have to get back up again, because getting up hurt almost as much as sitting down.

Jori arrived at her side with her crutches. "Looking for these?"

"Thanks." Rae took them and leaned on them, shifting her weight off her throbbing leg.

"Kaoli is something else," Jori said. "Is she really your girlfriend? Because she doesn't act like it."

"She's—"

"Please tell me she's not."

What could she say? She didn't want to continue lying to her. When she'd agreed to lie for Kaoli, she'd known it might interfere with any chance she had of dating anyone real, but she'd told herself she'd be too focused on rehabbing her stupid body to want to date. Rae reached down to rub the sore tendons around her knee. She *should* be more focused on rehab.

"She's not, is she?" Jori said.

Why was Jori pushing?

Rae straightened. She didn't want to lie, but there was a lot of wiggle room between lie and truth. "She'd probably sleep with you either way."

Jori's mouth fell open. "You think I want to know if she's your girlfriend because I want to sleep with her."

"It wouldn't be the first time a fan had her on their to-do list," Rae grumbled.

"She's not the one I want to sleep with," Jori said, herding her toward a narrow stretch of solid wall near the back of the band shell and crowding her against it until there was nowhere for her to go. Her voice—always hoarse from cheering on her aerobics students—was rougher than usual. The sound reverberated up and down Rae's spine. Jori could make love to her with only her voice and it would be a high point of her life.

Oh God. Jori wasn't joking, was she.

"Are you propositioning me?"

Jori stepped closer. She planted one hand on the wall next to Rae's head, boxing her in, then shifted forward onto her forearm, narrowing the distance even more. "You want me to be, don't you?"

Rae licked her dry lips and shrank back against the wall even though it already pressed into her spine. Jori's tough-dyke attitude was doing funny things to her insides. She'd never heard her I-eat-problems-like-you-for-breakfast, and-I-do - not - mean - *eat* - the - way - you - want - me - to - mean-it voice—never thought of her as someone who might have one. And now she could think of nothing else, except for how it would feel to have Jori's mouth on various parts of her anatomy.

But she wasn't going to fall for someone who had red flags plastered all over her very attractive…uh…personality? No, really, that's what she meant. Personality. She had a very attractive personality. Except, of course, for the red flags. The main red flag being that Jori could stand the thought of being with a man.

Jori reached for Rae's hair and stroked it. Gently, like Rae was precious to her. Rae's breath hitched. Jori's did, too.

"But if you're really dating her…" Jori stared into her eyes with an intensity that made Rae shiver. "Maybe I shouldn't touch you."

She should. She really should touch her.

Jori didn't move. Didn't pull away.

They were standing so close that all Rae could do was keep looking into her eyes. All she *wanted* to do was keep looking into her eyes. Breathing was optional.

"I…" Jori's voice failed her.

Rae swallowed hard, as if she were the one who couldn't speak.

"I don't…" Jori cleared her throat. "I don't think you should date her."

Rae was glad there was a wall supporting her spine, keeping her upright. "Why is that?"

"Because she's about to get married?"

Oh, Jori. "That's not why."

"She'll disappoint you. She'll hurt you."

Rae shrugged. It was a little too late to worry about Kaoli disappointing her. "I don't know about that. She's made it pretty clear she's going through with the wedding. It's not like she's stringing me along."

Misleading, even if it was all true. But what was she supposed to say? *Don't worry about who I'm dating, it won't change anything?*

"And you're okay with that?" Jori's voice sharpened with disapproval.

Great. Now Jori thought she had no standards. "I have my reasons."

"Fine," Jori said. "Go have unsatisfying, uncommitted sex with her."

Jori was annoyed. She cared enough to be annoyed.

Rae took a deep breath. If Jori was another straight girl tempted by a fleeting urge that would lead to nothing… No. She wasn't going to go down that road. She wanted this to mean something. She wanted this to be real. She wanted…this.

"I was lying before," Rae said. "I'm not dating Kaoli."

The pulse at the base of Jori's throat jumped.

God, that pulse. She wanted to close the gap between them but couldn't move.

"Good."

With an uneven breath, Jori thrust her fingers through Rae's hair and cradled her head. Their foreheads touched. Rae closed her eyes. The band shell, the boardwalk, the passersby who might or might not be near—all of it disappeared, her entire existence reduced to the delicious scent of Jori's skin and the warmth at the spot where Jori's forehead touched hers, a warmth that grew and spread downward, outward, everywhere. Rae shifted her hips closer, pressed her body into her, whispered her name. Jori was going to kiss her, and this kiss wasn't going to be about revenge. This kiss would be sweet. Beautiful. Pure.

Their lips met and Rae stopped thinking about what this kiss would be because she was too busy opening her mouth to her and letting her in. Jori's tongue touched hers and she reeled from the welcome shock of it. And then she couldn't think at all, because Jori tasted better than she'd imagined possible, and the gutsy optimist kissed like kissing her was the only thing that mattered. Jori kissed without guarding her emotions. She kissed like she was already in love with her.

Rae's heart pounded out of control. Her crutches clattered to the floor.

Jori's hands moved to her neck, her shoulders, her chest, sliding over the rise of her breasts as if she had every right to. And she did. If Jori wanted to touch her, Rae was more than happy to let her, because everywhere she touched her, she came alive. As a dancer, she thought she knew everything about her body—every ache, every soreness, every joy of every one of her muscle fibers—but Jori was giving her a whole new perspective on how her body could feel.

Was this what it felt like to be wanted? Was this was it did to her? Or was this what Jori—Jori and no one else—did to her? She hadn't reacted like this to Kaoli. Not even close. She hadn't reacted like this to anyone. Hadn't known anything was missing. But Jori…Jori's touch was a rush. A revelation. It made her feel not just full of wanting her, but wanted in return.

Her knee, though…her knee was giving out. She clutched at Jori's shoulders as her strength failed her, and Jori pinned her to the wall with her hips, the force of her sudden thrust stopping her fall. Jori adjusted her balance and their hip bones jutted into each other again, hitting her with another wave of heat. She felt so good pressed against her, their bodies finding where they fit.

"It doesn't bother you that I lied to you?" Rae asked.

"Nothing bothers me when you're kissing me."

They were so close she couldn't see her whole face, just her blond eyelashes as they fluttered downward. And her lips.

"Will it bother you later? When we're not kissing?"

"No. I'm sure you had your reasons."

"You sound so positive."

"Let's never stop. Then we won't have to find out."

Jori met her lips again, and it was just as good. Better. Rae wanted it to last forever and at the same time she desperately wanted to get underneath her clothes because this ache wasn't going to be satisfied by mere kissing. This ache demanded an all-out, full-body commitment to getting as close as physically possible. This ache was not going to go away until she slid up Jori's bare legs and tasted her in a whole list of places that couldn't possibly be appropriate in their current, not-all-that-hidden location.

Jori was perfect. She was supposed to *not* be perfect, but

at the moment she couldn't for the life of her remember why.

"Where is everyone?" Kaoli's voice carried from somewhere not far behind the other side of the wall.

Rae's eyes flew open and she broke the kiss, cursing Kaoli's bad timing. Jori sighed.

"Go away," Jori told Kaoli under her breath.

Jori stroked Rae's hair, her fingertips lingering on the side of her face. A spark lit inside Rae's heart and glowed, expanded, spilled out, made the world shine—even made her forgive Kaoli. Her timing could have been worse, after all. If she'd returned earlier they might not have had this moment alone together at all, and that would have been unbearable.

"Promise me this isn't over," Jori said, closing in for one last kiss.

Rae tried to answer, but all that came out was a moan. Jori had obviously meant for this kiss to be chaste or at least brief, but it was already spiraling out of control.

"Rae? Jori?" Kaoli sounded much closer.

Jori gently pulled away, then licked at her lips and kissed her once more. And then she was sauntering across the stage, away from her, intercepting Kaoli and greeting her like nothing had happened.

But something had happened. And now Rae was slumped against the wall, unable to take her eyes off the woman she wasn't supposed to want, burning in places that hadn't ever burned with this kind of intensity, wondering how long she was going to have to wait before she could trust her legs to hold her and risk pushing away from the support of the wall. And how long she would have to wait before she could have that bliss again.

13

Sitting all morning in Jori's passenger seat for the long drive to Washington, DC, for Kaoli's concert shouldn't have been awkward, but somehow the easy conversation Rae had looked forward to never materialized, and instead she was watching the highway fly by and enduring hours of study review podcasts on accounting practices while she tried to figure out why kissing had thrown them both off-balance. For a while, she rested her hand on Jori's knee, and Jori covered her hand with a sweet gentleness that was an affirmation that her gesture was more than okay. But Jori never clicked off her podcast, and Rae didn't ask her to.

Jori was the only one attending the concert with her—Sierra had begged off at the last minute because of an urgent but vague problem requiring her attention at the lodge, and Melanie wasn't coming, either. Which was too bad, because Rae had hoped the tickets would be a small token toward thanking them for their generosity. But there'd be other opportunities.

Right now, her plan was to stop by afternoon rehearsals to catch up on whatever ongoing changes were being made to the choreography. Her friend Sylvie—who, during the months they weren't on tour, shared an apartment with her in New York—had warned her that while she was away, Lorenzo had been up to his usual perfectionist ways and was tweaking and re-tweaking the material they had supposedly already learned until it was difficult to remember which version he wanted. She didn't want to find herself ready to dance but unable to jump in because the show she had lived and breathed for months had moved on without her.

Her other, even more important reason for dropping by was to remind Kaoli she was still one of her dancers and to remind Lorenzo she still existed. She didn't want out of sight to become out of mind and end with her not getting her contract renewed.

Jori pulled up behind the unmarked back entrance of the massive concrete-and-steel building that was Kaoli's concert venue, and Rae stepped out of the car onto the oil-stained pavement. The building wouldn't open to the public for a few hours, so Jori drove off with her backpack full of accounting textbooks and left Rae to walk up to the door by herself. A middle-aged man wearing a long-lensed, expensive-looking camera around his neck leaned against the wall snacking on cheese curls.

"Kaoli Morgenroth coming in for rehearsal today?" he asked between mouthfuls, licking artificial cheese powder off his fingers.

How did he even know who she worked for? He didn't. He was fishing. Or worse, he'd done his research, which meant he was professional paparazzi. According to Lorenzo Marziliano, their choreographer, the correct word was technically *paparazzo* if there was only one them, but whatever. It sounded pretentious coming out of the mouth of someone who didn't have Lorenzo's authentic Italian accent.

"I have no idea," Rae said. He must get bored out of his mind, stalking celebrities who never showed. So bored that he either hadn't recognized Kaoli's supposed girlfriend or couldn't be bothered to take a photo of her. Unless it was all an act calculated not to scare her off before she led him to the real money shot. "She usually doesn't."

The rehearsal space was hidden deep inside a warren of administrative offices most people had no idea existed behind the public portions of the music venue-slash-sports arena. When Rae found it, her coworkers were busy practicing a new sequence Lorenzo had come up with for "Wildcat", the song Rae had been injured performing.

Kaoli was not there. The line she'd been trained to feed the press—that she had no idea where Kaoli was—was frequently true.

"Welcome back," said Lorenzo from his perch on a stool at the front of the studio while the dancers continued their run-through in time to recorded music, sweat flying from their hair as they spun. "Are you fixed?"

"Almost." Rae did her best not to limp as she made her way toward him, but it had to be obvious to him that she was struggling. She'd chosen not to wear a brace into the studio because she didn't want to remind anyone she was out of commission, but it made it that much harder to move. She wasn't graceful and she wasn't comfortable, but if she was lucky, Lorenzo wouldn't notice.

"I see." He turned dismissively to his notes. "Then you are not needed here."

Of course he'd noticed. What was she thinking? He spent hours a day watching his dancers and clearly had no trouble at all detecting her condition.

"I thought I could watch rehearsal and catch up on changes."

"Don't bother," Lorenzo said. "You're no use to me like this. Go home."

"I'll stay."

Lorenzo spit out some choice, angry words in Italian that she didn't need to understand to get the gist of. No one challenged Lorenzo, not unless they wanted to be yelled at. "Enough of this. Go. You scare the others with the bad luck."

"You won't even let me watch?" How could he do that? She was still part of the tour, wasn't she?

"Rest. Heal. Return when you are ready to dance."

Rae was sick of being away from the action. She collapsed on the bench beside him and faced the dancers, her back to the steamed-up mirror. "I'm watching."

Lorenzo raised his hands to the saints and deplored the world's overabundance of female stubbornness. Of which there was a lot in his life, because unlike many female stars who surrounded themselves onstage with only buff male eye candy in order to appeal to the female fans, Kaoli didn't assume that was what her audience came to see. Sure, she had the buff men, but two-thirds of her dancers were women, and she wasn't afraid to show them off. Which was part of what made this a great job.

"Fine. Watch." Lorenzo turned his back on her and rose to give corrections to the dancers one-on-one.

Rae memorized as much as she could. She flexed and pointed her feet, endlessly rotating her ankles, antsy to get off the bench and join the others but unwilling to provide incontrovertible proof that her body wasn't ready to dazzle.

Eventually her friend Sylvie came over. "I'm so glad you made it. We missed you."

"I missed you guys, too."

"How's the leg?"

"Better. I'm planning to be back here dancing before the tour ends."

"Sylvie. If you please," Lorenzo said. "Catch up on your social life later."

Sylvie shrugged and returned to Ralph, who was paired up with her for some lifts. They whipped through a series of steps that were not remotely like the ones Rae was expecting. Then Sylvie stretched her arms out to the sides, preparing to jump, and Ralph lifted her overhead.

"You weigh a ton," Ralph complained, lowering her beautifully to the ground. "What have you been eating? Doughnuts and rocks?"

"Don't blame me if you're slacking off with the barbells," Sylvie retorted.

"I'm not slacking off. It's you."

"I weigh the same number of pounds I did last week."

"Lose a few of them."

"Don't be a wimp."

"You think I'm a wimp? Not a lot of guys who can lift two hundred pounds of bitchy ballerina over their head."

"I do *not* weigh two hundred pounds, you jerk."

"A hundred and seventy-five?"

"A hundred and two!" Sylvie shrieked.

"You lie."

With Ralph's hands on her waist, Sylvie bent her knees and jumped straight up to practice the lift again. He raised her over his head and paraded her in a circle as she split her legs and extended her arms in a line that looked too balletic to be what Lorenzo wanted. Most of the dancers came from a ballet background, because it was excellent training, but dancing for a rock star was a whole different art form. More earthy and gymnastic.

Ralph gave an unnecessary grunt of effort meant to annoy her. "You do not weigh a hundred and two pounds."

Sylvie finished the move with an extra stretch of her long legs as she landed. "I should tell your adoring fans you can't do an easy lift."

"I did the lift."

"And you were so manly about it, too."

"Hey, Chloe," Ralph said to the dancer next to them. "How much does Sylvie weigh?"

"A hundred and twelve," Chloe said.

"Ha." Ralph planted his hands on his hips in a very unmanly fashion.

Sylvie planted her own hands on her hips and glared at Chloe.

Chloe turned a pirouette. "What, is your weight some big secret now?"

"Ha." Ralph tossed his head, flipping his nonexistent tresses over his shoulder.

"Be a man," Sylvie ordered.

"He's not unmanly," Chloe said, meeting Sylvie's eye in the mirror. "He's a misogynist."

"He's unmanly *and* a misogynist," Sylvie said.

"What's a misogynist?" Ralph said, sounding bland but balancing on the balls of his feet, prepared to dodge if they attacked.

Neither woman took the bait.

"He wouldn't be complaining if he was doing that lift with Preston," Chloe said, eyeing her own buff—and very straight—dance partner.

"How depressing." Sylvie turned to Ralph. "Go lift Preston a few times and build up your delts."

Preston smiled evilly at Ralph. "Come here, Ralphy-poo. Let me show you what it's like to dance with a real man."

Ralph thrust his hips in a rude, suggestive dance move

that might have made another guy nervous, but Preston only laughed.

"Rae!"

Kaoli appeared at the door to the practice studio and everyone paused to look, some turning their heads, others surreptitiously flicking their gazes in her direction and pretending they weren't. No doubt they were all up-to-date on the details of Rae's new status as Kaoli's love interest and were curious to see the two of them in action. Her closest work friends knew it was a sham, but since Kaoli was paranoid and had insisted that no one, not even her coworkers, know the truth, they hadn't shared the scoop with the others. Sylvie said the group was evenly split on the issue of whether the relationship was for real, so everyone would be watching for clues.

Seemingly oblivious to the attention, Kaoli headed straight for Rae, assaulting her with a blinding smile, her sexual charisma bullshit on full blast. Rae didn't react. Did Kaoli really expect her to keep up their act in front of the people she had to work with?

"Were there paparazzi out there?" Kaoli leaned over for an awkward hug, refusing to let her rise from the bench.

Rae hated that even though she didn't bring her crutches and she wasn't wearing a brace, everyone still seemed to think of her as injured. Honestly, she was almost completely healed. Not enough to nail a spectacular leap, but close.

"Just one."

"Did he see you?"

"Yeah. I don't think he recognized me, though."

"That's not good. We need people to know who you are." Kaoli checked herself out in the floor-to-ceiling mirrors and tucked a wayward hair into place. "Why don't we run across the street together for coffee."

She should have known Kaoli would want a photo op. Because that was show business. It wasn't all about the music. It was about image. Gossip. Publicity. Dragging a fake girlfriend outside to pretend to get coffee when word got out that there were photographers waiting in the vicinity.

"Won't he wonder why you didn't send an assistant to do it?" Rae was stalling, even though stalling would make no difference. Kaoli wasn't going to drop this, and their camera-toting stalker would be waiting no matter how long it took.

Kaoli smoothed her crimson leotard over her bust, tugged the neckline down, and cinched her belt an extra notch over her red stonewashed dance pants that were meant to look like jeans but wouldn't rip a seam on the off chance she was in the mood to do high kicks. "They don't think. All they care about is getting the shot."

"All right."

Rae followed her into the maze of narrow hallways that led outside and quickly fell behind. Her ankle, which had not been feeling too bad, started aching.

"Rae?"

Kaoli finally noticed that Rae wasn't keeping up and turned back and took her arm. Jori would have offered a supportive shoulder to lean on, but Kaoli seemed to think the most helpful thing to do was to pull on her arm to make her go faster. Rae did her best to keep her balance. She should have worn her brace. At least an elastic sports wrap. She would have, if she'd known she'd be hustling at this pace.

"Thanks for doing this," Kaoli said, still tugging. "All of it. I keep waiting for you to ask me to buy you a car or introduce you to your favorite movie star, but that's not the kind of person you are."

"What are you talking about?"

Kaoli stopped dragging her down the hall and faced her with that laser-like intensity that used to always fill Rae with yearning. Even though they were alone and no one was going to take a photo, Kaoli gave her a peck on the cheek.

"You would be so easy to love, Rae. You're the only person I've ever been interested in who wasn't more in love with my fame than with me."

Rae recoiled. "I'm not in *love* with you." Geez. Hadn't she been paying attention? Rae had refused to sleep with her. Sure, she'd been enthralled in high school, but she'd changed. They both had.

Kaoli squeezed her arm. "Don't say that."

"And what about Griffin? He loved you before you were famous."

"Griffin's whole life revolves around celebrities. Who's doing what, who's doing whom…" Kaoli raised her eyebrows with a haughty where-are-my-grammar-bonus-points look that would have had Rae swooning back during their tutoring days. When it didn't have the desired effect, Kaoli pouted and went back to making her point. "Who's popular, who's trending, who's on their way out. I doubt he'd have asked me to marry him if I weren't someone he could put on the cover of his magazine."

"I'm sure that's not true."

"Don't be naïve."

Before she knew it, Kaoli was kissing her. On the mouth. What was she doing? She knew Rae didn't want this. And Kaoli didn't really want her, either. Because if Rae had said she *was* in love with her? This kiss wouldn't be happening. The only reason Kaoli dared was because it was safe. All those years Rae had ached for a kiss, even a tiny one on the cheek or the nose or gosh, maybe something even more harmless like her kneecap? Kaoli had made her believe she'd have her one day, but she'd never followed through. Only when it was finally clear that Rae no longer wanted her did Kaoli feel safe crossing the line.

Rae jerked away.

"Don't do that in front of the cameras," Kaoli warned.

"Don't do that in private," Rae shot back.

"Come on, Rae, I didn't mean—"

"Let's get out of here."

She didn't wait to see what Kaoli would do. All she cared about was getting outside and making sure her leg held her upright for as long as Kaoli was watching.

Kaoli's bodyguard was waiting by the door and joined them as they exited the building. Cheese Curl Guy was still there and perked up immediately and started snapping away even as Kaoli's bodyguard loomed over him. Hey, there were two guys with cameras—even better. With a carefree photo-worthy smile, Kaoli barked at her bodyguard to step aside. He did, just barely, not looking too happy about it.

Showtime. Kaoli grabbed Rae's hand with a determined, almost desperate grip and posed using Hollywood's favorite waist-slimming trick, swiveling her shoulders in the opposite direction from her hips with the ease of someone who had practiced endlessly in front of a mirror. Rae dredged up her dancer's acting skills and did her best to look poised and proud to be a rock star's girlfriend. Kaoli puckered her lips for the cameras and leaned in. Good thing Rae saw it coming so she had time to brace herself and not flinch, because she was supposed to smile and look like she was in love, not let her true feelings ruin the photo that was going to make their careers. At least Kaoli was smart enough to go for her cheek this time.

Except, whoops, no, she wasn't going for her cheek—she was going for her lips. Instinctively, Rae whipped her head to the side to avoid her, and then suddenly Rae was on the sidewalk, rough concrete digging into her palms. One of the photographers laughed. She'd bent her legs to duck, but the unplanned deep knee bend had thrown her off-balance and her legs had collapsed.

"Are you hurt?" Kaoli said, doing a decent imitation of a concerned girlfriend, but it was her bodyguard who loomed over Rae with arms outstretched to help her to her feet.

"We should turn back," Rae said.

She couldn't make herself kiss Kaoli, so there was no point in staying. They'd have to find another solution.

14

Kaoli chewed her out as soon as they reached the building and were out of the public eye, but Rae didn't care. She was glad she'd done it. She watched the rest of rehearsal, and, after the dancers had been dismissed to rest and prepare for the evening's performance, Jori returned and they drove to a charming, hole-in-the-wall tea shop.

Rae didn't eat much because they had plans to meet up with some of her dance friends for dinner after the show, but they stayed busy killing time sampling the custom tea blends, especially the caffeinated ones.

A few hours later they were driving back to the concert venue. Jori pulled up to the curb at the front entrance to let Rae out so she wouldn't have to walk.

Rae kept her seatbelt fastened and pointed to the sign for parking. "It's not far."

"It is if your leg hurts."

"It doesn't hurt." Well, not enough to stop her from putting weight on it. As a dancer, something always hurt, so pain was relative. Besides, her knee was doing pretty well and she was wearing her ankle brace thanks to that run down the hall with Kaoli. "My joints lock up when I sit for too long. I'd rather walk." If she was going to survive sitting through the whole concert, she needed to move.

Jori grumbled something about it serving her right if she had to carry her, but she merged back into traffic. They found a parking garage a few blocks away and circled several levels underground before finding an available spot. Rae stumbled out, her knees and hips already stiff. She held on to the car's roof for balance and swung one leg behind her in a stretch.

"Do you want your crutches?" Jori asked, getting ready to pop open the back, where they'd stashed the wretched things just in case.

"I was fine without them this afternoon. I'll be okay."

"Are you sure? I know you've been managing on your feet, but I have a feeling most people wouldn't be walking this soon after such a bad injury."

"That's what everyone says." Everyone who wasn't a dancer, anyway. Rae stretched her other leg, then flexed her feet to make sure her ankles were working right. She couldn't imagine. In her own mind, her progress felt agonizingly slow. But at least it was progress.

"Your call." Jori frowned at her ankle and locked the car.

They exited the garage and followed the flow of pedestrians toward the venue, bright enough to light up a whole city block in the distance. Car exhaust hung low to the ground in the humidity and mixed with the rancid smell of fried food wafting from an unseen restaurant. A large crow waddled across their path. Another crow followed, holding something unnaturally orange in its beak.

"Cheese curls?" Jori angled their path to avoid the two crows. "Those birds have better taste than I thought."

"Oh yum. Empty calories with artificial flavor."

"How can you not like cheese curls?"

Before Rae could reply, a catcall pierced the air. The crows rose from the pavement in a huff. Rae glanced across the street in the direction of the sound, and sure enough, a man was leering at her. He stuck his fingers in his mouth and let loose another long, drawn-out wolf whistle. He hopped on one foot, clutching his leg like a clown, making sure she knew that out of all the other pedestrians on the busy sidewalk, she was the one who was the object of his attention.

"Jerk." Rae placed her weight carefully on one foot and then the other. She'd thought she was doing pretty well without crutches, but if a guy all the way on the other side of the street could tell she was limping, it had to be bad. Because surely he couldn't see her brace under her jeans. "I'm not unattractive enough? What do I have to do, wear a bag over my head?"

"Maybe he was whistling at *me*," Jori said.

Jori *was* pretty damn cute in her lavender overalls with the cuffs rolled up and quite the figure-hugging dark plum tee, but it wasn't a look that would draw the typical male's attention. Still, if it weren't for the man's stupid pantomime, Rae might have taken the proffered out. Leave it to Jori to be gorgeous *and* nice. "I guess you have to put up with that crap, too, huh?"

Jori shrugged. "I wear shorts a lot. It's like pouring blood into shark-infested waters."

The thought of that rudeness being directed at Jori was worse than remembering all the times she'd endured it herself. "I hate that they do that."

"It doesn't bother me. I wear whatever I want and to hell with them."

"It doesn't make you insanely angry?"

"They don't all do it to be rude," Jori said. "Some of them, yeah, but some guys, they're just loud and clueless and having a good time. They think they're paying us a compliment."

"They know they're not."

"You can't see their side of it because you don't want them to look at you at all."

"Please don't tell me you do." Because...yuck. Did Jori honestly not feel her skin crawl when a man looked her up and down? Yeah, okay, she knew the answer to that. She just didn't like the answer.

"Kaoli did this exact same thing to those shirtless guys in town, right?"

"Minus the catcalls," Rae grumbled, although Jori did have a point. But all it meant was that Kaoli was rude, too.

Jori stared straight ahead, her hands thrust in her pockets, almost like she was embarrassed to look her in the eye. "You're beautiful, Rae. People do stupid things around women like you."

Rae's stomach fluttered. Jori thought she was beautiful.

"I'm average." She didn't think she was hideous, but she wasn't the kind of person who got told she was beautiful. A good dancer, yes. A hard worker. Nice. Skinny enough to be a model, but too smart to throw her intelligence away on a career like modeling, which, considering her grades in high school did not mark her as highly intellectual, was a polite way of saying she wasn't pretty enough to succeed at it. Which was fine, because she didn't *want* men to think she was beautiful. She didn't want anyone to think she was beautiful, except maybe Jori, and maybe even Kaoli—but only because she wanted Kaoli to know what she was missing.

"You're not average," Jori said. "You're way, way sexier than that."

That was a stretch. "Not today, I'm not. I'm limping."

"Not that much." Jori's pace slowed like she was thinking too carefully about choosing the right words to focus on walking. People behind them on the sidewalk sped around them to pass. "It's hard to explain, but even when you're hurt, you still move like a dancer. There's something in that highly trained body of yours, some unconscious *oh my God she's hot*, that doesn't go away. I know you think you're not graceful or attractive right now, but you are."

Wow. She wanted people to admire what she could do with her body onstage, admire her grace and her athleticism and her artistry and not turn it into something sexual, but when Jori crossed that line, it didn't feel slimy. It felt good.

Jori wasn't done. "The way you move..." Her voice softened, became a little too much like a lover's. "It's hard to look away."

Oh God. Her legs weakened just like they had against the wall of the band shell, except this time she had nothing to lean on. If they weren't in the middle of a well-lit sidewalk with people all around, she'd be tempted to cling to Jori's shoulders and kiss her. Where was a private, dark alley when she needed one?

Their friend whistled again and broke the spell. Rae cursed under her breath. Wasn't he done intruding?

"How old do I have to be before I'm not young and nubile enough for them? Forty? Sixty-five? Ninety? When does it end?"

"Menopause," Jori said confidently.

"How would you know?" Jori and her theories. She had one for every occasion.

"Would you be more convinced if I asked around? I have some older students in my water aerobics class who would tell me."

"Oh no, I wouldn't want you to sully your theory with actual facts."

"Here's a fact. Researchers have found that strippers get

better tips when they're ovulating. Men sense it, somehow. Pheromones, is my guess."

"No way." Was she making that up? She had a way of sounding authoritative whether she knew what she was talking about or not.

"Just one of life's little jokes," Jori said. "You don't want to have anything to do with men, but your eggs are busy sending out the Bat-Signal to all sperm within a five-mile radius, signaling that they are ready for action."

"That doesn't explain the guys who catcall out the windows of a moving vehicle." Jori had to be making this up. "There's no way pheromones could carry that far, that fast."

"You must have an exceptionally strong Bat-Signal."

"Lucky me."

"And since all the straight women are on birth control pills that drug their eggs to sleep, *your* Bat-Signal is the only one around. Totally unfair, but true. I'm sure the men don't appreciate it, either, constantly drooling over attractive lesbians like yourself who won't let them fertilize your eggs. The whole system is whacked."

"I think you're getting a little carried away with your theory. Men do date straight women who are on the pill."

"They do," Jori said. "But they wish they didn't."

"You are so full of—"

"Maybe." Jori caught her gaze and winked. "Maybe not."

She was cute the way she considered herself an expert on the heterosexual dating mind, she really was. She had an opinion on everything, and every single one of her opinions was disparaging. It was enough to make a person think she didn't like men. That she *wasn't* straight, or even bi.

"And this theory is based on dating a grand total of how many men?"

Because why sleep with men at all if she found them so disappointing? Then again, she knew plenty of straight women—her coworker Chloe was a prime example—who seemed to get an incomprehensible sexual charge out of fighting with members of the opposite sex. Rae snuck a sideways glance at Jori as they continued walking. The truth was, she didn't want Jori to be one of those people. She didn't want Jori to like men.

Even though the existence of Jori's daughter suggested she'd been with at least one man. Unless she'd gone the turkey baster route. But why do that if she didn't have to? Anyway it was unlikely, since conceiving anything other than a boy through artificial insemination was the closest thing to a miracle a lesbian was likely ever to see.

The self-proclaimed pheromone expert skimmed a hand across the back of Rae's shoulders, barely touching the thin fabric of her blouse. Rae tingled beneath her hovering fingertips, waiting for her to make full contact, yearning for something more than this almost-touch, shaking with nervousness at being out in the open where people could see. So different from performing for the photographer with Kaoli, where she hadn't felt nervous because it wasn't real.

Please say zero.

"I don't believe in labels, sunshine, and if I tell you how many men, you're going to slap a label on me." Jori drew her into the protective circle of her arm as if to shelter her from the stream of passersby.

Rae didn't need protecting, but the thought of letting Jori take care of her made her feel so safe that her legs became unsteady and she swayed into her.

"Is Axel one of them?" she said into Jori's shoulder, acutely aware they were touching.

Jori hesitated. The word *no* vibrated through Rae's mind, filling the silence that dragged on and on. *No, Axel is not one of those men. No, absolutely not. No, no, no.* Because if Jori said yes, that would mean the number she didn't want to tell her was not zero.

"We're not dating," Jori said. "I told you, we're pretending."

That was the answer it had taken her so long to think about? What was she not telling her? Rae looked her in the eye. It was none of her business what Jori did on their dates, fake or not, but she didn't want to be lied to.

"Are you pretending to sleep with him?"

Jori smiled. "Are you pretending to be shocked?"

"I'm not shocked. I'm…" Rae shook her head. She still didn't understand why Jori would pretend to date a man she wasn't on some level attracted to. She was certainly flirtatious enough to get a real date. With someone who didn't care that she hopped up and down the sexual continuum. "Why are you doing it? He's going to want to sleep with you for real."

"I doubt his boyfriend would put up with that."

"Oh." The flood of relief caught her by surprise and she almost twisted her ankle.

Jori tightened her hold on her shoulder until Rae was stable, then moved her hand firmly to the small of her back. Warmth licked at the tension in her lower back and her spine arched subtly under Jori's hand. It was a struggle to keep the reflex under control, to not do more. Not long ago it had been a joke, arching her back like a cat in heat to see if she could make Jori laugh, but now her body's reaction was real. She was almost glad her ankle was unsteady, because it meant Jori would stay close to make sure she didn't fall. As a dancer she'd been taught to push through pain and smile no matter what, to create the illusion that the contortions she put her body through were effortless, so she felt guilty showing weakness. But if showing weakness meant Jori would stand by her side and offer a steadying hand, she'd live with the guilt.

"If I ask if you sleep with women, you won't tell me that, either, will you?"

Jori brought her lips close to her ear. "Maybe someday you'll work your wiles on me and find out."

15

Someday?

The concert had wrapped up half an hour ago and Rae was still obsessing over what Jori had meant. Maybe someday she'd work her wiles on her? What did she mean, *someday?* Someday she'd sleep with her? Someday she'd figure out her secrets?

Whatever she'd meant, that day was coming soon. She wasn't going to wait forever to kiss her again. Kissing her was all she could think about—when she wasn't thinking about sleeping with her. It had made it hard to sit beside her all through the concert without doing anything more than surreptitiously brush her knuckles against her thigh or lean over to make unnecessary comments so she'd have an excuse to hover at her ear. They'd had front-row seats, and she wasn't going to do more than that where her boss—or a fan with a camera phone—might notice.

The situation was no better now that they were on the street with Sylvie, Chloe, and Preston and heading for a nearby Ethiopian restaurant, because a late-night dinner meant it would be another couple hours before she and Jori were alone and jumping her would become a possibility.

Their group was quickly seated at a round table and Rae snagged a spot beside Jori. She could behave. She repositioned her leg on her low, ottoman-like stool and wished her fashionably tight jeans weren't quite so restrictive as she tried to find a comfortable position without accidentally kicking anyone.

When the communal platter piled with mounds of mashed lentils, spicy beef, chopped collard greens and other colorful purées arrived, Jori and Preston dove in, tearing off strips of injera, the spongy Ethiopian flatbread, to scoop up the meat and vegetables. Rae helped herself at a more civilized pace to some chickpea mash while Chloe and Sylvie held back from the feeding frenzy and sipped cardamom tea.

Preston reached across the table enthusiastically for the garlicky lamb. "This is why I enjoy going out to eat with you girls—more food for me."

Preston was right. Female dancers did eat, but no one wanted to eat in front of witnesses. No wonder he seemed happy when Ralph had begged off, apologizing for being exhausted. No Ralph meant less competition.

"Mmm. This is sooo good," Preston taunted, waving the food in the air and smacking his lips. "I think I'll have as much of it as I want. *More* than I want. I'm going to eat until I'm stuffed."

"You're disgusting," Chloe said.

"I know I am," Preston said happily. "But you can't deny the food is amazing. And this bread... Do you know what this bread always reminds me of?"

Rae's eyes widened. She hoped she wasn't blushing, but she knew she was—her cheeks were burning. She didn't dare look at Jori. No one else was reacting at all. No one except Chloe, who glanced from face to face, confused, before taking a cautious bite of injera to check it out.

Preston laughed at Rae's discomfort and pointed at her. "The lesbian knows."

Chloe stopped chewing and did not take a second bite.

"If that means what I think it means…"

"He's trying to put you off your food," Rae said, wondering just how red she was. "Ignore him."

She probably couldn't get any redder than she already was, so she risked a peek at Jori's face. Nothing. She couldn't tell if Jori knew what he was talking about. Was she as oblivious as Chloe? Or did she just have a better poker face than Rae? And what did that say about her?

"Don't you just love the texture?" Preston waved a piece of bread in Rae's face, daring her to…what? Catch it in her mouth?

Rae pushed his hand away. "I can't decide whether you're being a jerk or if this is your way of proving how straight you are."

Preston popped the bread in his mouth with a smirk, chewed, and swallowed. "Hey, if I was being a jerk I'd say I hated the texture."

"Unless it's your way of bragging about how good you are in bed," Rae said.

Preston reached in front of Chloe and snagged her injera. "Are you eating that?"

Chloe gave him the evil eye.

"There's this theory that you can predict how good a woman is in bed by how she eats," Preston said, returning to his favorite topic. "If she chows down and doesn't hold back, it means she's uninhibited."

Oh, Jori was going to love this. She could add it to her ever-lengthening list of all the ways in which men didn't understand the opposite sex. Or was it a list of reasons why straight sex was not worth bothering with? No, oops, that was Rae's list. Jori's list was about being attracted to the wrong thing and going for it anyway. Or something. She was sure Jori would be happy to clarify. After Jori was done chowing down on their late-night meal. In an uninhibited manner.

Thank you, Preston, for that visual.

Rae forced herself to stop watching Jori eat and turned to Chloe. "Remind him of this the next time you practice lifts and he complains about your weight."

Preston continued, undeterred. "If she won't eat, then…"

"Are you trying to make a point?" Chloe said, her usual hostility toward her dance partner ramping up.

Preston laughed and gave a shrug. "I didn't say I agreed with the theory. If you ask me, it's all bullshit."

Rae stared, amazed that he would back down from an argument with Chloe. He loved arguing with Chloe. She suspected it turned him on. Why else would he even have mentioned this theory that was guaranteed to set off everyone at the table? Even Jori appeared to be ready to come to the defense of picky eaters everywhere.

Preston shoveled more food into his mouth and swallowed. "Hotness isn't about how she eats or what she weighs. All I want to know is, is she a dancer? Yes or no. It's as simple as that. If she is a dancer, she'll be great in bed. If not, forget it."

"Good save," Chloe said, "but I don't believe you."

"I'm serious," Preston said. "Although I will admit I prefer ballet-dancer thin. I want a woman who dreams about *me*, not about a hunk of hamburger."

Sylvie shuddered at the mention of red meat.

Jori reached across the table for the beef, which had mysteriously migrated to Preston's end of the table. She didn't seem to mind being lumped into the not-a-dancer, not-great-in-bed category.

"You honestly want us to believe that in your opinion, women like us are sexier than the thousands of big-breasted non-dancers you've slept with?" Chloe said.

"Thousands of big…?" Preston sputtered. "Is that what you think of me?"

"Yes."

"I don't do big."

"You're an embarrassment to biological evolution," Jori told him, helping herself to more beef. "Didn't anyone ever let you in on the secret that you're supposed to like big-hipped, big-breasted women who look like they can give you babies?"

Preston smiled boyishly, jumping at the chance to turn on the charm for the next potential mother of his children. No wonder he was able to convince so many women to sleep with him. "Not too many hourglass shapes in my formative years. I grew up taking ballet with stick-skinny, flat-chested bunheads in leotards. I'm warped."

"He is warped," Chloe agreed.

"Speaking of warped," Sylvie said, turning to Rae, "we think Kaoli's flirting with the new sound technician."

"Tom?" As far as Rae knew, only two techs—Tom and Graciela—had been hired when the previous ones left at the end of last year's tour after a big blowup that had kept everyone talking for months.

"Guess again."

"Not Graciela."

Sylvie nodded, looking pleased with herself. "Graciela never flirts back, but…"

A woman? No. Kaoli would never have tried to get Rae into bed if she already had a woman in her life. And she could say so, because her friends knew her very public relationship was a lie, and they knew the drill: say nothing to anyone about the boss or risk losing your job. So she said it. "Kaoli's not gay."

"Just because she won't sleep with you doesn't mean she's not gay," Preston said.

"I don't want to sleep with her," Rae said.

"Preston, leave Rae alone," Sylvie said. "Or at least thank her for the bonuses we all got when ticket sales went up after Rae agreed to play along with Kaoli's stunt."

Jori drew an audible breath. "You really aren't her girlfriend."

Rae turned to her in disbelief. "I told you I wasn't."

"You did," Jori agreed.

"You didn't believe me?"

"I wanted to believe you. I knew you didn't really like her, but there was something between you, some weird vibe, and I didn't know what that meant."

"Rae and Kaoli have a weird vibe?" Preston asked. "A sexual vibe? Since when?"

"Since never," Chloe said.

Because Rae had done an excellent job of suppressing those old feelings, even from herself. None of her coworkers had ever known she and Kaoli had been anything more than childhood friends. Only Jori had been able to spot it.

"No offense, Rae, but Kaoli's just not into you," Preston said. "Her sexual vibe is all about Graciela."

Rae scowled. "All about Griffin, you mean."

"The boyfriend? I don't think so. We never see him. And why else would she hire a female sound guy?" Preston smiled. He knew he was being obnoxious. Again.

"That doesn't make her interested in her, it makes her not sexist," Rae said.

"Why else would she hire a *gay* female sound guy?" Preston said.

"Because the gay female sound guy knows how to do the job?" Rae replied.

"You think Graciela's gay?" Chloe asked Preston. "Based on what?"

"Yes, please enlighten us, Preston." Rae didn't know Graciela well—she'd been injured soon after Graciela was hired—but she hadn't gotten that feeling from her. Then again, her success rate at identifying women's sexual orientation wasn't all that great.

"Number one, she introduces herself as 'the sound guy,'" Preston said.

"I think she does that to make a point," Rae said.

"What point is that?"

"Haven't you ever noticed how everywhere we go, everyone's always saying stuff like 'Get me your sound guy' or 'Where's your lighting guy?' Guy, guy, guy."

"I don't think she minds it," Preston said. "I think she likes being ones of the guys."

"Being one of the guys doesn't make her gay," Rae said. "It makes her a techie."

"Why are you arguing? You should want her to be gay. More people on your team," Preston said.

"What I want," Rae said, "is to understand why I'm sacrificing my integrity for my career if there's someone else. I know it was that photo of the kiss by the swimming pool that started it, but if Kaoli's interested in Graciela, she could have publicly dumped me and switched to a new girlfriend. Why is she sticking with me if she has someone else?"

"Maybe Graciela doesn't want her," Preston said.

"Rae doesn't want her either," Sylvie pointed out.

"Rae's good for her image," Chloe said. "Graciela's just a sound guy that Preston *thinks* might be gay. Rae we know is a lesbian. She's photogenic, she's not afraid to be lovey-dovey in public, she knows how to perform in front of an audience, she makes Kaoli look the part."

"True," Preston said. "Rae's a good actress. All Graciela knows how to do is look sexy moving her hands over a soundboard."

Great. Now her friends thought her highest achievement as a performer was her willingness to hold hands with Kaoli in public.

"Maybe this Graciela person, whoever she is, can afford to say no," Jori said. "I'm no expert, but I imagine sound technicians have an easier time finding jobs than dancers do."

Sylvie gasped. "Did she threaten your job, Rae?"

"Of course she threatened her job," Preston said, as if he were the one who'd thought of it. "Have you not noticed how easy it is to get fired around here?"

Rae shrugged. "She mentioned it."

"That's outrageous," Sylvie said. "You should quit."

"Hard to get another dance job when my leg's out of commission," Rae said.

Sylvie glanced down at her leg and winced. No dancer wanted to be reminded of how easily a career could be cut short. "It's not right."

"It's not that big a deal," Rae said.

It hadn't been, at first. But now? Now she was starting to wonder what it had all been for. And how much longer she was willing to do whatever she could to ensure Kaoli's success.

"I'm almost more worried about Lorenzo," Rae said. "Did you hear him today?" He was never exactly friendly, but this afternoon he'd been borderline rude. "He thinks I'm not coming back, doesn't he?"

"No one thinks that," Sylvie said.

"He doesn't want me in rehearsals. He must think there's no point in my keeping up with the choreography. Because I won't be performing it."

Sylvie put up a hand to stop her. "Don't say that."

"Kaoli will make him keep you," Chloe said. "She has to, after everything you've done for her. Like that swimming pool kiss? That was huge."

"Don't forget the photos we did this afternoon," Rae said.

"You mean when Kaoli dragged you out of rehearsals the minute you said there were paparazzi outside?" Sylvie shook her head in sympathy. "How did those turn out?"

"I didn't look." She'd been putting it off all evening because she didn't want to be reminded.

"You didn't?" Preston clucked disapprovingly and whipped out his phone to tap out a search. "Got it." He peered at the screen. "Wait a minute. What happened here?"

Everyone looked at him, but he didn't explain, just turned his screen toward Rae.

It was a dramatic shot. Kaoli had her lips partly puckered, moving in for the kiss. Except Rae wasn't there. Instead, her hair was a blur of movement near the ground.

"Can I see?" Jori said.

She leaned across Rae to get closer to the phone and Preston angled the screen toward her. Jori snaked her arm across Rae's back and clasped her shoulder, hanging on for balance as she leaned even farther. It was like a dance hold, only better. Better because it was real—something she was doing because she wanted to, not because a choreographer had told her to. She could have seen the photo without sprawling across Rae's lap and claiming her with the warmth of her body. She could have simply asked Preston to pass the phone.

"I'm impressed," Jori said.

"What happened?" Sylvie demanded.

"They immortalized her good side," Preston said.

"Shut up," Rae said.

"Looks to me like Rae kissed the pavement to avoid a lip-lock," Jori said, moving away, giving Rae her space back.

Rae didn't want her space back.

Sylvie sucked in her breath. "What did Kaoli say?"

Rae shrugged. "She didn't fire me."

Jori stole a roll of injera from Rae's plate. "She wants you, Rae. She's throwing herself at you. Just like all the girls."

"Yeah, right." If Jori only knew.

"One day that'll be you and me, Chloe," Preston said, draping an arm over Chloe's shoulder.

Chloe removed his arm the way she would pick off a spider and flicked invisible germs off her shirt. "You mean I'll be avoiding you?"

"Avoiding?" Preston said. "You'll be dropping to your knees in front of m—"

Chloe snatched the phone out of Preston's hand and suddenly no one was paying attention to Rae anymore. No one but Jori.

As the others picked apart the photo, Rae bent her head toward Jori and lowered her voice, low enough that even Jori might not hear. "You should have seen me in high school. I was so desperate for some girl—any girl—to notice me, and…that's why it was so easy to fall for…" *Kaoli*. She wasn't saying *that* in front of her coworkers no matter how quiet she was or how much they seemed to be ignoring her. "…for confused, unavailable straight girls."

"Forget those girls," Jori said softly. "You have better options now."

Rae stared into her lap and fought the heat that rose to her cheeks. Why had she spilled that? She'd never told anyone. Although she hadn't given away any details, even that vague admission made her uncomfortable.

"I make an excellent boyfriend," Preston was saying, pressing his case and yanking Rae's attention back to the table. "It's just like being an excellent dance partner. I know how to make my partner look good. I'm strong, I'm considerate, I'm respectful."

"Until you open your mouth," Chloe said.

"Verbal skills are overrated," Preston said. "There's no need to talk when you're dancing a horizontal *pas de deux* with me."

Chloe made a rude noise.

"Your dancer's body and my dancer's body? I don't see the problem here."

Poor Chloe. Maybe she should step in and help. Rae cleared her throat. "What about wanting someone for their personality?" Wait, that was Jori's theory. Okay, so she agreed with her. So what? It was okay for her to agree with Jori. Especially if it meant needling Preston.

"Those people have never had sex with someone who can do the splits," Preston said.

"Can we not talk about this while we're eating, please?" Chloe said.

Preston gave her a huge grin. "Oh, I'm sorry. Was someone at this table actually eating? I think I missed it."

Chloe looked like she wanted to kill him, but Preston

kept grinning.

"It's not about acrobatics," Rae said. "It's about love."

"What would you know about it?" Preston said. "You're a dancer. You're incapable of being non-acrobatic."

"I'm capable of it right now," Rae pointed out. "I can barely walk."

"No need to do any walking," Preston said. "Let lovergirl carry you around."

Rae leaned forward. "She's not—"

"Show her how high you can get your toes over your head and she'll be all yours," Preston added.

Rae covered her ears, then covered Jori's, worried about what might be coming next. "I don't need relationship advice from you, thank you very much."

"More like sex advice," Chloe grumbled.

"What? That wasn't sex advice," Preston said. "Sex advice would be—"

"I have to go the ladies' room," Rae announced, sliding out of her seat. It was the only way out. She figured her friends didn't know Jori well enough to tease her if Rae wasn't at the table, and a few minutes away would give them time to change topic. Because she couldn't listen to this. What she had with Jori was confusing enough without their well-meaning input, and turning a spotlight on their as-yet-nonexistent sex lives was only going to make things awkward later in the night.

Jori stood up, too. "Is your ankle okay? Do you need help walking there?"

"She definitely needs something," Preston said.

Rae pushed Jori toward the restrooms.

"Sorry about them," she told Jori when they were out of earshot. "After a show, we're all kind of high on adrenaline."

"They're sweet."

They wove their way around tables to the far end of the restaurant. Rae reached for the restroom door, but as she did, the door punched open from the inside. She hopped out of the way, but after sitting at the table, and sitting through the concert, and sitting in the car, her body was stiff, and she stumbled. Jori grabbed for her to keep her from falling and Rae slammed into her. They both lost their balance. Rae put her weight down hard on her bad leg and somehow twisted it wrong. She gasped. Then Jori was steadying her, locking her into the support of her body as Rae instinctively threw her arms around her neck. Chest pressed to ribcage; hip jammed against thigh. Rae's breath came loud and fast, and she pretended to herself that the reason she was panting was that her ankle hurt, pretended to them both that it hurt more than it did so she'd have an excuse to stay in Jori's arms.

There was no excuse for her to rest her forehead on Jori's shoulder or turn to bury her face in her neck, but that didn't stop her. She couldn't get enough of how good she smelled. She shifted more deeply into Jori's warmth. If this was Jori's Bat-Signal, it was working.

Once Rae had her footing, Jori should have let go. Instead, Jori became noticeably still, her only movement the rapid rise and fall of her ribcage. Rae could guess what she was thinking, because she was thinking the same thing: That when they left this restaurant, they were staying at the nearest hotel they could find. And neither one of them was going to fight too hard to get separate rooms.

16

The hotel room had two beds.

When Rae emerged from the bathroom after brushing her teeth, Jori was settled in the closest of those beds, slouched in plaid pajamas against a stack of inviting, soft-looking pillows, the covers pulled to her waist.

Jori's gaze lingered on Rae's bare legs. "That's what you're sleeping in?"

Rae tugged at the fraying hem of her faded black *Kaoli Morgenroth: Alpha in Heels: the Tour* T-shirt to make sure she was decent, but no amount of tugging was going to help. It barely covered anything. "What did you expect? A tutu?"

"I was picturing shorts."

And Rae would have brought some along if she'd thought of it.

"With or without a—"

"With a shirt," Jori said quickly, correctly guessing how Rae had planned to finish that question.

"You've been picturing what I look like in bed?"

Jori slid down the headboard, sinking farther under the covers. "Not every night."

Oh God. Rae flipped off the light by the door and made for the empty bed by the dim glow of the slacker bulb in the bedside lamp. She was sure there was some way she could finesse her way into sharing Jori's half of the room, but her blood was beating too loudly in her head for her to figure out how. Maybe it was just as well. In a few weeks she would be rejoining Kaoli's tour—sooner, if she was lucky—and sleeping with Jori would only make it harder to leave.

Unfortunately, Jori's shapeless plaid pajamas looked comfortable and homey and way sexier than a straight woman would ever understand.

"Shouldn't you keep your brace on?" Jori asked.

Weren't they done yet with discussing what she was wearing? "I'm not sleeping in an ankle brace."

"Were you planning on sleeping?" Jori snagged a free pillow from the mound on her bed and used the pillow to cover her face as if she expected to have to duck out of the way of a projectile.

Rae reached the gap between their beds and paused. Jori peeked out from behind the pillow. Smiled. This was crazy.

"You think you can say whatever you want and I won't take you up on it."

"Actually, I'm dying over here, waiting for you to make a move."

Rae swallowed. She wanted Jori so much, and at the same time she didn't trust herself to want the right thing. "Sweetie, only straight girls lie back and wait for it."

A wrinkle appeared between Jori's eyebrows. She looked serious and intent. Almost as serious and intent as Kaoli, trying to convince her to give her another chance.

Rae kept her sigh to herself. "Good night."

"If you dream about me tonight, feel free to come up with a good pet name for me. You know, to protect the identity of the innocent party when you moan my name." Jori wasn't ready to quit, was she? And yet she wasn't crawling out of bed to come get her, either. "I like *sweetie*, by the way."

Yeah. That had slipped out, hadn't it? Great.

"Although I also kind of like the sound of *love muffin*."

"I'm not going to dream about you." She was pretty sure that wasn't a lie, if only because she wasn't going to be able to fall asleep knowing Jori was in the other bed. No chance of dreaming if she was awake.

"Just keep it in mind."

"Not necessary." Rae hesitated at the side of her bed. Why hadn't she detoured around to the other side rather than into the gap between the two beds? She could have squeezed around the dresser and the bed and the armchair and put a little distance between them, even if it was only for a minute. She needed to just jump into bed and get it over with, but the love muffin was watching, and she couldn't move.

"You say that now, but—"

"Believe me, there is no way I am going to cry out your name in my sleep."

"That's just as well," Jori said. "Women who want a man to scream their name when they're making love? That's just weird."

A *man*? "Women who want a *woman*," Rae corrected. And how did they get from talking about dreams to talking about sex?

"Whatever," Jori said.

Rae shook her head in disbelief. Substituting *man* for *woman* wasn't a *whatever* to her. "Saying your lover's name proves that you're not fantasizing about someone else, or hung up on an ex," she said, not sure why she was letting Jori lead her down this road. The thing to do was get into bed and pretend she was asleep and not talk about…what they were talking about.

Jori turned to her side and propped herself up on her elbow, eager as always to discuss another one of her theories.

"Anyone who sleeps with me knows exactly who I am. I don't need to hear my name. I don't *want* to hear my name. If you're coherent enough to remember my name and you're capable of forming actual words, then the sex is just not that good, sunshine."

Rae's mouth went dry.

Jori's gaze locked on to hers and Rae got the disconcerting feeling that Jori was picturing her naked and breathless beneath her.

"If I'm doing my job right," Jori continued, "you won't remember your *own* name, let alone mine."

She didn't mean *you*, personally. She meant *you*, a random girlfriend.

Or maybe not. Because the way Jori was looking at her—eyes dark, pupils wide, like she could see through her and read her thoughts, and those thoughts were turning her on—it felt like she meant *her*.

Rae needed to sit down. She needed to get into bed and shove a pillow under her head and remind herself she didn't sleep with women who said *man* when they should mean *woman* and then dismissed it with a *whatever*.

She meant to do all those things. Really. Which was obviously why she yanked the covers off Jori's bed and scrambled on top of her on her hands and knees.

———

Jori sucked in her breath so hard she might have strained her lungs. Rae was on top of her, one knee on either side of her waist, smiling down at her in the shadowy darkness like a demented angel.

Her blood pounded in her ears as she stared up in awe,

unable to move. Rae was finally in her bed. On her. With her. And she didn't want it to end. Ever. She wanted to appreciate every rise and fall of Rae's ribcage and every burning point of contact for as long as possible. They could stay motionless like this all night and she'd never get tired of it.

Rae laughed. "You look shocked."

Jori stroked Rae's lean, strong legs in wonder, soaking in the warmth of her bare skin, discovering every curve, finding the crease where her thighs ended and something even more interesting began. "Not shocked."

Rae squeezed her thighs together and trapped her with a strength Jori wasn't easily going to escape, even if for some insane reason she wanted to. She was never going to watch Rae do that open-and-close leg exercise the same way again. Seeing her coworkers wrap their legs around stripper poles that descended from the ceiling during the concert had given her some idea why Rae needed strong inner thighs, but feeling her strength in action brought it home. She'd imagined Rae up there in mid-air, moving her torso in ways Jori couldn't manage even on the ground, wiggling the way she'd wiggled against the doorframe, performing in front of thousands instead of flirting for an appreciative audience of one. She hoped one day she'd see her dance up there. She'd look amazing. Almost as amazing as she looked right now.

"Shit." Rae rocked back on her heels and hissed in pain, knocking Jori out of her reverie.

"Your ankle," Jori guessed.

"Knee," Rae said. "Damn it, I thought my knee was okay."

"Are you all right?" She didn't need to be straddling her, for God's sake. She should be on her back or something, taking the pressure off. "Don't you want to—" *put on your knee brace,* she was going to say, but Rae was pulling her T-shirt over her head and the words died in Jori's throat.

Rae was incredible. The graceful curve of her neck. The vulnerable boniness of her elbows. The glint in her eyes, daring her to look at her breasts. And then there was that sexy navel...

"Rae," she breathed, forgetting her own theory about names. Maybe, just maybe, she'd been wrong about what it meant to use a person's name in bed. Maybe she'd never understood what it was like to feel smiled upon by the gods and want to put a name to the miracle in her hands.

Rae leaned forward and got rid of Jori's clothes, got rid of the last scrap of her own. Then she was straddling her again, rising on her knees and arching effortlessly into a backbend. Her breasts thrust skyward, her head dropped back, and her hands reached behind her, landing on Jori's thighs. *What the...?*

"You don't have to..." ...*do all that bendy stuff,* she tried to say, but seeing her so open made it impossible to speak. What was it Preston had said at dinner? That he liked being in bed with a dancer who could do the splits? All she cared about was Rae, not her flexibility, but that didn't mean she didn't look amazing. The splits were nothing compared to this.

But hadn't Rae replied that acrobatics weren't important? Apparently her definition of *acrobatics* was a bit different than Jori's.

"Your knee, sunshine."

"My knee's fine."

That was hard to believe, but if Rae was going to insist on crazy circus moves, the least Jori could do was make her forget the pain, obliterate it with something more pleasant.

She had a pretty good idea how to do that.

She reached between those flexible legs and Rae's hipbones jutted forward in invitation, her knees skidding out, her breathing harsh with anticipation. Jori stroked into her moist heat and her own breath came faster, matching Rae's rhythm. Rae moaned and arched her back even more, arms stretched behind her, the hollow of her navel taut, her fingers digging into Jori's thighs. Jori's core pulsed with need. Heat shot upward and without even meaning to, Jori's hips rose, straining against the pressure of Rae's hands.

It ought to have been impossible, but Rae dragged her palms up Jori's thighs as easily as if she were right-side-up. She wasn't seriously going to...

Jori tensed, bracing herself, wondering how close Rae was planning on getting. Could she really reach anything? Rae hit her goal and Jori gasped. Yes, she could. Yes...she...holy fuck, she totally could. Jori panted. A wet, aching urgency welled up. Except this wasn't how she'd meant this to go...

With Rae rocking above her, Jori shuddered and pushed her way farther in, past slick, contracted walls that relaxed and welcomed her in a rush. Rae's smooth, sensuous rhythm became jerky and uncoordinated. She was no longer in control, no longer graceful. Rae's hand between Jori's legs flailed, missing its target. Her focus was shot.

Jori's body went tight. Just knowing that Rae was losing it was enough to make her clench so hard she almost came. She needed to be on her, under her, inside her. She couldn't get close enough.

Rae's hips jerked forward and Jori pressed her advantage, grinding into her, staying with her as Rae convulsed uncontrollably, spasming on her fingers.

Rae straightened from her backbend, trembling the whole way up. She collapsed forward onto her hands and knees, her ribcage heaving with frantic gasps for air.

She was so beautiful. Jori pulled her into her arms, melding their bodies together, forgetting her own unreleased tension as she relaxed into the pure joy of holding her. Rae's warm cheek rested on her shoulder, and their breaths synchronized and slowed. Peace radiated from Rae's flushed face and enveloped them both. It felt profoundly right.

"Don't get too comfortable," Rae said, breaking the silence too soon, recovering her energy with an athlete's speed.

Before Jori could protest, Rae scooted all the way down and took Jori in her mouth. The tense need she'd thought she could put aside came roaring back and she bit back a cry.

Her knees drew up and her legs fell open, but they didn't get very far. Unlike Rae, Jori was never going to be able to do the splits.

Rae raised her head with a rough, uncontrolled breath that proved she wasn't as recovered as she seemed. "I've never been with a woman whose knees didn't flop apart all the way."

Jori had never been with anyone whose knees *did*. She groaned. "I can't do a backbend, either. That's not going to stop you, is it?"

"I like it. I think it's sexy. Like you won't let everyone in." Rae rubbed her hands up and down Jori's thighs and wedged herself more firmly into place. "Only someone special."

Rae lowered her head. Jori thought she felt her smile, the arrogant little shit. And then her tongue darted out. There was no mistaking *that*.

"God." Jori's hips bucked off the bed. "That feels…" …*like you love this. Like you love* me.

Jori caressed the top of Rae's head. With the way her

hand was shaking, she worried she'd catch at her hair, so she drew back, because maybe she was projecting, but no woman liked to be controlled.

But then Rae was reaching for her, clasping one of her retreating hands, interlacing her delicate, fine-boned fingers with hers with unimaginable tenderness as her relentless tongue made the trembling worse. Rae wasn't trying to make her grip on her hand gentle on purpose, like a caring brute; she was just being herself, and it was exactly what Jori had always wanted. She'd never known what it was she wanted until this moment—never known such a feminine touch would excite her to mindlessness—but it was perfect. Rae's touch was so full of love and so heartbreakingly sweet that she almost couldn't bear it.

I *love this. I love you.*

"Oh God..." A gentle, sublime ecstasy shot up her spine and overwhelmed her, making her shake so hard that she sobbed, desperate for it to stop, desperate for it to never stop.

"Rae," Jori whispered helplessly, barely able to suppress her screams.

Rae's murmur of encouragement vibrated against her skin and seeped into her bones, and deeper still, touching the barrier that guarded her soul, breaching it, breaking her apart.

You won't let everyone in, Rae had said. *Only someone special.*

She was right.

———

Rae woke in the dark, cold. She was sprawled diagonally across most of the bed, leaving Jori curled on a corner of the mattress. The sheet and blanket they'd been too heated to need at the beginning of the night had disappeared off the foot of the bed.

Silently, she slipped out of bed. Pain shot through her knee. She stifled a gasp and pressed her hands to where it hurt, flashing back to how she'd straddled Jori's body, her knees digging into the mattress, her back arching as desire shot up her thighs and lodged deep inside her. She could still feel Jori's touch on her skin, warm and exquisite. In the heat of the moment she hadn't felt any limitation from her injury, but she must have put too much stress on the joint. It had been worth it, though. She'd recover.

She tripped over the pile of bedding and caught her footing with another stab of pain. Well, at least she'd found the sheet. She hauled it off the floor and settled it over Jori as gently as possible and leaned down to kiss her forehead with a soft, slow, quiet touch that wouldn't wake her.

Definitely worth it.

Next stop: ibuprofen. She felt her way to the end of the room and clicked on the bathroom light, leaving the door ajar so she'd have some illumination to search for her bag and avoid making too much noise knocking her way around in the dark. She checked the bedside table, the floor…oh, there it was, against the wall.

She rooted around in her bag but couldn't find the breath mint tin she kept her pills in. Not by feel, anyway. She returned to the sting of the brightly lit bathroom and set her bag on the edge of the counter and somehow everything tumbled onto the tile floor. Yikes. So much for being quiet.

She listened for any sound from the other room, but there was nothing. Good. She found the tin and snapped it open. It was empty. Empty? She'd forgotten to replace her last pill right before she needed one in the middle of the night?

"You okay, sunshine?"

Great. She'd woken Jori.

"You don't happen to have any ibuprofen, do you?"

"In my purse," Jori mumbled, sounding not fully awake. "Can you find it yourself? You knocked me into such a good sleep, I don't think I can move."

"You're a lifesaver." Jori's purse, Rae had already noticed, was on a shelf underneath the bathroom sink next to her toiletries bag.

"In the zippered pocket." Jori's voice faded like she was falling back asleep.

Rae opened the purse. It was a lot smaller than hers and a lot more organized. She found the zippered pocket and nabbed the travel-size pillbox. And saw what else was in there and froze.

A square foil wrapper. She'd never seen one up close, but really, what else could it be? Cautiously—even though there was no need to be cautious, it wasn't going to attack—she touched it. The squishy hard ring inside felt exactly the way she imagined it would.

"You carry a condom?"

Jori groaned. "Please don't be upset about this." She didn't sound sleepy anymore.

Rae left the bathroom without swallowing the painkiller that had started this and approached the bed. Her knee didn't hurt anymore. She was too numb for anything to register.

Jori sat up, wrapping the sheet around her chest. Had it only been a minute ago that Rae had covered her with that sheet?

"I carry it in my purse just in case. I never think about it. It's been in there forever." Jori shook her head like she couldn't believe she had to defend herself. "It's not like I was planning on meeting up with a guy tonight."

"Then why do you need it?" Her purse was so organized. And so small. She didn't have room in there to keep things she didn't need. If she kept a condom handy, it was because she thought she might use it. Rae kept a ton of things in her bag "just in case", and not a single one of them was a condom, because she didn't sleep with goddamn men.

Jori pressed her lips together in a stark, angry line and tugged the sheet more tightly across her chest. "Is this really a surprise?"

No, not really. She knew this already. She just…wanted Jori to change her mind. About who she was. And how selfish was that?

Rae threw on her clothes and stomped to the second bed, the one they hadn't touched, and ripped off the sheets. She grabbed a pillow and threw it against the wall.

"What are you doing?"

"What does it look like I'm doing? Making sure housekeeping thinks we slept in separate beds."

"Rae—"

The cleaning people weren't going to care. They wouldn't even notice. But Rae needed to do it, needed to erase their night together. It was childish, and she hated that she was acting this way, but emotions were physical for her. She threw another pillow against the wall.

"I didn't plan on using it," Jori said.

"I don't date bisexuals."

"Date? You just slept with—"

"I don't sleep with bisexuals, either."

"Thanks," Jori said. "It was good for me, too."

Rae stumbled over the sheets she'd yanked to the floor,

knocked into the hard, industrial-grade armchair beside the bed, and fell into the seat. Shit, that was her bad leg.

"What are you so scared of?" Jori said. "That I'm going to leave you for a man?"

"It doesn't matter." There was no need to explain, because explaining would just be hurtful. And for what? Their relationship wasn't going to work. "I can't be with someone who's not a lesbian. This is a deal-breaker for me."

The bed creaked and Jori made an impatient, irritated sound as she sat up straighter against the headboard. "You knew what I was before you got into this bed."

Rae clenched her teeth. "I convinced myself you weren't. That you were really a lesbian but just wouldn't admit it." It was high school all over again. She'd thought she'd learned and matured, but somehow, she hadn't. "I wanted you to be what I wanted you to be. I was wrong."

"Why do I have to be—"

"Because men always win! Because eventually, women like you—"

Jori choked. "Like me?"

"—always end up with a man."

"That's not true."

"I need someone who feels comfortable calling herself a lesbian. Not bi, not curious, not questioning, not *I used to like boys but now I've seen the light but oops it's just temporary*, not *I sleep with girls right up until I marry a man*, not *I screw with people's feelings because I'm too confused to know what I want*, not *I prefer to hover in some doorway instead of choosing a side and being fair to the people I date*. Just lesbian."

"Whoever hurt you," Jori said gently, "I'm not her."

The fight almost seeped out of her at Jori's steady calm. Almost.

Rae drew her feet onto the chair and hugged her knees. "No one hurt me."

"Are you sure? You're this angry at me for no reason? No one who wasn't quite lesbian enough ever rejected you?" Jori shaped her hands into a letter K and raised her eyebrows. "No one we know?"

"Kaoli has nothing to do with this."

Jori shook her head, looking disappointed that Rae didn't trust her enough to tell her the truth. How did she know? How could she know? None of the dancers Rae worked with had ever figured out that she had once had a painful crush on Kaoli, even though they saw them together every day. If Sylvie and Chloe and Preston didn't suspect, how did Jori?

Because Jori knew her. Jori paid attention to little clues no one else noticed and put them together.

"Kaoli did hurt me," Rae admitted. "But it was a long time ago and it doesn't matter anymore."

"It does if it's preventing you from trusting me."

"It's not about Kaoli."

"Lesbians change their minds and marry men, too, you know. Sexuality is fluid. People change. Relationships fail. You want a guarantee? I'm sorry, but anyone who pretends they can give you one is lying."

"At least my odds would be better," Rae said.

Jori was right, though. God knew there were no guarantees. Not in relationships, not in show business, not in life. Rae could tolerate uncertainty in her career, but she deserved at least a little bit of certainty in the person she gave her heart to.

"I'm not going to lie about who I am just to make you trust me," Jori said.

Unlike Kaoli. Jori really was nothing like Kaoli.

Didn't change anything, though. Because Rae was going back to her real life where she spent half the year on the road, and Jori was going to land a respectable, well-paying job in a claustrophobic office where she'd meet some open-minded, inoffensive guy and marry him, and Baylee would become a big sister to a couple of little kids who were just as adorable as their mother. And Rae? Rae would dance her heart out until her body fell apart and she couldn't do her job anymore, and she'd spend the rest of her life searching for someone who made her forget what she'd once felt for a woman who flirted with men and made a swimming pool noodle look like fun.

"What if you decide you want Baylee to have a father?"

"Baylee already has a father."

"She does?" Rae blinked. Of course technically Baylee had to have a father, but the way Jori had said it, it sounded like she meant a real parent—someone who was involved.

"Axel." Jori winced like she was embarrassed to say his name. "Not that anyone would notice. But he does love her in his own distant way."

Axel. How could Axel be...

"You told me he was gay. You told me you were pretending to date. You told me it wasn't real."

"All true."

"You couldn't tell me you slept with him?"

"I didn't think it was important."

"You didn't want me to know."

Jori sighed. "Yeah, okay, I didn't want you to know. I was afraid if you knew I'd slept with a specific guy, if it wasn't just theoretical—even though I *did* tell you, lots of times, that I'm open to the idea of sleeping with men—you'd think differently of me."

Jori *had* told her. She'd been nothing but honest about not wanting her sexual identity to be boxed in. What difference did it make, really, to know she'd slept with Axel? If there was anyone Rae should be angry with, it was herself. Jori may have lied about Axel, but she'd told her the part that mattered. Rae was the one who'd seen the red flags and ignored them.

"Why does it matter so much?" Jori said, eyes cast downward, strength draining from her voice until it was no more than a hurt whisper. "Why is what I am so awful?"

Acid burned Rae's throat and she swallowed it back down, sick to her stomach.

"It's not," Rae whispered.

Jori clenched the sheet bunched in her lap.

Rae crawled out of the armchair and hobbled over to the bed. As much as she wanted to comfort her, she had no right to—not when all of this was Rae's fault. Jori should hate her. It wasn't fair of her to hope she didn't. She held out her arms anyway, braced for Jori to push her away.

That deal-breaker? That was before she met Jori. Now she wasn't so sure.

"Jori?"

Jori looked up at her as if Rae's fumbling whisper had made a difference—as if maybe her open arms counted as an apology—so Rae sat on the bed and wrapped her arms around her.

Jori leaned into her touch. Just a little, but that small movement was everything.

Rae's heart sped up and she buried her face in Jori's neck.

"I'm sorry," Rae said, her lips moving on Jori's skin.

Maybe she was wrong about there only being one acceptable, safe location on the continuum. Maybe she was wrong about herself—about what she was willing to risk.

Or maybe she was right.

Or maybe...

Jori tucked a stray strand of Rae's hair behind her ear like it was the most important task in the world. It was more than she deserved.

"Why do you have to be so nice?" Rae said. Didn't she know Rae was messed up? That Rae was a terrible person who didn't know what she wanted and who was going to end up hurting her worse than she already had? "So..." *Loveable.* "...nice."

"What...evil people like me can't be nice?"

"That's not what I mean. I just..."

"Don't decide now." Jori's thumb traced the line of her cheekbone with a softness tinged with sadness, a touch so wistful it was almost unbearable. "We don't have to decide now."

17

The sunshine was blinding when Rae arrived at the pool in her ratty terrycloth cover-up, glad to be back at this place she used to think she couldn't wait to leave. There were dozens of women in the water, but her gaze went unerringly to Jori, finding her without consciously being aware of looking for her, as if part of her needed to know where she was at every moment because knowing was vital to her survival. Jori was standing in the middle of the pool where it started to get deep, only her head and shoulders above the surface, helping her daughter swim.

Water dripped from Jori's hair and clung to her face. Rae held her breath, captivated by the planes of her nose, her cheekbones, her lips. Maybe if Jori looked at her, she'd remember to breathe. Or maybe eye contact would make it worse. She wrenched her gaze away from Jori's mouth but only got as far as the tight straps of her swimsuit and the sculpted slope of her shoulders, which really didn't help.

What am I doing? She closed her eyes and clasped the wrought-iron gate for balance. The metal burned after having been heated by the sun all morning and she bounced off, more out of reflex than from any conscious sense of self-preservation.

What *was* she doing? This wasn't logical. This was lust, and lust was not a healthy basis for a relationship.

It's not lust, a tiny voice whispered in her head.

Of course it was lust. Because if it wasn't, that meant it was love. And if it was love, she didn't want to hear it. She had a history of falling in love with the wrong people. Of making bad choices. Of believing the object of her affection would choose her over a man. Of being wrong.

Like the Valentine's Day dance in their high school gymnasium when Kaoli made the out-of-character choice to get drunk. When Kaoli whispered "I don't feel so good" and covered her mouth and bolted for the restrooms, Rae had run after her. Well, not run—walked really fast. She didn't want the teachers to notice something was up and decide to investigate.

Kaoli's pale folded legs and the soles of her valentine-red heels had been visible under the door of the first stall. When Rae asked if she was okay, Kaoli answered by vomiting.

Rae touched the stall door and it swung open. Kaoli was gripping the germy toilet bowl, her knuckles white. She must have barely made it in time and not bothered to lock the door. Rae squeezed into the cramped stall, careful not to step on the hem of Kaoli's skirt.

She leaned down and swept her hands through Kaoli's long hair and held it back from her face, struggling not to lose the contents of her own stomach from the smell. Kaoli trembled. Her head was hot, feverish. She puked again. Rae handed her a wad of toilet paper to wipe her mouth.

"How much did you have to drink?"

"Not that much."

Rae smoothed her hand over Kaoli's flushed forehead in an awkward attempt to be soothing. Kaoli didn't tell her to stop, so she stroked her again, amazed at her own daring. Kaoli nuzzled her hand, and Rae closed her eyes, overwhelmed by how perfect it felt. She didn't like that Kaoli had made herself sick, but taking care of her was heaven.

"Can you do me a favor?" Kaoli asked.

"Anything."

"Can you go see if Griffin is waiting for me outside? He's probably standing by the door worrying about me, thinking he's not allowed to come into the girls' restroom or something dumb like that. Can you get him? Please?"

Rae released Kaoli's hair, stunned.

Kaoli didn't want her help. She wanted Griffin. Griffin, who had stayed put, hanging out in the gym and joking with his buddies about girls and alcohol while Rae ran after her. Griffin, who was totally oblivious. Not Rae, who was right here, being her friend. She backed out of the stall, bumped into the door, banged into the walls of the confined space.

Kaoli wanted Griffin. The shock lodged in her chest as she stumbled out of the restroom. How could she want a boy when she had Rae? Rae would do anything for her. And Griffin, who did nothing, was the one she wanted?

Rae blinked herself back to the present. She'd been wrong about Kaoli, but that had been years ago. And Jori was not Kaoli.

Rae ran her fingers through her hair and watched as Jori raced Baylee to the edge of the pool and boosted her onto the tile, then hauled herself out with one fluid motion, ignoring the stepladder that Rae didn't use, either, but that normal people did—normal people who didn't have Jori's athleticism and strength. Baylee didn't wait. The moment her feet hit the ground she escaped on fast little legs and hugged one of the heavy stone planters that overflowed with white roses that were gorgeous in a look-but-don't-touch kind of way, their hidden thorns lying in wait for anyone unwise enough to get too close. Baylee swung one leg onto the lip of the planter to scramble up but couldn't quite make it, and her leg slid off.

Rae started instinctively toward the child to keep her from getting hurt. If that thing toppled over on her...

"Baylee, no." Jori had a bit more difficulty weaving between deck chairs and people than her munchkin had, but she was closer, and she beat Rae there.

Just as Jori reached her, Baylee pressed her face to a rose and took an exaggerated sniff. "Pretty."

"Don't take that flower, Baylee. Leave it so others can enjoy how pretty it is."

Reluctantly, Baylee released the rose. Jori swung her around singing *whee!* until she got a giggling shriek out of her.

Rae clutched the knotted ends of the drawstring at the drooping neckline of her cover-up and backed away. She wasn't sure if Jori had even noticed her.

"Rae. Don't go," Jori said.

Okay, she *had* noticed her.

"Cover your ears, Baylee." Settling her daughter on her hip, Jori approached and angled in close. The little girl squeezed both hands to her ears and Jori overlaid one of them with her free hand, trapping it in place.

Jori smelled of chlorine. Her wet hair dripped onto Rae's shoulder as she spoke directly into her ear, her voice barely audible. "I should still be mad at you, but your cover-up turns me on."

Rae's cheeks burned. "It does not."

Jori didn't pull away. "Oh, but it does."

It would help if she could stop feeling the remembered rush of Jori's bare thighs sliding underneath her, forcing her own legs wider. Maybe then she could think. Maybe then...

But then Baylee became impatient and her fussing broke

the spell. Jori rushed off with her daughter, and Rae finally released the terrycloth strings. Now that Jori was gone, she'd have a better chance of forgetting the sound of her gasping as she shuddered helplessly in her mouth.

The problem was, she didn't want to forget.

Not that she had much choice. Her knee still hurt a little, and each time it twinged she was reminded of exactly what she'd done to overstretch it, how she'd straddled her and arched back and...

She should have been more careful of her knee. She hadn't wanted to, though. She had wanted to lose herself in the moment and not think about her problems and fill her mind with Jori so completely that there was no room for anything else.

It had worked. For a while.

And then reality came crashing down and Rae said things she shouldn't have.

Although Jori still seemed to be flirting with her, so maybe Rae hadn't completely ruined everything. She hoped she hadn't ruined everything. She didn't understand why, because the kindest thing would be to walk away, but she couldn't help feeling that if she did, she'd regret it forever.

One of the clusters of women standing beside the pool broke apart and Rae noticed that Sierra was among them. A knot of familiar guilt stuck in her throat. Sierra had done so much for her, providing her with free housing and a pool to exercise in. She was glad she'd soon be able to free up her room in the lodge for someone else's use.

Sierra wandered over. "Holding up okay?"

Rae nodded. Maybe Sierra could help her come to her senses. "Can I ask you something?"

"Sure."

Rae swallowed. "Would you ever date someone bi?"

Sierra's eyebrows shot up and her arms sliced the air. "Hell, no."

Her response was so vehement that Rae rephrased. "I mean, if you were single, would you—"

"I'm clear on what you meant." Sierra dragged over two deck chairs and set one at Rae's side, treating her like she was still injured even though she was perfectly fine. "Developed a crush on my water aerobics instructor, have we?"

Rae dropped into the chair, too flustered to protest. "Is it that obvious?"

Sierra positioned her own chair to face the pool and leaned back in the sun, way more relaxed than Rae was. "Pretty much."

"Is she really bi? Have you ever seen her with a man? I mean, Axel, sure. But that was a long time ago. So aside from him, does she really date men? She's so disparaging, it's hard to imagine why she'd want to have a relationship with one— unless she can't help being attracted to them physically and she's only in it for the sex." The sex Rae had a feeling she wasn't having. "Which would be completely bizarre, but..."

I wanted you to be what I wanted you to be.

She was doing it again. Rationalizing. Again. Wanting Jori to be a lesbian—a lesbian in denial, but close enough— instead of accepting her for who she was.

"She was with Axel for two years, I think, if I remember correctly, but I doubt it was for the sex." Sierra wrinkled her nose in distaste. "They're still close. I could see her going back to him. I could also see her, long-term, with a woman. It's a tough call. I'm not sure even she knows the answer."

"But if she doesn't like them for their personalities and she doesn't want to sleep with them, what does that leave?"

Rae asked.

"Whatever it is, you have a better chance of finding out than I do."

By seducing her, she meant. It was obvious from the look on her face. Great.

"What does Jori have to say for herself?" Sierra asked.

"Nothing convincing."

Sierra laughed. "Really? I would have suspected that she would say just about anything to get you into bed again."

"Again?" Rae protested. How did Sierra know, anyway? Had Jori told her?

"Yeah, don't pretend you haven't already slept together. I've seen the way she looks at you."

"How does she look at me?"

Sierra flashed a knowing smile. "You're not denying it?"

"How does she look at me?" Rae insisted.

Sierra stared thoughtfully at her for a long time, her smile fading until all that was left was a small glimmer of sympathy. "Like no man will ever touch her again because the only person she wants is you."

18

It was a good thing Baylee loved coloring books, because Jori had to study for finals. They were down in the yoga barn where Baylee could run around because they were both tired of being cooped up their room, but so far, all Baylee wanted to do was color, sprawled next to Mommy on a pile of yoga mats with Jori's textbooks and notes spread on the floor and crayons rolling everywhere.

"Look who's here."

Rae's voice drifted from the open doorway and jolted Jori from the chapter she'd been poring over. Rae was in dance clothes—when was she not?—and a pair of ballet slippers dangled from her fingers.

"Are you here to play Twister?" Baylee asked.

"Baylee," Jori said. Rae was clearly planning to exercise.

"I don't think we have the game here," Rae said.

"I know how to make our own Twister," Baylee said. "We have paper. Mommy, can I have some paper?"

"Miss Peters might have things she needs to do."

"I'll draw the circles," Baylee said.

"Another time, Baylee," Jori told her.

As Baylee ignored her and gathered her crayons, Jori pushed to her feet and picked her way through the debris field. "Baylee and I will camp out somewhere else."

"You were here first," Rae said. "You're staying."

"We were just leaving."

Rae pushed past her. Her ankle might have wobbled, but there was nothing unintentional about the way her breast nudged Jori's arm, and there was no Baylee-appropriate explanation for why Rae's sharp hipbone should make contact with anything.

Jori caught her breath. Turned toward her touch. Ached to hold her and keep her wedged close, heat pressed to heat, until Rae confessed she hadn't really meant those angry things she'd said in the middle of the night. But Rae had already moved away, and now wasn't the time.

"You get back to your books," Rae said, as if nothing had happened. "Baylee and I have plans."

If Rae was offering to help out of guilt for how things ended at the hotel, there was no need. "Really, we were on our way back to the—"

Rae turned her back on her. "Come on, Baylee." Rae snagged a crayon off the floor and off they skipped to another corner of the barn, their footsteps echoing under the vaulted ceiling.

Jori gave up. Baylee seemed excited and Jori did need to get some work done, so she tore some blank paper out of her spiral notebook for them, dropped it off in their corner, and settled back down with her books, sneaking occasional glances at Baylee to make sure she was behaving.

What had Rae been thinking, brushing against her like that? Not that Jori was complaining, but she'd thought the *I don't date people like you* accusations would have set their relationship back to a point where touching wasn't going to happen.

Rae had just been scared. Angry, yes—but angry was okay, because it meant there wouldn't be any bad surprises down the road—the kind of surprises that came from thinking they'd never disagree about anything and then being unprepared for the truth.

Maybe Rae had reacted so emotionally because she had feelings for her. Or maybe Rae was just emotional. Emotional wasn't a problem, though, because Jori enjoyed building nerves of steel—as long as it was for the right payoff. And the right payoff might just be Rae.

Rae—her bright, imperfect ray of sunshine—was playing an improbable version of do-it-yourself Twister that involved hopping like a frog and flapping like a butterfly and twirling like a horse—which Jori had to have misheard—she hoped—until Baylee knocked into her and they both collapsed on the floor, giggling.

Rae couldn't be that scared—not if she was here.

When Rae finally said she had to go, Jori had gotten a lot more material covered than she'd hoped, and Baylee was so worn out she was sure she'd fall asleep early, freeing up even more study time later. Amazing.

"Do you have to go?" Baylee asked Rae.

"Unfortunately, yes." Rae scooped Baylee up and set her down next to Jori.

Jori drew Baylee into her lap to keep her from running off. "Remember to say thank you."

"Thank you," Baylee said.

"Thanks from Mom, too."

"Don't even." Rae swept the air in a dismissive gesture. "It's the least I can do after all the time you've spent helping me with that dumb wedding dance."

"You don't have to pay me back for that," Jori said.

Rae shook her head and waved goodbye.

Baylee waved back. "Bye!"

"Bye!" Rae said, waving again.

Baylee waved harder, her whole body wiggling from the force of it. "See you tomorrow!"

Jori cupped her hands around her mouth and joined in. "Or another time."

"Or another time," Baylee said.

Rae winked at them both and retreated toward the door, waving one last time.

Jori hitched a shoulder and shook her head, smiling. "No pressure."

––––––

Rae only had to put up with Griffin for one afternoon. He'd agreed to just one rehearsal, so he was learning all his steps today whether his memorization skills cooperated or not.

As soon as they all reached the yoga barn, Kaoli made a beeline for the sound system, belting out the opening bars of "Alpha in Heels" while her fiancé stood awkwardly by the door.

"Griffin, come on." Kaoli doubled back to retrieve him, wiggling her hips and serenading him until he cracked a smile. Well, good. If Kaoli could charm him into staying relaxed for the rest of the day, this might work.

With Rae taking Griffin's role and Jori standing in for Kaoli, they demonstrated how Rae wanted Kaoli to spin, first one direction and then the other, away from her soon-to-be husband and then back into his arms. All Griffin had to do was stand there. He didn't even have to remember to raise his arm because Kaoli knew her part and basically led herself into the spins, dragging his limbs where they needed to go.

"Doesn't my sexy hunk get to dance at all?" Kaoli asked.

Rae knew what she meant. Not about Griffin being a hunk, but about the fact that he looked like a rigid bystander. A professional could make anything look good, even if he was doing nothing more than standing in one spot and leading his partner into her turns. But not Griffin. Having a big step of his own would force him to move his feet and get involved. Make him look like he was dancing.

"Let's make him twirl," Kaoli suggested.

Rae had toyed with that idea earlier, wondering with vicious satisfaction if Griffin would find it unmanly to spin, but ultimately decided against it because she wanted this to look good and she didn't think he'd be smooth enough to pull it off. She and Jori had practiced it a few times, though, experimenting. It would be easy to put the discarded move back in.

"Jori, do you remember how we did that spin?"

"Sure."

Jori took her hand and Rae whirled away, demonstrating Griffin's part. They started out perfectly, but as Rae rotated through the spin, she realized too late that she'd moved before Jori finished dredging up her memory of what to do, because Jori forgot to release her hold on her shoulder blade. Which meant that as Rae spun, Jori's steady hand was now under her arm and now on the side of her breast and now on the front of her breast, the flat of her palm accidentally in firm, full contact with a part of her that wasn't meant to be touched in public. And then gone.

Rae's jaw dropped in shock. And amusement. Had Kaoli seen? Had Griffin? Did Griffin think Jori was feeling her up on purpose? *Was* she feeling her up on purpose?

"Sorry!" Jori laughed, not looking sorry at all. "That was unintentional."

Rae flushed. Unintentional or not, she could still feel where Jori's warm palm had trailed across her breast leaving aching lust in its wake. She wanted to grab her wrist and place her hand on her breast again. She belonged there. They should do all their dancing that way.

In private.

But they weren't alone, so she got Kaoli and Griffin started on practicing the step on their own—with the hand in the proper place—and gathered Jori back into dance hold—the real hold—to review what came next.

"Let's fine-tune this," she told Jori, pretending all she wanted was to avoid another hand-on-the-breast mistake, when really she just wanted to hold her hand and not ever let go.

She loved partnering her. She'd danced all her life, but she'd never known the rush of pleasure that came from guiding her partner into the right position, or been overwhelmed by a sense of awe that a woman would move confidently into her arms, trusting her to lead her into the next movement, waiting for her to show her the way. She'd never known that holding her would make her feel so protective, or that feeling protective would feel so good.

But their time together didn't last nearly long enough, because it soon became apparent that the only way Griffin was going to learn was not by struggling with his critical girlfriend, but by working one-on-one with Rae while Jori split off to practice with Kaoli.

"I can't believe Kaoli asked you to go to all this trouble," Griffin said, dragging his feet and eyeing the exit. Clearly what he really couldn't believe was that he'd agreed to Kaoli's plan to force him to dance in the first place. "Your skills are wasted on me."

Rae took his hand and showed him where to place his arms. She hadn't expected him to be quite this civil, but then again, high school was a long time ago. "Just smile and try to make her look good. And don't step on her."

Griffin nodded. "Heard the latest rumor?"

"Which one?"

"Seems you girls got into a screaming match because Kaoli won't call off our wedding." He bestowed an annoyingly superior smile on her. Maybe high school *wasn't* that long ago. "Is that true?"

"Who knows?" Kaoli needed to update her if she wanted her to not look like she was making things up. Not that it mattered in front of Griffin. Griffin was just jerking her chain. He couldn't possibly believe she knew more about this than he did. It was funny, actually, that he was the one asking. If there really was a rumor going around, she'd have expected reporters from other news outlets, not him, to be in touch. Especially if news of their wedding, which no one was supposed to know about, had leaked.

"Must have been quite the scene," Griffin said. "Do you miss each other? What's it like, dating long-distance and knowing she's lost interest?"

"What are you talking about?"

"'Kaoli Morgenroth's girlfriend won't confirm she misses her. Could their relationship be on the rocks? You decide.'"

"Are you trying to get me to say something so you can quote me in *Celebrity Crush*?"

"Of course not. If I need a quote from you, I have no problem inventing one."

Somehow that didn't surprise her. "So this is all a joke to you. Does it ever bother you that you're being unethical? I mean, you're Kaoli's fiancé. Some people might consider that a reason not to publish stories about her."

"Those people are called journalists, and they already think I'm scum, so what do I care? The general public doesn't care. They don't know who I am. I'm just the schmuck Kaoli Morgenroth's going to leave at the altar so she can run off with some second-rate backup dancer. Which reminds me…hmm…let me think. Last I heard, *you* were the one lying to the public."

Her face burned. That was different. *Kaoli* was the one lying to the public. Rae was just along for the ride. "I'm helping her." Surely he understood that she wanted to make Kaoli as popular as possible, and their so-called relationship was doing just that. "I want her to succeed as much as you do. We're on the same side."

Griffin tightened his grip on her shoulder blade. "You're helping her because you want her."

"That's ridiculous." It might be time to extricate herself from his arms before he left bruises. His hands were stronger than they looked.

"Don't you understand why she asked you to dream up our wedding dance? Because she wanted to prove she was over you."

"Who is she proving it to? To you? Or to herself?"

"To you, Rae."

Oh sure. He wanted her to believe that Kaoli had left her own tour and traveled several hours out of her way to a small town in the middle of nowhere to prove she didn't want her? He was too smart to think that made any sense.

"Kaoli warned me you were in denial. She was right."

Ah, now she understood what was up. Kaoli was trying to make Griffin jealous. So rather than reassure him that spending a day alone with Rae was nothing to be concerned about, she'd told him Rae still wanted her.

And he believed her.

He didn't know Kaoli had propositioned her in her room. He didn't know how hard Kaoli had tried to get her to sleep with her. He didn't know what he was marrying.

Rae broke free and threw up her hands in exasperation just as Kaoli appeared at their side, Jori trailing behind.

"Getting hot and heavy over here?" Kaoli said.

Rae wondered how much she'd overheard.

"I think it's time for you to dance with your husband-to-be," Rae said.

"Is Griffin telling you about the video?" Kaoli asked.

"What video?"

"You didn't see it?" Kaoli seemed surprised. Like Rae had nothing better to do with her time than stay on top of every up-to-the-minute development. "A fan recorded us rehearsing in that band shell the last time I was here. It's bad. It makes it look like you and I broke up. You're going to have to make an announcement saying you're not dating Jori, you're dating me."

Now Jori was caught up in this mess, too? That was not okay. Rae was going to have to find this video as soon as she could and figure out what happened.

Whatever it was, though, it obviously wouldn't have involved Jori if Jori hadn't been there in the band shell dancing with them in the first place. It was Rae's fault that Jori was involved. Rae should never have taken her up on her offer to help.

But what had Kaoli said? It looked like they broke up? Sylvie's comment that Kaoli was flirting with the new sound person echoed in her head.

Why *not* break up? If the pieces were already in place…

"Couldn't we just use this as an opportunity for you to move on and date someone else?" Rae said. "Someone more convincing?" Like Graciela the techie? Or a fan who would do anything for the chance to kiss a rock star in front of the cameras?

Kaoli scowled. "Your contract's up for renewal in an couple months, Rae. Don't be difficult."

Rae clenched her hands together and twisted her fingers in a nervous ball. What was Kaoli's problem? This could work!

And if they continued this way, what would next season be like? Rae would be back onstage, traveling from city to city with the other performers, back in the spotlight, making appearances with Kaoli at public events to maintain their charade. Would Jori still be in her life? If she was, and Rae was still "dating" Kaoli, they'd have to skulk around in secret to see each other. And she didn't want that. She didn't want her life to revolve around cameras and rumors and damage control. She didn't want to make a public announcement that Jori meant nothing to her.

She just wanted to dance. How had just wanting to dance turned into such a mess?

It turned into a mess because she hadn't been clear in her own mind about her priorities.

Now she was. She was clear.

"I can't do this anymore," Rae said. "I quit."

"Excuse me?" Kaoli looked stunned.

Rae felt a little stunned herself. Her heart pounded steadily, though, and her voice held strong. "I'm done. The dating, the paparazzi, the job, everything."

Jori jumped to her side. "Rae, don't. You love your job." She touched Rae's shoulder.

Rae shrugged away from her and shook her head. Her job was important, but there were other things that mattered more. "I'm sick of pretending."

But Jori wasn't, was she? Jori was still messing around with Axel.

It didn't matter.

"I'll finish teaching you this dance," Rae told Kaoli and Griffin. "And that's it."

Rae spent the rest of the afternoon shouting dance instructions and driving everyone so hard that no one had the energy to talk about anything but which foot was supposed to go where. By the end of the day, Griffin seemed confident he'd memorized all the steps. She hoped he wouldn't forget everything before the wedding, but if he did? Not her problem. She'd done the mature thing and not stomped out, but if he or Kaoli needed anything after today, they were on their own.

She ran them through the routine one last time. Then Kaoli and Griffin took off.

Rae breathed a sigh of relief. Later, she'd remember the downside of being unemployed, but for now, she was going to feel good about her freedom. She sat on a bench and changed out of her dance shoes into flats.

Jori could have left. She should have left, because she'd lost enough of her day already, helping out. But she joined Rae on the bench.

Rae finished with her shoes and straightened. "What are you—"

"I'm looking for that video," Jori said, fussing with her phone. "Here. Want to see?"

Jori scooted over until her shoulder bumped into Rae's side. Their arms were bare and they were both soaked with sweat, but the sweat didn't bother her. She liked it—liked the raw intimacy of it. Did they really have to watch the video? There was no point anymore, right? No announcement to make, no Kaoli to appease. Instead she could lean closer and take that phone out of Jori's hand and—

The tinny sound of Kaoli's singing burst from the phone.

Rae sighed. She should watch.

The video began in the band shell with Rae at the far edge of the screen, her back to the camera as she watched Jori attempt to position Kaoli's arms in the correct configuration for a weave combination. It was a relatively simple move for the feet, but the arm pattern was complicated, and Jori had struggled with it.

This was their breakup video? Rae remembered feeling bad for Jori and going over to help, but how would that…

In the video, Rae was shaking her head. Her awkward gait as she made her way over to them looked more like angry stomping than injured hobbling, and the amateur videographer had made sure of it by adding a voice-over.

"Get your hands off her," said the fake voice of Rae on the video. The voice sounded nothing like hers, but who would know? "She's mine."

The words *Kaoli Morgenroth's girlfriend makes a big mistake* appeared along the bottom of the screen.

Rae covered her face and continued watching through the gaps between her spread fingers. She knew what came next— she'd pulled Kaoli away from Jori to teach her the step herself. How that could possibly be construed as breaking up with her, she had no idea, but she was about to find out. But instead of zooming in on that moment, the video cut seamlessly to many minutes later, when Rae was dancing with Jori, making it look like *Jori* was the one Rae had pulled into her arms.

"You're the one I want," Rae's fake voice told Jori on the screen. "I love Kaoli's music, but you're the one who rocks my world."

"'Who rocks my world?'" Rae groaned. "That is the worst line ever."

But the way video-Rae was looking into video Jori's eyes, smiling and lost, no one would ever believe she wasn't in love.

The clip ended and Jori started it up again.

"Once wasn't enough?" Rae asked.

"I could watch you all day," Jori said absently, engrossed in her screen.

"You...what?"

Jori's head jerked up. "I mean..." She cleared her throat and paused the video. "I mean, what a great routine. I should teach Axel these steps. We'd wow everyone at his cousin's wedding."

Rae rose from the bench and threw her dance shoes into her carryall with more force than necessary. "You're still going to that?"

"Yeah. So Baylee can get to know her cousins."

Rae slung her bag onto her shoulder. She should admire Jori for staying on good terms with the father of her child. But the thought of her dancing in Axel's arms made Rae's fingernails dig painfully into her palms. Jori should be dancing in *her* arms.

"I'm not going to sleep with him," Jori said, ending the playback and putting her phone away as she stood. "I'm not going to sleep with any of the men there."

Rae schooled her face into a blank expression. Really, she wasn't jealous. It wasn't like she had a right to be. They hadn't promised each other monogamy. They hadn't promised each other anything.

"I'm not going to sleep with any of the women there, either," Jori said. "I already have a girlfriend."

Rae's bag slid off her shoulder and thumped to the floor. Her stomach clenched. Jori had called her her *girlfriend*. Was she her girlfriend? They'd slept together and Rae had freaked out but not completely run away, and Jori had assumed that meant they were dating? No, not dating—committed. Committed enough that Jori wasn't going to sleep with anyone else and was going to go around telling people she had a girlfriend.

Which was pretty presumptuous.

And felt nicer than she wanted to admit.

Jori wanted to be her girlfriend. Rae had pushed her away and Jori still wanted to be with her.

"That doesn't make me a lesbian, okay? That's not how it works."

"I remember," Rae said. "Sexuality is fluid. People change. No labels. No guarantees."

Even though *none* of those were true for *her*.

But somehow that didn't upset her the way it used to.

"I may have been a little harsh about there being no guarantees," Jori said.

"No, you were right. You shouldn't pretend something is true if it isn't."

Jori shook her head. "When I said people change and relationships fail, I didn't mean I wasn't willing to try." She stepped around Rae's bag and came closer.

"Don't say that." Rae's vision blurred with the threat of tears. Her throat closed. "I'm the one who needs to apologize. Not you. And I'm sorry. I'm very, very sorry for everything I said to you that night."

"You were being honest."

"And hurtful."

"I'd rather you were honest than protect my feelings."

"You can't mean that."

Jori reached for her waist and Rae wrapped her arms around her.

"I do mean that." Jori's warm breath caressed her cheek. "I love you, Rae."

"Don't." Rae's voice cracked.

Jori could have said *I love your hair. I love hanging out with you. I love dancing with you.* Thrown the word *love* out there like a test to see what kind of reaction she got before she threw in her soul. But not Jori. She had to be the bravest person in the world. Or the dumbest. No, the bravest. Telling her she loved her when she didn't know for sure whether Rae loved her back.

"But all those things I said about how I could only be with a lesbian…"

"Don't think of me as not a lesbian," Jori said, her head bowed close, planting kisses in her hair. "Or bi. Or whatever. Think of me as a human being."

"I do." And when she thought of Jori as just herself, she loved her, and nothing else mattered. And that scared her, because it meant she was sticking her head in the sand and ignoring reality.

She didn't want Jori to love her.

Rae moved her hands up and down Jori's back, wanting to protect her, to tell her this wasn't safe, to tell her it *was* safe. She slid one hand to Jori's head, smoothing her baby-soft hair.

Jori rested her head against Rae's. "Think of me as me."

She wanted to. All her reasons for why Jori's sexual identity should bother her seemed trivial compared to all the things she liked about her. All the things she loved about her. Maybe it didn't have to bother her. Jori was a better person than Rae was, and Rae was clinging to her stupid rule? Maybe she could change her rule, drop it completely. She wanted to drop her rule. It would be worth it.

"Jori—"

"Think of me as the woman who loves you."

Jori pressed her lips to the hollow just beneath her collarbone, and all that mattered was the feel of Jori's lips on her skin and the scent of her in her arms and the heady feeling of being wanted. Rae's grip loosened and Jori licked her way across her chest along the bare skin exposed by her tank top, leaving a trail of sensation that built with each deliberate kiss until Rae was shivering with anticipation and arching her upper back, helpless to do anything but urge her on.

Jori's moan rumbled against her chest. Her kisses grew more heated and her pelvis bumped forward, knocking into her at random intervals that rapidly sped up. Without thinking about it, Rae found herself grinding into her, rubbing against as much of her body as she possibly could. She probably shouldn't be doing it until they had more of a conversation, but she didn't care. It was insane how much she wanted her.

"Don't you have somewhere you need to be?" Rae asked, making one last grasp at rational thought before she lost herself fully to Jori's touch.

Jori kissed her mouth, cutting off further conversation.

Rae kissed her back with everything she had, desperate to erase the harsh things she'd said. Jori moaned into her mouth and shoved her hand between them to caress her through the stretchy fabric of her dance pants. The shock of it set Rae swaying, and she gripped Jori's waist and pushed forward into her hand, straining toward the unbearable pleasure. It was crazy. She wasn't even under her clothes and yet it didn't seem to matter. No barrier could stop her touch from burning through. Her touch was heat, and love, and home, and it filled her with a pleasure that built until she was shaking so hard she wasn't sure she could stay on her feet. And then she was over the edge, not caring that her legs no longer worked, spilling out words she didn't want to take back, whispering over and over that she loved her. She sagged and collapsed into the support of Jori's arms.

She loved her.

Her legs stopped shaking, but the sense of not being in control only got worse. How could she love her? But she did. God help her, she really did.

19

Zach Fourvel was contemplating lunch in front of his open refrigerator when one of his favorite tipsters phoned.

"Lots of celebs in town this weekend," the guy told him. "Diego Alvarez is flying into LaGuardia on Flight 1227 to flack his new movie. He's staying at Hotel Atlantico through Sunday."

Zach shut the refrigerator. "He's not bringing his rug rat, is he?"

"Not that I know of."

Too bad. A candid shot of a big movie star like Diego Alvarez would be marketable, but without the rug rat sitting on his shoulders looking barfably cute, the photo wouldn't be worth nearly as much. It was better than nothing, though. He did have a new movie coming out, so the timing was good.

"Anyone else?"

"Blue Detweiler is staying at the Marco. Should get in today from some shindig upstate, but no one knows when. Len Leppanen is rumored to be staying there, too, but I can't confirm that."

"Any women?"

"Kaoli Morgenroth. Performing downtown tonight."

Hmm. Kaoli Morgenroth. Most people would advise him to keep a calendar and look up venue schedules and shit like that, but calendars and schedules were for nerds. Give him last-minute tips and unexpected run-ins any day. Those were the exciting shots. Scheduled appearances weren't his thing. But Kaoli Morgenroth might be good. He could only be in one place at a time, so choices had to be made, and photos of women paid more than photos of men. A lot more. Go figure.

Although that dynamite shot he'd sold of her—the one of her kissing the chick in the swimming pool—hadn't paid nearly as well as he'd hoped. *Celebrity Crush* hadn't been an option for reasons that were obvious to anyone who'd ever done business with the lovestruck guy in charge over there, and the other big-name news outlets hadn't been interested because a kiss on the forehead didn't sound newsworthy to those idiots, but he'd kept at it, firing off messages to every buyer on his list until finally a start-up online gossip site that paid crap started nibbling. Crap money was better than no money, he always said, so when it looked like he wasn't going to get a better offer, he sealed the deal. Two hours later, his shot went viral. That would teach people not to turn up their noses at his hard work.

He'd stalked her for a while after that, but nothing much had come of it. That second kiss had been interesting, but another photographer had swooped in out of nowhere and beaten him to the sale. Not being first had cost him.

He'd give her one more chance. He couldn't shake the feeling she was going to pay off big.

He downed three slices of cold pizza and packed up his camera, his backup lens, his backup battery, and a bag of cheese curls. And a paper napkin, because last time he'd gotten cheese powder on his camera and almost damaged the lens, so he was trying to be more careful.

A little while later he was on the platform waiting for the commuter train that would take him into the city. A torn copy of *Soundstar Magazine* lay abandoned on a bench. He picked it up and paged through it. His gaze landed on a shot of Anatalia Gold, and he squinted, homing in on the photo credit.

Brian Washington. Brian? Brian got a shot of Anatalia Gold coming out the front door after her last concert? While yours truly was waiting like an idiot out back? Damn him. What was Brian doing at the front entrance, anyway?

Thinking outside the box, that's what. He needed to do more of that himself if he didn't want to go broke. He did okay in this business that rewarded patience, luck, and good instincts, but recently Lady Luck was sleeping with the other guys instead of him.

What he needed was that one shocking, hard-to-get, once-in-a-lifetime photo that sold all over the world and made him rich.

Or at least saved his house.

Because if he didn't get some cash soon he was going to lose his home to foreclosure, and then how was he going to find a cheap rental that would let him keep his dog? Hard to hide a barking, eighty-pound German shepherd from a landlord. He'd find a way if he had to, though. Him and Fetch were a team. Wasn't nothing gonna split up him and Fetch.

All he needed was one good shot. Then he could relax.

He continued to study the magazine, ignoring the professionally edited publicity photos for the out-of-focus crap cell phone shots made by amateurs who happened to be in the right place at the right time, updating his mental database of who was popular right now, who was selling.

Hey, what do you know, another photo of Matt Gosri throwing a punch at some photographer. Wonder if he knew the guy who'd pissed him off?

A small news item caught his eye. Kaoli Morgenroth was rumored to be cheating on her on-again, off-again boyfriend. Again. With a different chick.

> *While Rae Peters—rumored to be the girlfriend (or is it ex-girlfriend?) of superstar Kaoli Morgenroth and recently sidelined from the tour with extensive injuries— recuperates alone at a secret vacation hideaway, Kaoli is all smiles as she autographs the bra of a shirtless fan at last night's birthday celebration for music legend Anatalia Gold. Is Kaoli back on the prowl?*

Hmm…

Kaoli Morgenroth.

Just where he was headed right now.

He always knew one of these days Lady Luck would end up back in his bed. She couldn't stay away.

Zach waited in the shadows of a parked semitruck and listened to the strains of Kaoli Morgenroth's concert bleeding into the familiar nighttime sounds of the city, counting down the minutes to the start of his timetable.

Finally. He swallowed his last cheese curl and let the crinkling empty bag drop to the ground where it joined the cigarette butts that littered the asphalt until a gust of wind blew it away.

Aside from the semis, the parking area he'd snuck into held a small fleet of buses plastered with oversize images of Kaoli Morgenroth's face, but the star's private bus was easy to identify: it was the only one with a guard. A local rent-a-cop, judging by the uniform. Her personal bodyguard would be inside the venue with her, not out here sneaking coffee from a takeout cup.

Zach crept closer, stopping every two steps to reassess, gripping his oversize camera in both hands. In order to do his job, he had two major strategies—either hide and let his high-powered telephoto lens do the work, or get in the target's face. It wasn't photo time yet, but the same rules applied. Zach went for option number two and strode straight for the slouching guard.

"No visitors allowed," barked the guard, suddenly no longer slouching.

"Kaoli in there?" Zach asked casually, even though it was obvious from the sounds coming from the venue that she was onstage.

"I'm afraid I'm going to have to ask you to leave."

"I'm afraid you're going to have to make me."

No self-respecting freelance celebrity photographer ever left because he was asked to leave. They left only when forced to, and everyone knew it. It was all part of the game.

What he was about to do next, however, was not part of the game, and could get him arrested. But only if someone saw him do it. With no one else around but this one security guard—if there were others, they were inside the venue, ready to escort the star to her next destination—he figured he was safe. He clenched the sleeping pills in his sweaty palm.

The guard did that thing with his shoulders and pecs that guards always did to make themselves look even heftier than they already were. He was pretty good at it, although the coffee cup in his hand did detract from the effect.

"I said, time to leave."

"Tough guy," Zach said blandly. Sometimes acting bored was the best way to get these guys riled up.

"Start moving," ordered the guard, stomping toward him.

Zach didn't budge. He needed him close. "Too bad you're not a real cop so you could arrest me."

The whites of the guard's eyes went wild with the need to grab his arm and haul his ugly ass out of the area without being sued for assault. He managed to control himself and reached for his two-way radio instead and called for backup.

Now he was close enough—and distracted. The coffee cup was at hip level. No baby-ass plastic sippy top to protect against spillage. Zach casually moved his hand and dropped in the sleeping pills. Double dose. He wasn't happy about it, but the guard left him no choice. If he'd been friendly and invited him to wait for Kaoli's arrival together, things might've been different. Besides, he was a security guard, for cripe's sake. If he couldn't keep an eye on his own frickin' coffee he deserved to be drugged.

"Get out of here, paparazzi."

"I'm going, I'm going." Zach raised his hands and backed off. Cripes. The guy was an amateur if he thought the paparazzi *ever* backed off.

Zach turned a corner and tucked himself out of sight behind a truck, and the guard called off the backup. Honestly, he was making it too easy.

Fifteen minutes later, the guard was yawning. Right on time. The guy leaned against the bus, closed his eyes, mumbled to himself to stay awake. Jogged in place. Did a lap around the bus. Like that was going to help.

On his second lap, Zach slipped inside the tour bus. Quickly he scanned the layout, hopped into the bathroom, and hid behind the door. He propped the door ajar with his foot, just wide enough for his camera lens.

Heavy footsteps entered the bus. The guard. Zach shrank into the shadows. If the guard had seen him come in, it was all over. But if he hadn't...well, then he had no reason to search for an intruder, did he? No reason to check the bathroom. Not unless he had to take a piss after all that coffee.

Or heard loud breathing. Zach held his breath. This was not a good time for his lungs to decide to get a workout.

The guard dragged his feet past Zach's hiding place and headed to the back of the bus. Party music kicked on. The pressure in Zach's chest eased. The guard was getting the bus ready for the boss's return. Or trying to keep himself awake. Either way, he was safe. *Good idea. Thanks for helping me out, man.* The music meant it was harder for Zach to hear the guard, but it also meant the guard couldn't hear Zach, not if he was quiet and didn't bang into anything.

As soon as the guard left, Zach double-checked that his camera settings were properly adjusted for the tricky lighting conditions. A few minutes later, the sound of female laughter set him on alert. He raised his camera to the crack in the door. Prayed no one would turn up the lights and screw up his shot.

Framed in the threshold was Kaoli Morgenroth. Jackpot. His heavy-duty equipment was no silent piece-of-shit camera phone, but over the pounding music, no one heard the shutter slam open and shut.

The star grabbed her companion's hand as they entered the bus. A chick. She was with a chick. And not the swimming pool chick, either. A new one. Zach clicked. Click, click, click. Who cared if the hand-holding was innocent or not? Either way, Fetch was going to get to keep his backyard in the 'burbs.

"That was an awesome performance if I do say so myself." Kaoli looked exuberant, still high from the show. Smiling. Great shot. Zach pressed the button again.

Her friend grabbed a sandwich from the kitchen area and put it in the star's hands, which meant she was probably a staff person, personal assistant, something like that. Who cared? Kaoli chowed down and the chick stared at her mouth, watching her chew and swallow. She needed to get a life, if watching the star eat a sandwich she'd made—or maybe only touched—was that interesting.

It was just a sandwich, lady. Toasted ham and cheese, by the looks of it. Not something the tabloids would want to run a photo of, not even on a slow week. Not unless the hand that held the sandwich had a freakish sixth finger. But the hand-holding...that was gold.

"I have to go back and take care of the sound equipment," the chick said. "I don't want anyone messing with it."

"It can wait."

Kaoli Morgenroth pulled the sandwich chick into her arms. Kissed her. God, there was tongue.

Jackpot. Zach clicked and clicked and clicked.

20

"We have to break up," Jori told Axel in the driveway outside his parents' house as she buckled Baylee into her booster seat in the back of his car. "Your mother's asking me why we're not married yet."

"When did she ask?" Axel demanded, ignoring the important part of what she'd just said.

Breakup? Hello?

"When I was helping her in the kitchen after dinner."

"What did you tell her?"

"That you blackmailed me into dating you and not to get her hopes up. She thought I was joking. I didn't have the heart to convince her I wasn't." She was Baylee's grandmother, after all. There was no need to be cruel.

Axel laughed like he thought Jori was joking, too. His laugh sounded a lot like his mother's, come to think of it. Or a dashing old-fashioned mobster's. "Don't think of it as blackmail, darling. Think of it as a business deal. Because it is."

"A business deal that was never intended to last indefinitely."

"Personally, I'm okay with indefinite."

"Is Gus?" Jori finished up with Baylee and got into the car on the passenger side as Axel slid behind the wheel. It would have been nice if the adult next to her was Rae, not Axel. Just being near her would have made this whole day more bearable. "If I were your boyfriend, I would not put up with being invisible forever."

"Gus is okay with it. If it means he doesn't have to show up for dinner with my folks and he gets to stay home and watch tennis instead, he's all for it."

"*I'm* not all for it." She hadn't been in much of a hurry to end it because they were Baylee's grandparents, after all, but this had gone on too long. Axel's mother, Gus, Rae...it wasn't healthy for any of them. And Rae deserved better than a woman who couldn't break things off with her pretend boyfriend. "We need to end this."

"One of these days," Axel agreed in a vague sort of way that meant it was never going to happen. He started the engine and it promptly sputtered and died. He kept his car shinier than she bothered to keep hers, but shiny didn't make it reliable.

"One of these days, like, today."

"Now is not a good time."

"Now is the perfect time. Step one: I break up with you. Step two: You say *Great idea.*"

Axel tried the ignition again and the engine coughed to life. "Please, Jori, you said you'd be my girlfriend."

"I *was* your girlfriend." Why was he so set on keeping her? "I've done more than enough to pay you back."

"A few more weeks? Until my cousin's wedding? You promised you'd be my date."

"I'm standing you up. Take Gus."

"Come on, Jori. You took those dance classes and everything. Wouldn't want those to go to waste."

Oh, they hadn't gone to waste. Not in the slightest. She'd never thanked him for bullying her into that and she wasn't going to now, but she did appreciate it. Dancing with him in a room full of soon-to-be-married couples had been a small price to pay for the opportunity to put her arms around Rae. It had been the first time she'd held her, and she'd never forget it.

But that wasn't the point. "I mean it, Axel. No more."

She frowned out the window at the driveway they were still parked in. Were they ever going to leave? Her hand brushed against the door handle and her arm encountered the edge of something soft—one of Gus's conservative neckties that had been abandoned and stuffed into the door's cupholder. She hadn't noticed it on the way over, but now she pulled it out, a sad reminder that she was occupying Gus's usual seat. She pressed the tie flat against her thigh in a futile attempt to smooth the crumpled silk.

Axel rubbed his hands up and down the steering wheel. Finally he nodded. "Let me be the one to break it to my mother."

Jori released the breath she hadn't known she'd been holding. She folded Gus's tie into a neat roll and returned it to where she'd found it, nestling it snuggly on top of a few spare coins. "Sure thing."

"The news will crush her. What do I tell her?"

"That we were lying?"

"She wouldn't believe me." He tapped a rapid drumbeat on the steering wheel. "No. I'll say you left me for another man."

"Fine with me."

Axel got into gear and pulled out of the driveway and onto the street. "They'll yell at me for letting you get away and everyone will move on. They'll reminisce about how great you were and I'll tell them you married a nice, impotent, much older gentleman who never managed to get you pregnant. Mom will feel bad for you and everyone will get over it. Win-win."

Until Baylee visited Grandma and let slip that she didn't have a stepfather. By why mention it? Axel was smart. He'd figure it out soon enough.

"You're really fine with this?" Jori said.

"We'll need a reason for why you left."

"Because the old guy was sexier than you?"

"A believable reason."

Jori let out a snort of laughter. "You stud. Why don't you have an affair?"

"Classy," he said. "I always hoped—prayed—that you would forgive my indiscretions."

The old Axel was back. She loved him when he was being reasonable. Or maybe she just loved that this was over.

"Whoa. You've been cheating on me?"

"Have I?" Axel mused. "I don't know. Maybe you should leave me for a woman. My brother would appreciate that."

"Maybe you should get tired of waiting for me to agree to marry you."

"I'm already tired of waiting for that."

"Then what are you doing? You should be drowning your sorrows in the arms of another man."

Axel's grin spread slowly across his face. "Not his arms, darling. A bit lower down."

———

Two days later around lunchtime, Rae pulled into one of the parking lots at Jori's college and found all the parking spaces were taken. Jori had lent her her car so she could run some errands in town while Jori was taking her last exam of her last semester, and now Jori and Baylee were supposed to be waiting for her to take them home.

She parked illegally in the fire lane, hopped out of the car, and started down the short path to the back entrance of the building where Jori had asked to meet. Voices from inside the building rose and fell, loud enough to be heard through the windowless steel double doors.

The doors banged open and there was Jori. Axel stalked at her side, checking his phone.

Jori spotted Rae on the path and broke into a big smile. She pumped her fists. "Done!"

At that, Axel took notice and sauntered up to her and shook hands. "Rae, right? I don't think we've been formally introduced. I'm Axel Nye."

She knew who he was. "Congratulations on finishing your degree."

"Thanks." His gaze drifted past her shoulder to where Jori's Corolla was parked, its hazard lights flashing. "You came in Jori's car?"

Rae nodded.

Axel looked surprised. "Quite an honor that she lets you drive it, piece of shit that it is."

"Watch what you say about my car," Jori said, coming up on Rae's side and taking her hand.

A warm glow filled Rae's chest. She rubbed her thumb over Jori's knuckles. "Congratulations to you, too. I'm proud of you."

Jori grinned and squeezed her hand. "Let's get out of here."

Once Axel had taken off across the parking lot and Jori had claimed the driver's seat, Rae leaned across the gearshift to give Jori a kiss.

"Where do we pick up Baylee? She's at the childcare center, right?"

Jori gave her a sideways glance. "I was kind of hoping to get you to myself, so I signed her up for a few extra hours. I'll come back and get her later." She looked away and stared straight ahead at the road. "Is that okay? I'll be looking for work and leaving town soon and..."

"How many hours do we—"

"All afternoon."

"Does this involve going up to your room?"

Jori laughed. "That sounds lovely, but I was actually thinking more like a walk. If that's not too tame for you."

"Who says a walk has to be tame?"

Jori grinned and shook her head. She was thinking about it.

Maybe Rae was being unfair, though, flirting when they had more serious things to discuss. Like their future.

In less than ten minutes they were back at the lodge and headed into the woods. Rae found a fallen tree branch like the one she'd used as a walking stick not long ago lying across the path. She picked it up and planted one end in the dirt, but rather than lean on it for balance, she danced around it like Fred Astaire with his top hat and cane, showing off because finally—*finally*—nothing hurt.

Her heart wasn't in it, though. In a few days she'd be gone. It was what she'd been working toward and looking forward to every single day since she'd been injured, and now that she was ready to dance, she wasn't happy. Because she didn't want to leave Jori.

"I have an audition in New York next week," Rae said.

"So soon," Jori said expressionlessly.

"You're leaving, too. You're done with school."

"I knew it was going to happen eventually—both of us leaving—but I've been trying not to think about it." Jori stared at the ground and folded her arms across her chest. She blew out a frustrated breath. "What are we going to do?"

"I don't know." She wasn't going to give up her career for Jori, and she couldn't ask Jori to follow her around the country and limit her own career before it even started. She wasn't even sure they had that kind of relationship. She was *sure* they didn't have that kind of relationship. "Maybe we can date long-distance?"

The thought of being apart made her sick to her stomach, but people dated long-distance all the time. It could be done.

"We'll figure something out," Jori said.

God, they should have talked about this sooner.

They continued along the trail in silence. Outbuildings gave way to unbroken stands of maple and oak and hickory, but Rae was too busy watching the ground to avoid twisting her ankle on knobby tree roots to pay much attention, and besides, Jori was leading the way so all Rae had to do was follow. When she did occasionally glance up it was not to admire the forest but to appreciate Jori's loping gait. Her gait—right. Because *gait* sounded better than *derrière*. She did love the way she moved, but this went beyond dancerly appreciation. She didn't know when she'd see her again, and her familiar shape was too good a sight to miss.

Did that make her shallow? Too bad. It would certainly be easier to live apart if she were one of those people who only had high-minded thoughts and loved on a non-embarrassing intellectual plane, like women were supposed to. But she didn't love that way. Her love was as messy and physical as all her emotions, and if that made her crass, so be it. If anyone thought that meant she didn't love Jori's mind and heart and personality and spirit even more than she did her body, they were wrong.

Jori turned and touched Rae's shoulder to get her to stop. "Look at that."

In the distance were two oaks that had grown together to form an arch. They had started several feet apart, leaned toward each other like they'd gone in for a hug, and never let go.

"It's a sign," Jori said.

"A sign of what?"

Jori bounded over to the twin trees—now really a single tree—and Rae followed, wading through layers of dry, crunchy leaves from years past and sidestepping the clumps of ferns that poked through. She didn't know why Jori was so excited, but she was willing to go along for the ride. Jori reached the tree and beckoned.

"A sign of our future together."

Rae joined her and touched the barely visible seam where the two trunks met and became one. "You believe in signs?"

"I believe in taking advantage of unexpected opportunities, and this, sunshine, is a natural door." Jori patted the tree trunk and smiled like she was issuing a dare. "Come on, show me your moves. If you can work a manmade doorway…"

Ah. *Those* moves. Those wiggling-against-a-doorframe moves she'd had so much fun with, not realizing the effect she was having. Jori must have thought she was a terrible tease.

Jori ducked under the arch and leaned against it, her back to the inner curve of the tree, and Rae squeezed in to join her on the opposite side, planting the back of her shoulders and the sole of one foot against the other trunk so they stood face-to-face. Jori propped her hands on the arch overhead, elbows flared, striking a casually sexy pose.

"I thought I was supposed to be the one with the moves," Rae said. "But look at you. You could get some with that."

Jori's eyes sparkled. "I can get some without it, because I have personality."

"You think so?" Rae pressed her chest subtly forward. There was no room to do anything blatant in the tight space, but some things didn't require any space at all.

Jori's gaze softened. She touched Rae's shoulder, trailed her fingertips down her arm, clasped her hand. Raised her hand to her lips. Kissed her fingers. "I love you."

Rae drew in her breath. The sun grew brighter and the lines of the tree's bark came into sharp relief.

"I love you, too." The trees blurred, and she had to blink until her vision cleared. "I really...I really do. So much. I should have told you sooner."

It was too late to worry about being safe. About rules, and deal-breakers, and heeding red flags to protect herself from hurt feelings or disappointment or rejection or heartbreak. She'd glimpsed a light in Jori, and what she'd seen, she could never unsee. She'd fallen for that light. She could try to forget, she could pretend it never happened, but no matter how good she was at lying to herself, part of her would remember, because seeing that light had changed her. There was no going back.

Rae touched Jori's face and traced her cheekbone. "I'm sorry I was so slow to figure it out."

"It's okay."

Jori brushed her lips against hers in an exquisitely beautiful slow-motion kiss that left her struggling to catch her breath, worse than if she had just done a series of leaps across the stage.

"I'll find a job where we're not too far apart," Rae blurted out. There was no guarantee she could land any dance job, let alone one in whatever city Jori ended up in, but she could try. With Jori as incentive, she'd be the best auditioner anyone had ever seen. "Wherever you move to, I'll—"

"I wouldn't ask that of you."

It was the right answer and the wrong answer all in one.

"You're so nice." God, *nice* was so inadequate a word. *Nice* wasn't enough to explain why her heart ached.

"You should tour with another singer. Do what you're best at."

And not be tied down. Jori didn't say it, but she had to be thinking it. Jori was allowing her to walk away. *That* was why Rae's heart ached.

"I suppose we shouldn't rush into anything," Rae said.

"Probably not," Jori agreed. "But I'm up for rushing if you are."

"You are?" Excitement bubbled up until Rae's chest heaved and her arms shook and she had to hold on to Jori's shoulders because Jori was the only thing that could steady her racing heart.

"Would you make me your home base?" Jori said. "Come back to me when you're not traveling?"

"Absolutely." Jori wanted to be with her. She wanted to make this work as much as Rae did. "You think I'd give you up?"

Jori pressed her into the tree, cradling her head with one hand to protect her from the rough bark. Rae slid her knee— the one she'd gotten so used to thinking of as her good knee, but which was now one of two good knees—up the side of

Jori's leg. Probably flashing the local squirrels in her skirt, but who cared? Jori certainly didn't seem to, not with the way she hooked her arm under Rae's calf and positioned it around her waist to run her hand up the underside of Rae's bare thigh.

Rae tightened her leg around Jori's waist and molded the length of her body to her, surrendering. Jori kissed her again, more thoroughly this time, making her feel wanted and safe.

When they finally pulled away, she could still feel the imprint of Jori's lips on her own, a tingling reminder of why she didn't want to leave.

"This isn't the reason I love you," Rae said.

Jori smiled and kissed her collarbone, then her neck, making her way upward until she reached her jaw. She paused, their faces touching. "Didn't I say I have personality?"

"Sounds vaguely familiar."

Rae slid her knee down Jori's body and pulled her to the ground. They tumbled into the leaves and rolled each other, both vying to be on top, neither one giving in, their laughter mixing with the rustle of crushed leaves. Their legs tangled and Rae pinned Jori beneath her.

"You're more invested in being up there than I thought," Jori said with a hitch in her breath.

"What, you want me to let you win?"

"Let me?"

With a surge of her hips, Jori flipped her over and flashed a victorious grin. Gently, carefully, like she hadn't just rammed their hip bones together, she eased Rae's shoulders to the uneven ground. The weight of her on her thighs felt so good that Rae lost the urge to fight back with a move that would actually work. Rae wiggled to prove this wasn't surrender, but it was. It was surrender. The best kind. Jori didn't budge. They stayed there as Rae fell still, as Jori stared into her eyes like she couldn't get enough of her. Rae slipped her hands between their bodies and stroked Jori's breasts.

"Rae," Jori whispered, her voice cracking. She shifted onto one arm to guide Rae's hands out of the way and lowered herself onto her full length.

Rae wiggled underneath her again, adjusting to the contours of Jori's body, finding the places where they fit. So perfect. Like they belonged together.

Jori picked a leaf out of her hair. "Is your back comfortable?"

Was she still worried about how Rae had stressed her knee that night? Because that was completely unnecessary.

"I happen to know where there's a nice soft bed," Jori continued.

"No, here. Stay."

Jori gave her a hesitant look, waiting for her to change her mind. Rae just smiled.

Jori scooted down and pushed Rae's skirt up and freed her of her underwear, her palms warm on her already heated skin. Rae trembled, her pelvis moving of its own volition, ready for Jori's next move. Instead of going for it, Jori arranged the back of Rae's skirt to make sure it protected Rae from the bare ground, and the care she put into that thoughtful gesture made Rae tremble even harder. When Jori finally flattened herself between Rae's legs and took her, the shock of her warm, wet mouth made her mind short-circuit.

Rae gasped. OhGodOhGodOhGod…

If you're coherent enough to remember my name and you're capable of forming actual words, then the sex is just not that good, sunshine.

Less amusingly egotistical now that…oh God…her vision was going white.

Jori kept going, driving her into a shivering, shuddering frenzy, bringing her to completion, grinding the brittle leaves beneath her to dust.

21

The endless rows of plastic folding chairs under the commencement tent were almost full. Jori was supposed to be halfway across the green with the other graduating students in their caps and gowns, finding her spot in alphabetical order, waiting to file in, but instead she was under the tent getting Baylee settled beside Axel's mother in one of the back rows. Jori's own mother had medical issues that made it painful to travel so Jori had told her not to come, and she wasn't close enough to her brother to invite him. Axel, on the other hand, didn't seem to have any shortage of guests. His whole family was in attendance as well as a group of men who seemed to know his boyfriend Gus.

Baylee stood on her flimsy chair, wobbling precariously. "Where's Rae?"

"Miss Peters," Jori corrected, grabbing the back of the chair and holding it steady.

"When is Miss Peters coming?" Baylee craned her neck to see through the crowd.

"Can't you tell that child to sit down?" said Axel's mother.

"She's fine," Jori said.

"I see her!" Baylee waved her arms enthusiastically and almost fell off her chair. "Rae! Over here!"

Jori lifted Baylee off her feet and plunked her down in her seat. The last thing she needed was for her to fall and prove her grandmother right. Baylee squirmed until Rae reached their row.

"Baylee saved you a seat," Jori told her, gesturing to the empty chair between Baylee and Gus. She wasn't sure Rae would want to sit with Axel's crowd, but there was no arguing with Baylee, and Rae had to sit somewhere.

"Mommy's graduating," Baylee told Rae. "She's going to find a job."

"She'll find a great one," Rae said, setting her bag down and accepting the seat. "Anyone would be lucky to have her."

Baylee nodded gravely like she understood that finding a job was a serious matter. "We're going to live somewhere new. Sierra and Melanie can't come."

Baylee was worried about that, wasn't she? Jori leaned down and swung her into her arms, unable to resist giving her a reassuring hug. "It's back to just you and me, kiddo."

"And Daddy," Baylee said, grabbing at the tassel swinging from Jori's head.

Jori bit her lip. Now that they were done with school and both moving on, there was no telling how interested Axel would be in parenting. She hoped he'd visit Baylee once in a while, but it was going to have to be up to him to make the effort.

"We'll see."

Axel's mother frowned and turned away, clearly unhappy with that answer but not willing to discuss it in public.

"And Rae," Baylee said.

Jori hugged her more tightly and exchanged a look with Rae. They'd agreed to *be* together, but living together under one roof? Was that decided? Rae smiled and shrugged as if to say she wouldn't hold her to anything she promised.

"You've got quite the interesting family structure there,

Baylee," Jori said lightly.

"Do you want to live with us, Rae?" Baylee asked.

Thanks, Baylee. Way to put the pressure on.

Rae laughed and joined them in a three-way hug, surrounding Baylee on all sides with people who loved her. "Of course I do."

"Really?" Jori grinned. "Next time I want something I'm siccing Baylee on you."

"Don't think it'll be that easy," Rae said, but her smile was all sunshine.

"Shouldn't you be lining up with the others?" Axel's mother interrupted. "They're waiting for you."

Jori looked over in the direction Mrs. Nye pointed. One of the college administrators was headed her way, scowling with exasperation. She had no doubt who that scowl was meant for. The mortarboard on Jori's head did make her conspicuous.

"Oops. Time for me to go."

Jori returned Baylee to her seat, and, easily evading the woman sent to round her up, escaped between the rows of seats and jogged to where she was supposed to be.

A little while later she was sitting at the front of the tent with her classmates, watching them walk across the stage one at a time to accept their diplomas and have their ceremonial hoods draped over their necks.

Then it was her turn. She walked up the three short steps at the side of the stage, waited for her name to be called, crossed the stage to shake hands with the college president and the dean of her program, smiled for the official photo.

As she headed for the end of the stage, she turned and gazed out at the sea of faces. Baylee and Rae were easy to spot—they were the crazy people on their feet, hooting and waving and clapping their hands overhead like Jori was a rock star. She waved back and made for the stairs that led off the stage.

"Jori!" It was Axel, yelling from the audience. He barreled from his seat, clambered over a row of surprised classmates, and jumped onto the stage.

What was he doing? It wasn't his turn. He snatched the cordless microphone from the startled dean's hands and dropped to his knees in front of Jori.

Oh no. He wasn't involving her in this prank, whatever it was. She started to back up, but he grabbed her hand before she could escape.

"Let me go," she hissed. Making a scene was not how she wanted to be remembered by the school.

"Jori Burgess," he said into the microphone, calmly and clearly, pausing for the powerful, nicely positioned speakers to echo his words. "Mother of my child and friend extraordinaire. Will you make my dreams come true? Will you marry me?"

Jori stared at him, dumbfounded, trying to make sense of what he was saying. Someone in the audience shrieked with happiness. She turned to the crowd and instantly, unerringly found Rae. Their connection steadied her. Axel's mother leaped out of her seat and clapped her hands over her mouth. Was she the one making all that noise?

"Jori?"

Maybe Axel thought proposing in public would make it harder for Jori to turn him down—that she wouldn't want to embarrass him. That making a grand gesture would make him look like a romantic guy and that if she rejected him, she was a rhymes-with-witch. And if she said yes, and got everyone's hopes up only to "change" her mind afterward, she was…again…a rhymes-with-witch. Although in front of fewer people.

Or maybe, just maybe, he was counting on her to reject him. Public humiliation would give him six to twelve months to nurse his allegedly broken heart before his mother dared nag him about his lack of female companionship.

Or not, because it was also easy to imagine her urging him to get back in the saddle as soon as possible.

Or maybe he was serious.

Was he serious?

Mother…friend… Those were words that rang true. He might even love her, albeit in a caring, friend-like way, although he hadn't gone so far as to used the word *love*. Would've been helpful if he'd announced he wanted to boink her brains out, because she knew he didn't want to do *that*, so that would have clarified things.

Still trapping her hand between his larger, stronger ones, Axel drew their hands to his chest, begging, apparently unaware that his beaming, confident smile ruined the illusion, because anyone who saw that smile would know begging wasn't in his nature. It was clear that in his mind, this was already a done deal.

This was what she got for being nice. For stroking his male ego and assuming that in return, he would do what she needed him to do. She did honestly like him—as a friend—but keeping up their charade, although it had started out fun, had taken a lot of effort. And this was how he thanked her. Did it even occur to him that she had feelings? That Gus did?

Jori yanked her hand out of his and stalked off the stage. As she returned to her row, Axel's mother dropped to her seat, hands still covering her mouth.

"My future wife is so happy she's in shock," Axel

explained into the microphone, remarkably undeterred.

Jori shook in her flimsy chair, hating the sea of sideways glances and outright stares.

"What do you say, cupcake? Marry me?"

It seemed walking away wasn't enough of an answer. He was like a pit bull with a bone, and he wasn't going to let it drop until she did some damage. So she'd have to do some damage.

Jori didn't have a mic, but she raised her voice the way she would in aerobics class to ensure her words carried over the crowd. "You're going to have to hire a new actress. I'm through."

Axel's mouth became an angry, flat line. With an excessive show of care, he returned the microphone to the dean. He did not return to the empty chair in the row where he was supposed to sit. Instead, he left. Just up and left the tent. Jori turned in her seat and watched. Gus swiveled in his seat, too, arms folded across his chest, slowly shaking his head. Axel didn't speed up and he didn't slow down, just kept going across the green until the campus buildings blocked him from view.

The dean cleared his throat and read the next name on the list.

Gus didn't get up and run after his boyfriend. And why should he? Axel had just publicly announced that the most important person in his life was someone else.

———

Later that night, with Baylee asleep in the adjoining room, Rae kicked off her shoes and stretched out behind Jori on the sofa, tugging up her comfortable worn capris at the hip to allow her full flexibility so she could hug her with not just her arms but also her legs and burrow her feet in Jori's lap.

Jori dropped her head back to rest on Rae's shoulder and traced the curve of her bare calves. "I can't even tell anymore which one was injured."

The not-yet-faded scars from the surgery made that a lie, but she knew what she meant—that the muscles that had shrunk so quickly after the injury had regained their former shape.

It should have been a relief. It *was* a relief. But it was bittersweet, too, because it meant her time living at the Mountain Laurel Center was over. And it was scary and exciting, because she had to find a new job. And it was everything she could hope for, because Jori wanted to move to New York with her.

"When do we pack for our new lives together?" Jori asked.

Love swelled in Rae's heart until the force of it made her chest ache. "Right now."

"Not right, *right* now," Jori protested, twisting in her lap to press a trail of kisses down her neck to her collarbone.

"Tomorrow morning, then." Neither one of them had much to pack, so it wouldn't take long. Their next move would be different, because she and Jori and Baylee would have a place of their own, with their own furniture and everything. A home.

"Tomorrow," Jori agreed.

Rae hugged her close. "Thank you for doing this."

"I was going to have to move somewhere anyway, right? So why not go where you're going?"

"But what if your dream job is somewhere else?"

Rae had thrown away the best job of her career, and she

ought to be worrying about what she needed to do to outshine the competition in all the auditions she was going to start going to, but instead she was holding her breath, waiting to hear what her girlfriend would say.

"My dream job is anyplace that will hire me that's close enough that you'll come home to me at night."

Rae let out her breath and rearranged their position to draw Jori into a kiss. If she was ever reinjured, or when the day came that she was too old to dance, her life wouldn't be over. She'd have this. She touched her nose to Jori's. "Sounds suspiciously like I might be in love with a lesbian."

Jori tensed. Just a slight little bit, the reaction so muted that she might not have noticed if Jori weren't wrapped so tightly in her arms. Crap. She hadn't meant... Was it too soon to joke about this?

"Uh..."

"You know I love you exactly the way you are," Rae said, "but God help me, if you say *no labels*, I'm going to...I'm going to...I don't know what I'll do." Sleep with her again and not feel bad about it later, most likely. Again and again for the rest of her life.

She should be so lucky.

"I—"

"So to compensate," Rae said, "I'm giving myself an additional label. PWLJBNMW. Person Who Loves Jori Burgess No Matter What."

"That's—" Jori shook her head and laughed. "I want to say *ridiculous*, but it's actually kind of nice."

"Good." Rae stroked Jori's cheek and felt Jori's tension disappear. "Because I have this theory that you might be it for me."

Jori captured her hand and kissed her palm. "Hey, I'm the

one with the theories."

"You're rubbing off on me."

"Am I?" Jori curled her hands softly around Rae's shoulders. Her voice, always a bit rough, became even hoarser. "You didn't even ask if I'd be a Person Who Loves Rae Peters. But, you know what? I am. I want a future with you. You're my ray of sunshine. I don't want to be with anyone else."

"Me neither," Rae whispered, her vocal cords suddenly as unreliable as Jori's. She didn't need Jori to define herself as *not bi* and *not straight* if she'd narrowed it down to one person—and that one person was her. She could live with knowing her identity wasn't black and white. Jori was a person, not a label. She deserved to be seen as herself, not judged by the box Rae had put her in.

Because it was too late. She already loved her. She could either acknowledge that and trust that they would do their best, or she could run away and spend the rest of her life regretting it. And if Jori didn't fit the box Rae had always thought she wanted—the *no boys allowed* box—the box that meant no history with men, no interest in men, no ex-husbands, no ex-boyfriends, no prepubescent crushes—the box she'd been so certain was her only acceptable option—so what? Being together made them both happy, so obviously she'd been wrong.

It felt great to be wrong.

She had no doubts anymore, only certainty—a bright, blazing, solid certainty that this complicated woman was the one she wanted to live the rest of her life with. She kissed her cheekbones, her jaw, her welcoming mouth. Whatever the future held, they'd face it together. She was ready.

ABOUT THE AUTHOR

Siri Caldwell began her career as a hydrogeologist wearing hip-high waders to slog through polluted streams and struggling not to tumble into the water in front of her older, more experienced colleagues. In addition to keeping her balance, she quickly learned that when collecting water samples on farmland and encountering an angry cow, it is best to back away. (Cows: not as docile and picturesque as you'd think.) Now she works at a desk, where the risk of falling or being surprised by interspecies encounters is low and she is not required to wear tall boots of any kind.

When not busy being a dutiful contestant in the rat race, she writes romance novels. Lesbian romance novels—because if anyone knows how to make a relationship complicated, it's a lesbian. And complicated is a good thing on the way to happily ever after.

She lives with her partner outside Washington, DC.

Visit her online at www.siricaldwell.com

Angel's Touch

Siri Caldwell

2014 Golden Crown Literary Society Award
finalist for Best Debut Novel

Kira has one goal: to make money by opening an exclusive spa in scenic Piper Beach. Megan agrees to help, but money is the last thing on her mind.

Kira Wagner needs a local expert to get her new hotel and spa up and running. Megan McLaren's name is at the top of her list. Megan isn't aware that the woman on her massage table is planning to offer her a job. She gives her healing touch as she would to anyone and turns down the invitation to dinner. But the persistent Kira awakens something else in Megan: memories of pasts they may have shared, none of which ended happily. When Megan realizes exactly where Kira plans to build her hotel, she agrees to consult, but her only goal is to make sure the new hotel doesn't ruin the sacred space nearby. She wishes she could tell Kira the truth, but she's deeply afraid that Kira will look at her like every other woman in her life when she explains about the powerful ley lines…and the angels…

Available in ebook and print from Bella Books

Earth Angel

Siri Caldwell

New England Chapter, Romance Writers of America
Readers' Choice Award finalist for
Best Contemporary Romance of 2013

People say Abby Vogel sounds like an angel when she plays her harp at weddings and other events in beautiful Piper Beach. They don't need to know that real angels—or possibly figments of her imagination—keep her company. They wouldn't understand.

Gwynne Abernathy blames herself for the deaths of her sister and mother. Her psychic gifts have brought her only grief, and she's turned her back on anything that isn't "normal". Abby's kindness and quirkiness are irresistible, but there must be a reason Abby is swarmed by angels, and she suspects that when she discovers it she'll want to stay far, far away.

Abby knows immediately that there is more to Gwynne than meets the eye. When she realizes she's not the only one who sees angels—that Gwynne sees them, too—she finally trusts that her glowing friends are not hallucinations. What's more, the angels desperately need something from her. If she answers their call, it means giving up the magic she feels with Gwynne. It means giving up…everything.

Available in ebook and print from Bella Books